D0710010

For Barbara and Adam, two very special people who have helped me so much on this story that they have every right to lay some claim to it. Without you both, this story would never have gotten into print. With you both, this story is much more than it ever would have been otherwise. I am deeply thankful for the input and constant support.

To all you other readers who have made Dark Justice a small part of your lives, many thanks.

Dark Justice

By

Donnie Light

Chapter 1

August, 1806

Tobias faced the bittersweet reality that he was probably living the last day of his life.

The escaped slave cautiously approached a small camp. Moving silently from tree to bush, he worked his way to a shallow ravine. He listened intently for the sound of baying hounds. He took his breaths in long, hard pulls that fully expanded his chest. His nostrils flared as he breathed and streams of sweat stung his eyes.

The slaves who inhabited this camp were still working in the fields. They exchanged their life energy for a meager amount of food and a place to lay their heads. Tobias looked at the neglected shacks of the camp. Their gray, weathered boards looked as old as the dirt path on which they sat. A half-dozen of these shacks lay in a rough semicircle at the base of a majestic hill, making them look much smaller than their actual size.

Three old women tended a fire in the center of the camp, preparing to cook a meal for the tired workers upon their return. A few children of toddling age and smaller milled about their feet, occasionally breaking the silence with a cry or a laugh that echoed through the hills.

Tobias gathered a bunch of crumbly, dried leaves from the floor of the forest, stirring up the rich, moist scent of the rotting matter beneath. He would rest until nightfall, and then approach those in the camp. His exhausting run had worn him down to a point of near collapse, but sleep had not come easily since his escape. Looking up through the thick canopy of the forest he saw only flecks of the reddish-blue evening sky between the leaves.

The runaway slave listened intently to the near-silence. He did not expect to hear the wailing dogs that were surely on his trail, but kept alert for the sounds just in case. He had done his best to confuse the hounds, knowing that it would only delay them. He figured he was a full day ahead of the slave-catchers, enough time to do what he needed to do here.

Please, give me this night. Let me have my wish this once, oh gods, and let my run end here. He prayed his silent prayer to the gods of his religion in his native tongue.

Tobias lay quietly in the darkening woods for another hour before noises from the camp caused him to stir. Peeking over the lichen-clad trunk of a fallen tree, he spied on the group of little shacks.

Four young black men had gathered around the well that marked the center of the camp. One was raising the bucket as others anticipated their turn at the water. Older slaves slowly entered the camp, herding children who were just old enough to begin working in the fields. Their bare feet raised a cloud of dust as they slowly trod into the camp. A couple of teen-aged girls with small babies slung onto one hip quickened their pace to reach the water ahead of the others.

Tobias would wait until things settled down before entering the camp. He watched closely as the slaves put large pots to boil on the cooking fires. Thick ropes of smoke and steam from the fires blended, snaking their way upward in the calm evening air. As the enticing scent of vegetable soup rose from the boiling cauldrons, darkness fell.

The fugitive slave again lay back and peered into the darkness. Painful memories, like poison-tipped arrows penetrated his mind. Tobias winced at these dark memories and a tear escaped from beneath tightly closed eyelids. He thought about Master Richards, the man he ran from. Pain jabbed him again at the thought of never seeing his children again; and his wife, now dead at Richards' hands.

2

Tobias had never experienced such total sadness. The sadness was so thick that it nearly suffocated him. His mind whirled in confusion as he pondered why his life had taken such an unfortunate turn.

Master Richards had generally been a good man during the years that Tobias had been in his service. He had been stern, yet fair. He had been determined that things would go his way, sometimes to a fault. Yet during those years, he had treated Tobias and the other slaves fairly and consistently. Herein lay Tobias' cause for confusion; how had things gone so terribly wrong?

After waiting for full darkness to fall, Tobias cautiously entered the camp. He prayed for acceptance by this group as he approached the fires. He prepared himself to run—his muscles like springs under tension—in case he was not accepted. He did not know what he would do if he were turned away. A slave on the run had limited choices.

The slaves, a surprisingly small group of about twenty, sat talking quietly among themselves until Tobias breached the ring of light cast out by the fires. All heads turned toward him, silenced by his sudden appearance. Their dark, shiny faces reflected the orange glow of the fires. The whites of their eyes glowed brightly in the light as tiny reflected fires danced in the wet, black pupils.

Tobias squatted before an older man and looked into his aged eyes. The man looked to be in his late fifties. He was scarecrow-thin, tall, and had short, graying hair.

"I'm needin' some help from y'all," Tobias said, never breaking his gaze on the old man. "I'm lookin' for a *Kuaar Muon*."

Tobias watched the old man's face closely for a reaction to his request for a high priest. The old man said nothing, but his eyes indicated he knew of what Tobias sought.

"I been hearin' that there's a mighty pow'ful leopard-skin priest in these parts, and I need him bad." As Tobias waited for a response from the old man, an older woman grabbed him by the arm.

"You be a runner for sure," she said, dragging him by the arm. Fear grabbed Tobias at the thought of the woman turning him in to the slave-catchers. "Let's get you a bowl and get you out of the light," the old woman said.

The tension within Tobias eased as the old woman led him behind a shack. "If a Master was to find you here, it'd be our hides," she said. She had Tobias sit on a stump of firewood that had not yet met the splitting ax. "Y'all just sit right here and I'll get you a bowl," she said, turning back toward the fires.

Tobias looked around for a few seconds, trying to readjust his eyes to the darkness again. He could still see the ghostly flames of the fire on the inside of his eyelids when he closed them.

A couple of minutes later, the old man appeared with a bowl of soup and handed it to Tobias.

"How long has it been since you last eat, runner?"

"I found me some berries yesterday," Tobias said, accepting the bowl.

"Eat it slow then," the old man croaked. "Men can't be livin' on berries."

Tobias put the small bowl to his lips and drank some of the soup. It ran down his throat, satisfying his hunger and warming his core.

"How long you been runnin'?" the old man asked as he pulled up a stump of firewood for himself. He sat heavily, and leaned against the shack.

"Six or seven days," Tobias replied, running his sleeve across his mouth to dry it.

The old man looked at him suspiciously, raising one gray eyebrow. "You mean to tell me that you been runnin' for that long, and you ain't dead or cripple yet?"

Tobias looked long and hard at the old man before he spoke. "You run hard, when you run for your life."

4

The old slave nodded, eyes full of thought and gazed into the dark woods. After a moment he spoke. "I'd say, you'll be runnin' some more." He stroked his face with one downward sweep of a skeletal hand. "You here right from Africa, ain't ya'?"

Tobias looked at the old man and nodded. "I was brought here during my sixteenth summer," Tobias said.

"Well, ya' can't be stayin' around here," he said, looking at Tobias. "If Master Browning was knowin' you be holed up here, he'd beat my po' black ass somethin' terrible."

Tobias finished slurping up the last of the vegetables out of his bowl. "Ain't meanin' to cause no harm," he said, and placed the empty bowl on the ground. "If I can see the leopard-skin priest, I'll be off runnin' again."

Tobias began kneading the tired muscles in his legs.

The old man looked up at Tobias. "What you be needin' a Kuaar Muon, fo'?" the old man asked. "Not that there's one here, ya' understand."

Tobias stopped the muscle-rubbing and stood up. "I think I be needin' to tell that to the *Kuaar Muon*."

The old man rubbed his face again, a look of worry in his eyes. He studied Tobias' eyes as if reading something there. "Keep on talkin' then and follow me."

The old man led Tobias into the woods where they would not be heard by the others. Tobias told the old priest his story. After an hour of listening, the old priest told Tobias to stay where he was until he returned. The old man got up stiffly, knees popping and other joints creaking with age and abuse. Alone, the old *Kuaar Muon* headed deeper into the woods.

Tobias sat quietly where he was, listening to the sounds of the night. Crickets serenaded their mates and the tree-frogs supplied a chorus. A half-moon cast a faint blue light down upon the forest. His mind raced with possibilities.

The old priest sat alone in the dark woods, chanting in the tongue of old Africa. As he sat on the dew-moistened grass beneath a great oak tree and became quiet, he let the sounds of the forest comfort him until he could no longer hear those sounds. His mind reached out into the ether, searching for the spirits of his elders, his god.

In his mind's eye, he saw the heavens; so glorious, so expansive. A smoky haze came into view, swirling, mesmerizing. This haze began to take shape, dividing into individual elements, resembling human figures. Becoming ever more focused, the haze resolved itself into the images of faces, shoulders and torsos.

In his mind, the old priest addressed the assembled spirits, in his native language.

"Oh grand ones, I seek your counsel. A troubled soul has come to me, seeking justice."

"Be at peace, my child. We have been following this one's journey toward you. All things are not as they appear," a spirit replied.

"Thank you, Grandmother," the priest said. "What this one seeks, I fear is beyond my abilities."

Another of the assembled spirits then spoke. "If you believe what he seeks is beyond you, then it is indeed beyond you. If you believe that it can be achieved, then it will be achieved. You must decide, and what you decide, will be."

The priest thought a moment, then replied, "Forgive me grandfather, I hear your wisdom. I only fear that I will not be able to fulfill…"

"What you fear are not your abilities," yet another spirit interrupted. "You fear the obstacles that stand before this tortured soul. I say to you, the obstacles before this one do not block his way; they provide the way."

The old priest reflected on his own troubled thoughts. "Your wisdom is great, and it is always trusted. This one seeks justice, but the unjust is not of our clan."

The spirits smiled at the old priest. "My son," one of them said, "is the unjust one not a man? Does he not belong to the clan of mankind? Does the color of his skin make his injustice less so?"

Another grandmother spirit spoke to the priest. "This particular injustice has set many things in motion upon your world. While certain paths through time have now been lost, other paths have now been cleared. The path that is chosen will depend upon the strength of man's will. You cannot choose the outcome, nor can we. In order for justice to exist, injustice must also exist. The gods favor justice, but in this case, injustice wields much power. The balance no longer exists. Many possibilities are now open to resolve this injustice. In the end, only one will become reality."

"Thank you, Grandmother. Your message is wise and clear," the old priest replied.

"To restore the balance will require much energy," one of the spirits said. "Justice is the stronger virtue, but justice has limited paths available in this case. However, the will of this soul who seeks your help is indeed strong. If his will prevails, it will give justice the stronger path for generations beyond his own."

"I do not fully understand," the old priest said, "but I trust your counsel. Please guide me as to your will, and I will perform as expected."

"Alas, my child, we already know you will perform well. Like a well-worn path, we see this clearly. Your task will be only to convince the others, to stir their passions, to make them believe it is so. Their energy is crucial to this mission to restore the balance of justice and injustice. There must be a ceremony, tonight, to see what paths will then be opened for justice to prevail."

After an hour the priest reappeared and sat next to Tobias. "You know that this is a mighty spell that you be askin' fo'," he said, and put a hand on Tobias' shoulder. "And you know that you'll be payin' a mighty big price for it."

Tobias nodded and swallowed hard. "So, it can be done?"

"It can," the old man said, "and I reckon it will, judging from what you have told me."

They sat in silence for a moment before Tobias spoke again. "I ain't got much to give," he said, "but I'd give my life to see it done."

A serious look fell over the old man's face. "I'm afraid your po' old life ain't worth spit right now," he said, and then lowered his head. "I'm afraid that what you'll have to give," the old man paused, "will be worse than dyin'."

．　．　．

Within a couple of hours Tobias found himself sitting in a small clearing just a few hundred yards from the camp. A small

7

fire glowed weakly in the center of the clearing and the old priest sat next to it. The entire camp population was also present, down to the smallest baby.

The priest had shed the tattered rags he had been wearing earlier and was now naked. His upper torso had been smeared with some kind of paint, and as he sat before the fire, he applied the same paint to his face.

There were several small bowls set before the fire and the priest applied the contents of each to some part of his body. From the last bowl, he slowly drank. Some of the contents dribbled from both corners of his mouth, running in dark, glistening lines down his neck. He rose and poured the remainder into the fire.

The fire hissed, as if in pain, and a column of black smoke rose from its depths.

The priest began to speak in the tongues of Old Africa. The rest of the slaves began to chant.

Flames from the small fire began to lick high up into the air. Crackling sparks flew wildly into the still night.

The gods were listening. Every eye in the camp watched the priest as he began to dance around the fire. Some of the men began to use their legs as drums, slapping a rhythm upon their thighs. The priest, wearing only the paint, raised his arms to the sky and began to dance faster. The chanting speeded up to match the rhythm of the priest. His body glistened with sweat. His eyes glowed madly. The Kuaar Muon was no longer in this world, but among the gods, begging for their approval, *for justice*.

The priest could see his body dancing around the fire, no longer under his control. His spirit sped through the night sky. He fondly remembered his own father, also a leopard-skin priest, who had taught him to mind-fly. He rushed through the night searching for direction from the gods. He heard their voices questioning him, asking of his worthiness.

The answers came. The gods explained to the priest the direction he was to take. Yes, the white man would pay for his actions. The unjust one must be punished for his sins against the children of Africa. The gods *would* unleash a power upon the white man as never before. And the runner *would* run again. He must. There was a mission to accomplish and a price to be paid.

The priest praised the wisdom of the gods and asked their blessing as he bid their will.

With a speed that could not be calculated, the old priest's spirit returned to his body with a *thud*, the impact knocking him down. He lay on the ground for a moment shuddering uncontrollably. The camp was quiet, except for the crackling of the fire. The old priest slowly rose to his feet. His body no longer glistened with sweat. Covered with the dust from the ground, it looked dull, flat. He turned to face the other slaves, their faces an ashen shade of gray. The slaves began to chant again, as the priest raised his hands over his head and began to speak his native language.

"Remember our brother, stolen by white men, as many were, and brought to this land! Curse the white Devil who beat him, who spat in his face, who took of his blood! Forgive not he who tore out the heart of our brother and made him run! Show this white beast what it means to run for your life! Let him run, and let him hide! Give peace to our brother, his run will someday end! Show the white man your power! Send your justice!"

The priest dropped to his knees, breathing hard. The fire blazed in one last glorious display and then died to a flicker.

The gods had listened. The priest walked past Tobias, motioning him to follow. He also beckoned two other slaves, both young men, to join them. They walked in silence to a tree stump near the edge of the clearing.

A splitting ax had been stuck into the stump and the priest lifted the handle, working loose its bite on the hard wood. The priest looked into the eyes of the younger men. With no exchange of words, they grasped Tobias, one on each arm, and bent him over the tree stump. The old priest lifted the ax and swiftly brought it down. The blade sliced through the cool night air and a horrible scream exploded into the night.

Chapter 2

August 1991

Lt. Galen Morris pulled open a cabinet drawer in the back of the ambulance.

"Hey, Bob, we need more tape and gauze over here," he told his fellow crewmember. "While you're in the supply room, you might as well bring more run forms; we've only got a couple left on the clipboard."

Galen checked over the rest of the supplies and was satisfied that his ambulance, 1-Charles-47, was well stocked and ready to roll on their next call.

Galen was one of four full-time firefighter—paramedics that staffed the mostly volunteer, Willow River, Illinois, Fire District, Station Number One.

Until a just a few years ago, Willow River had been a completely volunteer Fire Department. As the community grew, the township board decided to hire four fully trained fire fighters to staff the department during the daytime hours when most of the volunteers were at work.

Galen stepped out of the ambulance and headed for the soda machine. The cantankerous old machine had not been in a good mood lately, having cheated several people out of their money. This was evident by the number of fresh dents and shoe marks in the lower panel. Galen deposited his coins slowly, giving each a chance to register. Before he could make his selection, a call came in over the radio. The speakers popped with sudden energy and a hollow voice crackled out a message.

"Attention Willow River Station One. 3342 Old School Road. Possible heart attack."

As message repeated itself, Galen had already headed for the rig, his soda still in the machine. He climbed into the back of the ambulance while the volunteer driver and an EMT also climbed aboard.

The ambulance quickly left the station as the siren punched a hole in the quiet evening.

Galen knew the patient at 3342 Old School Road, having been called to this address on previous occasions. It was the address of his best friend.

Galen picked up the microphone from the mobile radio mounted in the back of the ambulance.

"Charlie-47 to dispatch"

"Go ahead Charlie-47"

"We are en route to 3342 Old School Road. Can you advise us of any details of the call?"

"10-4, Charlie-47. The caller complained of severe chest pain radiating to jaw, and left arm. The caller also requested that you come in the rear door."

"10-4 dispatch. Do you still have the caller on the line?"

"Affirmative, Charlie-47."

"Dispatch, please advise the caller our ETA is approximately four minutes."

"10-4, Charlie-47."

Hang in there, you old geezer, Galen thought as he prepared the medical kit that he would take into the house.

The resident, Professor Albert Gaston, had chronic heart problems. A wonderfully interesting old man, Galen and the professor had become close friends over the last couple of years. In fact, Galen had just visited Gaston a few days ago during one of his many "check-up calls." Gaston had been his bubbly self at the time and the two had talked for over three hours. The old man fascinated him, and Galen always felt better after visiting the professor.

Professor Gaston had retired a few years ago from a college out east and moved to Willow River to be near his ailing sister who had died a few months ago. As professor of anthropology,

11

he had traveled the world and had written several successful books including a string of bestselling novels. His large Victorian home was just outside of town. Interesting and rare artifacts from various cultures around the world filled his house. All it took to engage the professor in an extensive conversation was to show some interest in something from his collection of artifacts. The professor had many unique views on the world, especially concerning those two subjects that Galen always avoided talking about in polite company; politics and religion. Galen would sit for hours listening to Gaston explain how those two subjects were the major source of change in the world, most of it negative.

Gaston had been everywhere. From the Arctic Circle to the tropical rain forests of South America, Gaston could tell stories that would keep anyone engrossed for hours.

They had become more than just friends. Gaston had been Galen's first medical call after reporting to active duty at Willow River. He had been captivated by the old man's wit, his gentle disposition, and the brightness in his seventy-eight-year-old eyes. Their friendship had started after Galen's first visit and had continued for the next two years.

The professor, like Galen, had no family nearby since his sister had died. He did have a nephew in New York, but they never visited each other. The professor had never married and rarely had visitors.

Galen had thought of the professor as the grandfather he had never known. One of his own grandfathers had died before he was born, but to hear his mother describe him, he sounded a lot like Al Gaston. He had been kind and gentle, yet wise and opinionated.

Galen also told stories about some of the emergency calls he had been involved in during their frequent visits. Having been a five-year veteran of a station in south Chicago, Galen also had plenty of stories to tell.

The two men - one old and wise, the other young and strong - always enjoyed the company of the other. Many people would think Galen and Gaston, so far apart in terms of years and

12

background, made an odd couple indeed. But their friendship had only grown stronger over time. Galen and the professor had spent many hours together, sometimes sipping coffee, sometimes beer, talking about anything and everything. On more than one occasion the visits had not ended until the wee hours of the morning.

Hang on, Al, we're on our way, Galen thought again as the ambulance sped out of town.

Audra Winters was also preparing herself and the equipment for arrival at the scene. Audra had only completed her EMT training a few weeks ago, but commanded herself as if she were a seasoned pro. Only the slightest signs of nervousness fluttered about her face.

The ambulance reached the long driveway that lead to Gaston's home and the driver cut the siren. The sudden silence was deafening.

"You grab the O2 kit," Galen said to Audra as he opened the side door and jumped out of the rig.

Audra already had it in her hands.

Galen ran to the rear of the house and opened the back door. Gaston was leaning back in a kitchen chair, phone still clutched in his right hand. He was a small man, with short gray hair and a round belly. Upon seeing Galen, he dropped the receiver, which bounced noisily on the tile floor.

"There's a lot of pain, Galen," the professor managed to squeak, clutching at his chest.

"Okay Al, you hang in there, and we'll get you to the hospital."

The ambulance driver, Bob, appeared with a gurney.

Galen turned to Audra, "get him on 15 liters of O2, pronto."

Audra began to set up the portable oxygen and Galen began taking vitals.

Within minutes they were en route to Rockford Community Hospital, about 15 miles due east.

Gaston was wincing with pain, thrashing about a bit, and trying to talk to Audra. He lay on the gurney with his head and shoulders elevated. Audra sat on a bench to the patient's left and Galen, on a single seat to his right.

After establishing an IV, Galen was on the radio with the emergency room getting his orders from the ER Doc. A bag of IV solution swung back and forth on a hook above the patient's head.

Audra was doing her best to calm Gaston down. He was naturally very anxious. Although his heart problem had manifested itself years ago, it was not something you could just get used to. Gaston had been placed on several medications and Audra struggled to write them down for the emergency room physician.

Galen finished with the radio and began to hook up the heart monitor to his patient. The professor grabbed Galen's hand as he attempted to adhere the heart monitor leads to his chest.

"Galen," Gaston croaked, "I have to tell you something."Gaston's breaths were very labored and he was in a lot of pain.

"Don't try to talk, Al. Just try to calm down," Galen said as he busied himself with applying the monitor leads.

Gaston tightened his grip on Galen's arm. "I have to tell you *now*," he gasped.

Galen responded sternly, "Al, try to calm down. After the doctor fixes you up, we'll have plenty of time to talk."

Gaston looked into Galen's eyes. Galen saw there the look of the dying. Galen had seen that look more than a few times in his career. There was a certain look about people who were dying, and not just the obvious trauma victims, struggling in their last minutes of life. This look required no blood, no missing limbs and no broken bones. This look came from inside, from the core of their being.

Gaston started to talk again and reached up to remove the oxygen mask that hindered his speech.

Galen reached for the old man's hand and stopped him from removing the mask. "Al, you need this. It will help you. Leave it on, I can still hear you."

14

Gaston hesitated for a second and removed the mask anyway.

"Galen, I need you to...," his face tightened into a knot of pain, "...to do something for me."

"Sure Al. We're doing all that we can. Just hang on 'til we get to the hospital."

Audra was trying to get the oxygen mask back on his face. Gaston kept turning his head in an effort to avoid it.

"No, Galen... something else," Gaston said, still attempting to push the mask away. He was becoming agitated trying to communicate while in so much pain.

Galen continued to hook up the heart monitor as he listened to Gaston's raspy voice.

It is especially hard for an ambulance crew to work on someone they know and care about. Galen was trying to save the professor's life, while at the same time, trying to take the time Gaston wanted, but maybe did not have. Galen wanted nothing more than to talk to the professor and was doing everything he could to keep him alive. He was doing his best to ensure many lengthy conversations with his friend in the future.

"Galen, please," Gaston croaked, "Listen...to me."

Galen looked at Gaston again, trying unsuccessfully to avoid his eyes. The look was worse. Death was close.

Galen managed to get the monitor hooked up and began transmitting the readings to the hospital. Galen had done all he could for now and turned his full attention to speaking with his friend..

"Galen, you must do something for me, if I... die."

Gaston could only whisper now and Galen leaned close, holding his hand. "Don't you give up, Al. I'm not givin' up, so don't you give up!"

Gaston shook his head to indicate that he had not given up. "A box, on my...my bookshelf, in my...study." Gaston gasped for breath, "a wooden box, send it to...to." Gaston was struggling to speak and the expressions on his face changed in a random pattern of fear, pain and anxiety, like a kaleidoscope of emotions.

15

"Send it to...Paxon, Prof...essor Paxon, at Baxterrrr... College."

Audra tapped Galen on the shoulder and nodded at the heart monitor. The monitor indicated Gaston's erratic heart rhythm was steadily worsening.

Galen turned back to the professor, tears filling his eyes. "You stay with me, Al!" Galen choked out, "we're almost there!" Galen wanted so badly to tell Gaston he was going to be okay, but Galen had never lied to a patient and would not start now.

Audra put the oxygen mask back over Gaston's face. Galen held his friend's limp hand as he constantly checked the equipment. He leaned close when he heard Gaston begin to speak again. The oxygen mask muffled the professor's speech, but Galen could understand him.

Audra was on the radio with the hospital, who was asking for a patient update and an ETA.

"Galen," the professor groaned. A small squeeze from Galen's hand let the professor know he was there. "Call him; tell...him that ...

The professor squeezed his eyes closed in pain, and Galen could not understand what he was saying. The professor then took and deep breath and tried to continue.

"Eater...of...hearts."

Gaston's eyes looked glassy and stared straight ahead as he spoke. His lips were a pale blue and the look of death had washed the other emotions from his face.

Audra was taking another blood pressure reading. The look on her face was enough to tell Galen it was very low.

Galen wiped at the tears in his eyes then turned back to Gaston.

The professor looked up, meeting Galen's eyes. "Galen," he said, trying to focus, "I...I...love you." The old man squeezed Galen's hand then pulled it toward his cheek.

The ambulance was only two minutes away from the hospital when the heart monitor signaled a shockable pattern.

Audra, who had been intently watching the heart monitor, shouted that the patient was in v-fib. Knowing what was coming next, she changed her position in the cramped ambulance.

Galen tried to set aside his emotions and got back into his role as a professional paramedic. He was reaching for the defibrillator when an indicator on the monitor signaled that the patient was in ventricular fibrillation.

"Let's defib!" Galen shouted. He had trouble positioning the defibrillator unit paddles through his tear-blurred eyes.

"Clear!" Galen said, making sure Audra was not in contact with the patient.

Gaston reacted to the shock with a spasmodic jerk, heaving up from the gurney.

Galen leaned back, and looked at Audra, who closely watched the monitor.

"Nothing!" she shouted.

Again, Galen positioned the paddles.

"Clear!"

Gaston jerked again and the monitor signaled a weak heartbeat.

"Got it!" Audra shouted, intently staring at the monitor.

Galen replaced the paddles on the defib unit and moved to the professor's head. "Al!" Galen shouted as he checked for a carotid pulse. "Can you hear me?" Gaston reacted with only a twitch in his face. Galen knew it was useless.

The monitor still signaled a heartbeat, although very faint and erratic.

"Al, I love you too," Galen said, leaning close.

Galen would never know that Gaston had heard and understood because the professor could only react with another twitch.

The heart monitor flat lined this time as the rig was pulling into the emergency room gate.

Chapter 3

The old priest, (named Wilbur by Master Browning, Mendalla-Umba by his father) gave Tobias a drink of a medicine-brew he had concocted. He watched Tobias take the drink, then lay down on the priest's bunk, delirious and in a lot of pain. He moaned softly and his eyes rolled crazily behind their lids.

Wilbur, having no family of his own, shared a cabin with four other slaves. He had asked the other slaves to find another place to bunk down for the night, leaving him alone with the runner. He had also asked the rest of the slaves to try to get a good night's sleep. Mendalla-Umba did not want the field bosses to be suspicious that the slaves might have been up all night, doing that 'African mumbo-jumbo stuff' again. The old priest would probably be up the entire night himself, which would be bad enough.

He lit a couple of candles, which cast just enough light for him to see. His shadow moved upon the wooden walls of the cabin like a dark ghost haunting the night.

He left the cabin and retrieved a burlap sack he kept stored in a hollow tree at the edge of the camp. He kept his secret things in the sack, things necessary for his duties as leopard-skin priest. Among these things were various small bones, dried leaves, a few pebbles, and a coin.

If Master Browning knew he was still practicing the religion he had brought with him from Africa, they would undoubtedly beat him again. He had taken several beatings for his faith, refusing to drop the practice and have the white man's god forced upon him. Instead, he and the rest of the camp kept their beliefs a secret.

There was no name for his religion, for it was the only one his people had ever known and everyone abided by its rules. His people had called upon the same gods for millennia. It was their way of life. Their beliefs were the one thing the white man could not strip them of, though try as they might. In this camp, Mendalla-Umba kept the faith alive.

Master Browning wanted them to *pray*, to *Jesus*. He pressed his beliefs upon the slaves many times, forcing them to listen. He told them there was only *one* God, and Jesus was his son. Mendalla-Umba could not, *would not*, pray to Jesus. Jesus could not make his spirit fly and could not talk to him like the gods of his fathers. The old priest did not understand the white man's God, but understood his own as well as anyone. He had seen their power, and knew of their wisdom.

The gods had been powerful tonight, showing their dark powers to all present. The spell was mighty and required the energy from all of the camp to cast it. A spell such as this one was rare. The gods must look into the heart of the man asking for the spell, and judge that he is worthy. They must also determine if the priest is worthy, and his soul clean. They must settle upon the sacrifice to be given. When this is decided, it would be told to the priest. It is then up to him, to the extent of his knowledge and his powers, to call forth the justice of the gods. If all is in order, they would begin the ritual.

Mendalla-Umba's people had always lived by this system. They only used the spells to battle evil, never for personal gain. The old priest looked back upon his first spell. It had been cast upon the evil spirit-creatures of the sea. These spirits had eaten most of the fish from the sea and the village's fishing nets brought in little food. They depended upon the fish for nourishment and the empty nets caused much concern among the villagers.

The village elders summoned Mendalla-Umba to their council, directing him to speak with the gods.

Mendalla-Umba pleaded with the gods to help them, and used all of his powers to persuade them. He performed his ritual as his father had taught him.

The fish had been few before the spell, barely enough to feed the children, but within a few days, the fish were back. The villagers once again harvested their food from the sea. In return for their deed, the gods asked only that the first day's harvest be sacrificed to them for their great task!

Mendalla-Umba had cast spells against the evil spirits that caused sickness among his people. He had cast spells against the insects that ravaged their scanty crops, and against the evil spirits that dried up their land, holding back the rain.

If the cause was worthy, and if the heart of he who asked of them was honorable and pure, the gods would consider the request. The gods would then name their price, to be paid in the form of a sacrifice for granting the deed.

Mendalla-Umba did not know how the gods battled the evil, for he was merely a man. He knew only the outcome. The rains would come, the insects would die, and his people healed.

If his people died, then they would know their hearts were not noble, or their faith was lacking. If the rains did not come, it was because of some injustice his people had done to anger the gods. The gods were powerful, the gods were honorable, and the gods were *just*.

Mendalla-Umba retrieved a small crystal from his burlap bag. He had found it while working the fields for Master Browning. The gods had now asked him for it. The gods had told him of their plan to bring forth a mighty servant to carry out the task requested of them. The gods would call forth the *Eater of Hearts* to aid the running slave.

Mendalla-Umba had trembled when the gods told him of their decision. He had heard of the Eater of Hearts, but had not thought of it being sent here, for this spell. It was one of the most powerful of the servants of the gods and its power struck fear into the heart of the old priest.

The ultimate sacrifice was usually that of a human life. Mendalla-Umba had only cast one such spell, many years ago in his homeland.

At that time, the evil spirits that dwelled below the ground began to heave the earth. The sea had licked the land with a furious wave, destroying most of the village and killing many people. The crops had been washed away, threatening the remaining villagers with starvation. Huge cracks had opened in the rocks, threatening to release the evil spirits from below.

Mendalla-Umba had flown with the gods as he had earlier this night. They would require the sacrifice of a warrior to stop the evil spirits. The village had gathered for their energy. A mighty warrior had volunteered his life, just as the gods had said one would, to save the village.

The gods had asked a mighty price for the spell that Tobias sought. The gods had not seen Tobias' life as the ultimate sacrifice, for to Tobias, death would be no sacrifice at all. It would be a release. Tobias the runner was dead already, as the gods saw it.

Instead, Tobias had been given a mission; a mission that would prove to be more of an offering than immediate death. Tobias had also given of himself, his right hand, for the spell that he had called for. Mendalla-Umba had made the cut quickly, hoping Tobias would suffer as little as possible. The bones had yielded easily to the sharp ax. The potion would alleviate the pain for a while. The gods were pleased, and the gods were wise.

Mendalla-Umba took the small crystal, and placed it in a bowl. He then took Tobias' severed right hand, and like a hideous inverted udder, squeezed the fingers to milk them of their blood. The bloody stone was retrieved from the bowl, and placed in the palm of the severed hand. In a death grip like no other, Mendalla-Umba wrapped the fingers of the hand around the stone. Wax from a candle was then dripped between the fingers, sealing the stone inside.

Mendalla-Umba walked over to check on Tobias. The potion he had drank was working now, giving Tobias a fitful, though much needed, sleep.

The priest walked outside with the hand. The air was cool and dew had fallen over the camp. The fires had burned down to a bed of furious coals. Mendalla-Umba dropped the hand into the center of the coal bed and with a long stick, raked the coals to cover it.

The priest sat before the fire. The smell of burning flesh was immediately noticeable. He could hear a sound above the quiet crackling of the fire. Leaning closer, he heard a faint hissing and sizzling, as blood from the severed end of the hand dripped upon the hot coals.

The bed of coals had been smokeless before the priest placed the gift to the gods into it. Now, a column of smoke resembling a light gray snake, wriggled its tail as it climbed into the sky to meet with the gods.

The priest began to chant, quietly, almost to himself, but he knew the gods would hear. It was well past midnight and the woods surrounding the camp were completely quiet except for the sounds of crickets and an occasional toad. Mendalla-Umba sat with his eyes closed, chanting quietly, until he lost track of time. The chanting was automatic. He need not think about it to do it.

His mind wandered back to Old Africa. He remembered his father, one of the most powerful leopard-skin priests ever. He thought about the great pride that his father had known when Mendalla-Umba, his only son, had become the Kuaar Muon of the village. His joy had been mixed with sorrow, for his father knew the burden a priest carried upon his shoulders and how it weighed upon the mind and body. A priest must be strong to serve the gods and his people. A priest must be willing to kill to appease the will of the gods. Emotions must be set aside and not allowed to interfere with judgment. Now, Mendalla-Umba knew what it was to maim, to cripple, to the same end. Although his heart was heavy, he knew he had only done his duty.

Reflecting upon the events of the night, the old priest noticed a sudden brightness from the fire, just before he felt increased warmth upon his face. The brightness had been powerful enough to sense through closed eyes. Upon opening them, Mendalla-Umba was nearly blinded.

A small orb, about the size of a child's fist, glowed brightly about three feet above the ground, directly over the fire. With a light nearly as intense as that of the sun, Mendalla-Umba could barely look at it. Through squinted eyes, he stared in amazement. The priest hardly noticed the few, large drops of rain pelting his shoulders and the top of his head. Within a minute, the light rain turned to a heavy downpour. Mendalla-Umba could hear the hissing fire as the rain drowned it out. He could feel the heat upon his face decrease as the rain seemingly cooled the orb, dimming its previous brightness.

The bed of coals was soon a wet pile of ash. The orb maintained its position above the fire pit, but dimmed to a faint yellow glow. The rain continued, sending small streams of runoff throughout the camp. The priest was aware of the voices of some of the slaves, probably complaining about getting wet through leaking roofs.

Mendalla-Umba kept his eyes on the mysterious thing before him. After a moment, the orb dropped, all at once, as if some invisible hand had suddenly released it. It landed with a squishy *plop!*

The rain stopped as suddenly as it had started. The camp became quiet again. The rain had quieted the crickets and toads and now the only sound was the dripping of water from the roofs of the cabins in the camp.

Mendalla-Umba cautiously approached the fallen orb. He probed at it with a stick, trying to rake it from the muddy ashes. Upon getting it on open ground, he noticed it was no longer glowing. His heart pounded rapidly at the thought of what he had just witnessed. Without touching it, he held his hand close to see if he could feel any warmth. Sensing nothing, he cautiously picked it up. It was only slightly warm. He carried it over to the

23

well and rinsed it off in a puddle that had collected around its base.

Tobias groaned as Mendalla-Umba entered his cabin. The old priest studied the orb intently as he approached a candle for a better look. It was marvelous! The gods had shown Mendalla-Umba a power he had never seen before. He silently praised them for their awesome power and wisdom.

Mendalla-Umba placed the orb in a small leather pouch that he also took from his secret burlap bag. He placed the pouch beside the bed where Tobias tossed about. The potion was wearing off and he could see the fear and pain on the runner's face.

He took his burlap bag back to its hiding place and looked into the sky. The stars shone brightly and no trace of a rain cloud could be seen. In the east, a faint pink glow lined the horizon. Morning was near and Wilbur would soon be expected in the fields.

Chapter 4

Tobias awoke with a start, having been replaying the events of the night in his half-sleeping mind. He jerked himself upward, trying to support himself with his hands only to awkwardly discover the amputation of his right hand. He hoped it had all been a dream, a very bad dream.

His arm burned like rampant fire. Blood-soaked rags covered the stump, and Tobias shook it briefly to rouse the swarming flies that had gathered there.

Wilbur returned to the cabin, void of the body paint, dressed in the same tattered clothes he had worn the day before. "Time to run, Tobias," he said. "Time to get your pitiful ass as far away from here as you can." There was no sympathy in Wilbur's words, although there was in his heart.

Tobias had gotten exactly what he had asked for and now had to pay the price. The spell had been cast, and its completion depended upon Tobias' strength and will. Mendalla-Umba had bid the will of Tobias and the gods. To Wilbur the slave, his concern now turned to being caught harboring an escaped slave. The slave catchers would probably pass though here, led by their dogs, and suspicion alone would be enough to warrant severe punishment. Wilbur had to do all that he could to protect himself and the other slaves from being incriminated in any way.

Tobias stood, swaying slightly as he tried to regain his balance. His head swam and he felt weak from the loss of blood. He steadied himself by leaning against the wall.

Tobias held his stump-arm upward and studied it. Streaks of dried blood ran from under the saturated rags, like dark lightning bolts from a gore-soaked cloud. Flies continually swarmed the dressings, buzzing about in a frenzy.

"Here's you a little blade and a piece of flint," Wilbur said. "It might help you out some along your way." He pushed the small knife and flint into Tobias' pocket. He then took Tobias' left hand into his own, and tied the drawstrings of the leather pouch around his wrist. He looked into Tobias' tired eyes. Fear and pain were waging a battle to control the runner's face.

"Whoever ya' give this to will be cursed," he said, trying to avoid Tobias' eyes. "The gods say to give it to him as a gift, and yo' spell will be done. Ya' got to give it freely, and don't let anyone steal it from ya'. "Wilbur pulled a rag from his back pocket and used it to reinforce the dressing on Tobias' stump. "It's got to pass from the *giver* to the *taker*, and the taker will be cursed."

Tobias started to protest, feeling there was no way he could make the trek back to Master Richards' plantation. He decided against saying anything, only nodding his head in confirmation.

"What is it?" Tobias asked, bouncing the pouch in his hand, trying to get a feel of its weight and shape.

"This po' old man don't know. The gods call it *biit loac*, The Eater of Hearts." Wilbur rubbed his face, a now familiar gesture to Tobias. "Don't go lookin' at that thing in the pouch. It's a mirror of fear, *and it knows what's in the hearts of men*." Wilbur took Tobias' shoulders in his hands. "You just got to git it to yo' Master, that's all the gods say. The gods will take care of the rest. Now you go on and git. Remember, I ain't never seen ya', and you ain't never been here." Wilbur turned his back to Tobias. "You go on back into the woods," he said. "It'll be light soon, and if y'all gits caught here, the spell will never be done."

Tobias was too stunned to say anything, and didn't know what to say anyway, so he headed for the door. Swaying like a drunk, Tobias made his way to the woods. The morning light was still faint and the air was cool. A glow in the east gave Tobias his bearings and he turned northward.

Wilbur stood in the door of the cabin. Tobias looked back at him. They exchanged glances and then Tobias was gone.

The ways of the gods were sometimes strange, but their will had been done. Wilbur felt that his duty was over. He knew what Tobias was facing and tears filled his eyes. He had not even had the time to get Tobias some food for his journey. Although that couldn't be helped, Wilbur felt a tug at his heart for the runner. *Good luck, Karmanna, son of Harub,* Wilbur thought to himself. Tobias had not told him his African name, but the gods had.

The other slaves were beginning to wake up and they had a full day's work ahead of them.

.   .   .

Tobias slowly made his way north, keeping the rising sun on his right. After about an hour he came to a stream where he began to replenish his lack of body fluids. Drinking deeply of the water, Tobias wondered how he would ever make it back. That was the last thing he had expected to have to do.

Tobias had expected to die. He thought his life would be demanded as his sacrifice to the gods and had accepted it. Being asked to return to his plantation was something he had not anticipated. He felt he would never make it. His mission sent him straight toward the slave catchers instead of away from them. His arm hurt worse than any beating he had ever known.

Tobias lay next to the stream for a few moments, thinking. It had taken six days to find the priest. He had stopped at two other camps inquiring about a Kuaar Muon, and they had directed him to where Wilbur lived. He had been physically strong then, able to move quickly, to hide, and to run. He had been nearly exhausted by the time he had found the priest. Now he was beyond exhausted. He was also crippled.

He considered just staying where he was, never to face Master Richards. He also considered how that would just waste the spell, letting Master Richards go on as before.

No, he could not do that. Wilbur and his entire camp had risked helping him. He could not come this far and just let it go.

27

He must dig deep within himself, somehow manage to get back and carry out his task. He had vowed to the gods that Master Richards would know their justice and fear their power. Whatever the gods had in store for Master Richards, it started with Tobias' journey back home.

Still lying along the side of the stream, Tobias wondered what was in the pouch. He felt it again through the soft leather. It was round, and weighed as much as three or four hen's eggs. He wondered what it was that would carry out this spell.

Let Master Richards be the first one to see its power, he thought.

He stood up and looked into the stream. A crayfish was silently searching for food among the rocks in the shallow water.

"Hey, Mistuh Craw-Daddy," Tobias said, licking his lips, "you sho' look like a fine meal to me." Using his teeth, Tobias untied the leather pouch and laid it upon the bank.

Catching a crayfish with one hand proved to be quite a challenge. He managed to catch four of them. It was a meager meal, but he would find more food later. He spent about fifteen minutes wading in the shallows before moving on.

Before he left the water, he took a few minutes to wash some of the blood from himself. He sat down on a rock and managed to rinse off his right arm. A tendril of reddish-brown water snaked its way downstream from Tobias before diluting enough to run clear again.

Tobias retrieved the pouch from the bank and slipped his hand through the looped strings, drawing them tight with his teeth. He felt slightly better and the small gain in strength would carry him a long way before he stopped again.

Recovery from the exhaustion, hunger, and loss of his hand would require time. Time Tobias didn't have. He was moving closer to the slave catchers, and had a long way to go before his journey ended. He needed strength, sleep, and food.

He moved rather slowly that day, making his way through the woods. At least the shade of the trees kept the hot August sun off his back as he traveled. The woods were thick, almost shutting out the rays of the sun completely. Only a few narrow beams of light penetrated the leaves, spotting the ground beneath with round blotches of light. He felt safe in the woods. The chances of anyone finding him here were slim.

The same could not be said for the rest of the trip. After he left the cover of the forest, Tobias would be in the open more often. He would travel during darkness, trying to pick up a few miles each night, making whatever headway he safely could in the daytime.

Tobias reached the Northern edge of the woods about two hours before sunset that first day. A tobacco plantation lay in a valley to the north. About three miles to the west, Tobias noted a narrow strip of woods winding in an irregular path Northward, probably bordering the same stream he had crossed this morning. Tobias would rest here until well after nightfall. Then he would decide if he should follow the road or the stream.

He poked around in the woods looking for anything Mother Nature may offer in the way of food. After finding only a few edible roots, Tobias happened upon a wild apple tree. The tree yielded some small, bitter apples. The first apple instantly dried his mouth, but after gobbling three or four his stomach was temporarily satisfied. He wished his pants sported pockets, for he would have liked to take a couple of the sour apples with him. But, given the fact he had a hard time carrying anything, he would pass, hoping to find more food along the way.

Tobias began to move deeper into the woods when he realized he had left the apple cores lying on the ground, a sign that the slave hunters would surely notice when the dogs led them here. He picked up the cores, wondering what he should do with them. The only thing he could think of was to eat them. He ground the gristly cores between his teeth as he looked for a place to sleep.

Tobias found a dry creek bed and lay down between two large rocks. The base of the bed was mostly small pebbles with larger rocks scattered along its length. The large rocks were cool. Tobias moved close to feel the comfort.

He inspected the dressing on his arm. Except for the edges, which were wet with sweat, the dressing was dry. The blood had hardened to give the dressing a stiff, cast-like feel. The arm still hurt madly, but after so long, Tobias did not think about it. Pulling the bloody rags between his teeth and left hand, he managed to tighten the dressing that had loosened during the day.

He slept for a while in the creek bed, and then lay thinking about his next move. If he followed the stream, it would offer him the opportunity to wade. Wading through the stream would cover his scent, hopefully confusing the slave catchers' dogs. However, wading at night with low visibility could be dangerous. This area was infested with snakes, including cottonmouths, which were poisonous. Although the stream looked small, Tobias felt it could still harbor an alligator or two, which added to his concern.

He decided to follow the road. There was a better chance of being seen there, but it was a much safer route overall. He would make better time traveling the road and could duck into the roadside shrubs should someone come along.

After the cool darkness had fallen, Tobias made his way to the road. The dusty trail still felt warm to Tobias' bare feet, having absorbed the warmth of the day's sunshine. He moved quietly Northward, never breaking his stride until he heard a dog barking.

He panicked at first; diving into the woods, ready to run if necessary. He then realized the barking was not that of the slave-catchers' bloodhounds, but a yapping kind of bark from a smaller dog. Tobias came out of the woods and began to run. He was afraid that someone might be aroused by the dog and come to investigate the cause of its barking. Wherever it was, Tobias hoped it stayed there.

It took all of his energy, but he managed to run until he could no longer hear the dog. He slowed again to a walk and tried to catch his breath. The short run had caused a pain in his side, like the point of a knife working its way between his ribs. He began to get dizzy and sweat poured from his brow.

Tobias had to stop. He walked to the side of the road feeling queasy, and vomited before he could sit down. Dryness returned to his mouth, along with the taste of sour apples. He leaned against a tree and drew deep, staggering breaths. The pouch remained nestled in the crook of his right arm and it began to feel warm. Tobias felt the warmth in his arm and his side, still painful from running. He grasped the pouch in his left hand and felt the warmth course the length of his arm. It felt like warm sunshine and not only warmed his skin, but heated his insides as well. Like a hot liquid, the power from the pouch surged through him, renewing him. He looked upon the pouch and noticed small rays of light escaping from the pouches' loose bindings.

The gods are watching out for me, Tobias thought, *helping me along*. This thought restored some of his waning strength and again let him run.

Tobias alternated running and walking for the rest of the night. The pouch continued to radiate its healing warmth and he nestled it close, keeping it between his stump-arm and his side.

The area he now traveled was mostly farmland. Planted fields, almost ready for harvest, lay all around him. Far to the west, Tobias spotted a column of smoke. It was probably from the chimney of a farmhouse. Birds began to flutter about in the pre-dawn light. The sun had not yet risen above the horizon and Tobias began looking for a good place to hide.

For a long time, the only sound Tobias could hear was the whispering shuffle of his feet on the dirt road. Suddenly, a rattling, metallic sound from up ahead startled him. It sounded distant, and Tobias could see nothing past the curve in the road before him. He quietly bolted off the path, seeking refuge in a narrow band of trees and brush. He crawled into some low bushes, taking a position that allowed him to see without being seen.

The rattling sound grew louder in the quiet morning air. He thought it was probably a wagon traveling down the road. Next, Tobias heard the sound of a horse as it noisily exhaled. The slave watched the road closely, waiting for a glimpse of the approaching wagon.

The sounds grew ever closer, and Tobias could not believe he had not spotted the wagon yet. He heard voices, but could not make out the words. The sounds moved surprisingly close, yet he could still see nothing on the road. Tobias moved to a state of near panic. He heard people talking, but could see no one. As if they were the voices of ghosts, they came ever closer.

"Git that wagon over here!" a disembodied voice called. Tobias swung around. About fifty yards away, in the hayfield behind him, Tobias spotted the source of the sounds. Six slaves and a white foreman were there with a wagon, preparing to harvest the hay. They had traveled in the field, parallel to the road and Tobias had not seen them coming.

Tobias froze like a scared rabbit. He flattened himself against the ground in an effort to avoid being seen.

The foreman sat upon a large, gray horse. A pistol was tucked into the back of his pants. He was facing away from Tobias, shouting orders to the slaves.

Tobias was twenty feet from the edge of the field and the slaves would eventually work their way toward him. If he did not get out of there soon, he was bound to be discovered.

Half of the slaves carried sickles, with which to cut the hay. The other slaves would then load the cut hay onto the wagon for transport to the plantation.

Tobias planned to scurry away when the slaves were at the far end of the field. He would seek a safer hiding spot on the other side of the road, reducing his immediate danger. As opportunities allowed, he could slowly put some distance between him and the field boss.

The pouch began to grow warmer along Tobias' side. The heat ran through him like a tidal wave. His muscles trembled and his eyelids fluttered as he watched the slaves move away from him. The foreman walked his horse alongside the wagon. The slaves were working diligently, but making agonizingly slow progress. The morning sun had cleared the horizon and cast long shadows behind the working slaves.

Tobias' heart skipped a beat when he saw a large, playful dog come bounding into the field. The dog was exploring the edge of the woods, some hundred yards away. Tobias had to move quickly, before the dog realized he was there.

He turned as quietly as possible and moved toward the road. His heart pounded so hard he could feel his pulse in his eyes. He looked up and down the road to see if anything was coming, and then turned to see if he could spot the dog.

Seeing neither, he crouched low and crossed the road.

Ten yards of trees and brush separated him from the next field. He slowed as he approached the tangled growth, frantically searching for a place to enter.

He spotted a small dent in the thick brush a few yards to his right and ducked for it. Dropping to his hand and knees, he kept the pouch close as he entered the brush. He discovered it was mostly briars, a thorny cross between a bush and a vine. It clutched at him with a thousand tiny claws. Tobias pulled and tugged, trying to make his way through the tangle, hoping to quietly free himself of its grip. He dropped flat on his stomach and dug in with his elbows and feet, desperately trying to make progress. The briars hung on relentlessly, their thorns tearing his clothes and piercing his skin.

Just ahead of him the briars ended, giving way to a scattering of hardwood saplings and high weeds. He struggled against the tangle of thorns, making little headway. He turned and tried to free himself from his captor. It seemed that as he broke the grip of one of the barb-laden vines, two more snared him in another spot.

Tobias thought he heard something crunching in the brush across the road. He lay still, hoping he had imagined it. A joyous howl from the dog made him realize he had been discovered. The dog had picked up Tobias' scent from his previous hiding place. He made another instinctive howl, ready for the chase.

The scent was clear and fresh. It was as visible to the dog as a lighthouse to a lost ship.

The pouch pulsated as if it held a live animal. Tobias made a wild, tearing leap to free himself. Driving with his legs, he pumped furiously toward the edge of the briar patch. With a tremendous burst of energy he broke free. Bits of his ragged clothes stayed behind, forever entrapped by the thorny bush. The thorns cut deep grooves in Tobias' shoulders and down his back. His forehead was tattooed with a criss-cross pattern of cuts and scratches. Blood oozed down his brow and ran in tiny streams down each side of his broad nose.

He broke into the next field and bolted diagonally for the woods that bordered it. His heart pumped furiously and his legs felt weak with the fear of being caught.

The dog also had a difficult time making it through the briars, but had gotten through much quicker than Tobias had. He continued to howl and bark, nose to the ground, following the strong scent.

The foreman looked up from his work, eyes searching for the dog. *He probably flushed out a rabbit,* he thought, *or maybe a deer.* He entertained the thought of checking it out. Some venison would be nice if he could get a clear shot at it. He pulled the pistol from the back of his pants and jabbed the horse with the heels of his boots. The horse surged forward and the foreman pulled the reigns hard to the right.

Tobias was only a few yards from the woods, running hard, when the dog got its first glimpse of him. The dog bellowed again in his excitement, streaking across the field. He now tracked the slave by sight, allowing him faster pursuit.

Tobias entered the woods and began to look for a weapon. He frantically searched for a big stick, or a rock, anything with which to defend himself. A layer of brown pine needles covered the ground. He continued to move deeper into the woods, scanning the ground for a weapon as he went.

The dog entered the woods a few seconds later. A big, heavy mongrel, the dog darted quickly between the pine trees. Within moments, he was on Tobias' heels, teeth bared, massive jaws snapping.

Tobias sensed how close the dog was but could find no weapon. Rather than be caught from behind, he turned to face the beast. The pouch was hot, vibrating wildly at his side.

The dog was upon him.

It leaped.

Tobias raised his left arm in defense.

Chapter 5

The ride back to the station from the hospital was quiet.

Further attempts in the ER to resuscitate Professor Gaston had failed. The driver, Bob, and Audra, sensed the sadness Galen felt at the loss of his friend.

Any run that encounters death will be a somber run indeed. The members of the emergency crew will question themselves for days afterward, wondering if there was anything that they could have done differently. Within the next couple of days, the entire staff would critique the run discussing all of the particulars. This was routine for all runs that the ambulance made, regardless of the type of call. After the critique, the crew would think about what they had discussed and decide as a group if anything should have been done differently. This exercise was intended as a learning tool. It allowed less experienced crew members to learn what the more experienced ones would have done in similar circumstances.

Galen had stayed with the professor the entire time at the hospital. Audra had filed all of the necessary run forms and gathered supplies, bothering Galen only for his signature on the run sheet.

Galen had held back the tears as best he could. Normally, he was not a very emotional person, but thinking of the friend he had lost made him realize how much he would miss him. The long conversations, the interesting stories, and the advice were now gone. Galen no longer had the professor to lean on. He then realized he had lost the only person he could call a *true friend*. He buried his face in his hands and silently wept.

After returning to the station, Galen retreated to the radio room to do some paperwork. He needed to get his mind occupied with something other than his loss. On the way, he passed by the soda machine. He stopped and hit a button. After a mechanical groan and a couple of clicks, a can of Pepsi rolled through the little trap door at the bottom of the machine with a clang. *At least something went right today,* he thought as he reached for it.

Audra's heart ached for Galen, sensing how badly he felt. She had not known the professor herself; not well anyway. She had exchanged greetings with him on the sidewalks downtown, but no more than that. She thought she would give Galen some time alone, and then talk to him. Perhaps she could even cheer him up a little.

Audra held much admiration for Galen, as did everyone on the department. He was so *professional,* so good at what he did. His dedication to the department was obvious. Speaking at the school during fire prevention week, teaching first-aid classes, and participating in training drills were often done on Galen's personal time.

He also treated everyone as an equal. There were only four women volunteers, but Galen had made them all feel welcome; unlike some of the other guys who felt women had no place on a fire department.

Galen came out of the radio room and went to check out the ambulance

Audra was inside the rig, changing the linen on the gurney. She looked up when she saw him.

"Hi, Galen," she said, gathering the used linens. "How are you doing?"

"I'll be alright," he said as he climbed into the rig.

Audra dumped the linens on the floor outside of the ambulance and took a seat in the rig. She could tell Galen was still feeling the pain of losing his friend. His face carried an expression she had never seen there before.

"You must have been close," she said. "I'm so sorry, Galen."

Galen sat down next to her. "Yeah, he was a pretty special old guy," he said. "I'm gonna miss him."

Galen did not seem to be in the mood to talk yet so Audra decided to leave him alone.

"If there's anything I can do, let me know. Okay?"

"Yeah, thanks, Audra," Galen said rather absently.

Audra got up to leave, but Galen gently took her wrist in his hand.

"Audra, did you hear what Al was talking about before he died?"

Audra thought for a moment. "Some of it," she said, and sat back down.

"He said something about a box, and wanted me to send it somewhere?" Galen asked as he tried to replay the scene in his mind.

"Yeah, in his study, on the bookshelf," she said. "What was that all about?"

"I'm not sure. Do you remember where he said to send it?"

Audra put the tip of her index finger on her upper lip and stared fixedly at the floor. "Was it, Baxter College?"

"I don't know," Galen said. "It was such a strange thing for Al to be talking about. It didn't seem that important to me, but I think it was important to Al."

"I think it was a Mr. Paxon, at Baxter College," Audra offered. "It did seem like a strange conversation."

Galen shook his head, "You'd think I could remember the last request of a dying friend."

Audra chanced a brief smile and said, "I think saving his life was your foremost concern."

Galen nodded.

"I guess I can find out. There can't be too many 'Baxter' Colleges around.

"He probably has the name and address around his house somewhere," Audra volunteered.

"Yeah. I've got a key, so I can go check it out later."

"Good idea."

Galen fell silent again and Audra got up to leave. She was glad he was talking, but she could tell he was far from being himself.

Again, Galen stopped her.

"One more thing before you go," he said, "did you get the last part of what he said?"

Audra replayed the scene in her mind.

"He said that he loved you."

"No, before that, something about *eating...hearts?*"

Audra remembered that part, too. She could not make out all of it, but she remembered that part.

"It did sound like that," she said. "Like 'eater hearts', I thought he might have been referring to his condition, a heart attack or something."

Galen nodded again. "Yeah, I bet that's it," he said. "Probably something about a *better heart*. I wish he'd had one."

Galen sat in the ambulance for a few more minutes. Audra left for a short time, and then returned with clean linens. He looked up to her as she climbed into the rig.

Galen was fond of Audra. She had that "girl-next-door" look about her. She was attractive, but not in a stunning sort of way. She was a little spunky and had an *almost* tomboy way about her. She always wore her hair in an efficiently short pony-tail while she worked. Galen had only seen her a few times when she had worn her hair different. She worked at Rockford Community Hospital as an X-ray technician. He occasionally saw her there and would always chat with her if they had the time.

Audra began to put the clean sheets on the gurney. She was quite aware of Galen silently staring at her. It made her feel a little uncomfortable. Having completed her task, she turned to him.

"What are you staring at, Galen?"

Galen did not answer.

"Galen?"

Galen shook himself out of his trance.

"I'm sorry, I was just...thinking."

39

Audra blushed for what she had been thinking; almost wishing he *had* been staring at her. She knew by the tone of his voice and the look on his face that he had indeed been somewhere else, deep in thought.

"I was thinking, Audra," Galen started, "that you might go with me over to the professor's place tomorrow."

Audra thought for a moment, gently nibbling her upper lip. She wanted to help Galen get over this personal tragedy, but at the same time wanted to give him some room. She looked at him and saw the look of sadness and fear play across his gentle features. He was wounded, hurt and in pain. Audra could not let that go unchanged.

"Sure," she said. "What time do you want to go?"

"I'm off for forty-eight, after twelve noon. What time do you get off work?"

"I'm on the seven-to-three shift for the rest of the week."

Galen shrugged and said, "how about six or so?"

"That's fine with me. Want to meet here?"

"Sounds good," Galen replied. "How long are you on call tonight?"

Audra looked at her watch. "Just about long enough to wash up and get my purse."

Galen looked at his watch, too. "Jees, it's almost midnight," he said in disbelief.

"Yep, and five a.m. comes awful early when you're on call 'til midnight. So, I'll see you here at six tomorrow."

Galen nodded, "Okay, and thanks for everything, Audra. I appreciate it."

"Anytime," Audra said, not knowing exactly what she was being thanked for. She smiled warmly at him and disappeared, leaving Galen sitting in the back of the ambulance.

After Audra had left, Galen sought out an empty bunk and lay staring at the bottom of the bunk above him. No matter how hard he tried to think of something else, the events of the evening played across his mind. As if projected like a movie from the depths of his brain, visions of Al Gaston flashed upon the inside of his eyelids.

Galen tried to fight off the depression that had set into him. He had been around this business long enough to know about what many paramedics called 'The Wall'. This 'Wall', a kind of burnout state of mind, was just beginning to be understood. It usually took place after a particularly disturbing call, but not always. Often being attributed to the constant exposure to death, pain, and the gruesome scenes emergency workers often encountered on the job.

Galen had never experienced a head-on collision with the Wall, but had side-swiped it a few times. He struggled now to keep himself centered, and put things into the proper perspective.

To Galen, becoming a Paramedic created an instant conflict. Wanting to help people who were injured or sick required a warm, loving heart. It required getting involved with the patient, to share his pain, to feel his emotions.

On the flip side, a person could only withstand these emotional storms for a short time before seeking refuge. Refuge was a cold heart. Do your job, but do not get emotionally involved. Keep your distance.

The result was to bury those emotions. Keep them hidden away, stored in a dark closet somewhere in the hall of memories. However, when the closet was full, you faced The Wall.

Galen was at that point right now and he knew it.

.   .   .

At six o'clock the next evening, Galen stood talking to some other people on the department. He was dressed in civilian clothes; an Air Jordan t-shirt and jeans. A small group of people had gathered around the soda machine, smoking cigarettes and sipping cold soft drinks. It was the only area in the station where smoking was allowed and there was often a small group gathered there with their heads in a rolling cloud of smoke. The large overhead doors were open to take advantage of the northerly breeze. The newly waxed fire trucks gleamed under the station's fluorescent lights. Galen saw Audra's new red Mustang pull into the parking lot.

She waved at him from the car, as he walked toward her. "Want me to drive?" she said, smiling.

"I never turn down a good chauffeur service," Galen replied.

He walked around to the passenger's side of the car. "Nice rig," he said. He sat down, running his hand over the plush upholstery.

Audra backed up, and then sped out of the parking lot. Not in a reckless way, but very quickly.

"Whoa!" Galen said, grasping for a hand-hold. "I didn't picture you as the hot-rod type."

Audra slowed a bit. "Sorry," she said. "I guess I don't have passengers that often." A faint redness appeared in her cheeks.

"Hey, it's okay. It's just that we're not going to a fire or anything."

They both laughed.

"So, how are you today?" Audra asked, now very conscious of her speed.

"I'm a lot better," Galen lied. "It'll just take some time."

"Time heals all wounds, as they say." Audra's tone was more subdued now that they were talking about Galen's loss.

"Galen, I want you to know that I'm sorry about what happened last night."

"I know you are, and I'm alright," Galen said. He smiled at her, a smile that meant *"thank you"*.

Audra's right hand was resting on the stick shift. Galen placed his on top of hers.

"I'm glad you're coming with me, Audra. I thought about going over there alone, but I would much rather have someone along."

Audra looked at him sympathetically and nodded. Letting go of the shifter, she closed her hand around his.

"It'll be okay, Galen," she said in her most soothing voice. "Really, it will."

"I know," he said, "but I was afraid that going over there by myself...." He paused and looked intently through the windshield.

"I thought I might really break down over there. All those memories; all of his things," he finally blurted.

She squeezed his hand.

"I know, Galen, you don't have to explain."

They made it to Gaston's place and she turned the Mustang into the long driveway. The house sat back off the road further than she had realized. The expansive lawn was beautiful. The hedges were trimmed to perfection and beautiful flowers painted colorful lines and patches in several areas. The setting was park-like. The house was very large and well kept. The white brick structure featured four large columns in the front. It reminded Audra of a plantation house in the south.

"Park in the back," Galen instructed, pointing the way.

Audra hadn't noticed the view of the river during the call last night. In fact, she hadn't notice much about the place at all. She had been too focused on the call and doing the best she could for the patient.

"This is such a beautiful place," she said. "I had no idea this place was so big!"

"Yea, it's great isn't it?" Galen said. "C'mon, I'll show you around."

Galen led Audra to the far side of the house. Another building sat about thirty yards away.

"What's that building?" Audra asked.

"It used to be a stable before Al bought the place. He just stores stuff in it now." Galen realized his mistake, then added, "At least he used to, that is."

The house sat atop a large hill and the Pecatonica river wound a serpentine course about a half-mile away.

"It's such a pretty view from up here," Audra said.

Galen nodded and opened a door leading onto a screened-in porch that covered most of the backside of the house. The porch was equipped with white wicker furniture and a porch swing

43

hung unmoving at the far end. Audra moved to the swing, and merrily tried it out.

"I just love these things!" she declared, sitting down and putting the swing in motion.

Galen leaned against the wall and smiled. "Me too," he said. "My grandparents had one of these. We could fit six of us kids on it when I was little."

Audra patted the spot beside her, inviting Galen to sit down. He moved toward her, accepting her offer.

"Al and I used to sit out here a lot in the summertime," he said, gazing out into the yard. "We would bring a bucket filled with beer and ice and just sit and talk. Sometimes, we would go out into the yard on reclining lawn chairs and just look up at the stars." He pondered the thought for a moment and then looked to Audra. "Have you ever done that?"

Audra shook her head.

"Makes you feel small, almost insignificant," Galen said, looking out over the lawn. "You'll have to try it sometime." Galen leaned back in the swing, straightening his legs in front of him. "You get the feeling there are things out there man will never understand. You start to think about how big space really is, and wonder what part we play in the scheme of things. It's peaceful and scary at the same time."

They sat quietly for a moment, neither of them knowing what to say. Galen still brushed against the "wall," and longed for internal peace. He no longer wanted to be a Paramedic. After a brief silence, Galen straightened up in the swing and slapped his hands on his thighs. He closed his eyes to the "wall." "Let's see if we can find this dang box for this guy at Baxter College."

The back door to the house was locked, probably by the police, Galen guessed, although he didn't know. The professor had no family nearby, only the nephew who lived out east. Galen himself had called the funeral home in town and found out Al had pre-arranged his funeral and had paid for it in advance. The County Coroner's office - part of the Sheriff's Department - had asked Galen about any relatives and Galen told him what he knew.

Al had mentioned the nephew a couple of times, a stock broker in New York named Leonard Brewer. Beyond that, Al had not said anything more.

They entered the kitchen as they had the night before. The place was very tidy and painted a bright peach color. The room was large and windows lined one wall. Galen gave her a tour of the house as they worked their way to the study on the second floor.

Audra was agape at the furnishings and decorations in the house. It was more like a museum, but very well done. The walls were plaster, with beautiful hardwood trim and floors. The ceilings were quite high, giving the rooms a very open feeling. Interesting items sat everywhere but nothing looked cluttered. There were hand-woven baskets and rugs, hand-carved masks, and a few musical instruments of unknown origin. There were other things adorned by feathers that Audra thought to be Native-American. Large pieces of pottery sat in a couple of corners and small sculptures made of various materials were distributed throughout the house. The furniture was not too unusual, but very elegant. Some traditional art, mostly paintings, also added to the decor.

Audra's thoughts turned for an instant to the cedar chest in her apartment. The one in which she stored all of the things that would someday help furnish her own house. She had been saving things in this chest since she was a teenager, fantasizing about a small white house with blue trim. Someday, when she met the right guy, she would unveil the cherished things in her cedar chest. It would provide the finishing touches to a newly-weds love nest. *It wouldn't go very far in a house like this,* she thought.

The stairway to the second floor was massive. Made of a dark wood, it utilized beautifully turned balusters and handrails. A large chandelier hung above the stairs, adding to the grandeur.

"Al must have been rich to afford all of this," Audra said.

45

"Al obviously had a lot of money, but he never talked much about it."

Actually, Galen knew little about Gaston's financial status. Money had not seemed important to Al, although Galen observed Al as being very thrifty. For instance, he knew Al always traveled coach class in airplanes, drove a Toyota, and clipped coupons from the Sunday paper.

Audra's image of Al being a meticulously neat person changed when they entered the study. It was chaotic. In one corner was a huge desk, buried by an equally massive pile of junk. Papers, books, computer disks, photographs, a telephone, and various other things were strewn about in no obvious order. Books were piled everywhere, on chairs, small tables and windowsills. A smaller desk sat along one wall supporting a personal computer. Any wall space that was not occupied by windows or bookshelves, was covered with maps or charts.

Galen began looking on the bookshelves for a wooden box. He had no idea of how big it was and hoped he would find only one.

"This place is a pigsty!" Audra declared.

"Reminds me of my place," Galen said under his breath.

"Are all men slobs?" Audra asked, smiling, "or just the ones I know?"

"Give the old guy a break," Galen said, good-naturedly. "This is where he *worked*."

"Worked doing what?" Audra asked.

"Writing and research mostly," Galen said.

Galen spotted a wooden box on the bookshelf behind the desk.

"Not to fear," he said, "I think I might have found it."

Galen retrieved it from the shelf. About the size of a cigar box, it looked rather plain. The top was hinged, and clasped in the front with a small brass hook.

Audra walked over to Galen as he sat the box on the desk.

"Let's find out what's important enough for a man to use his last earthly wish for," Galen said as he examined the clasp.

He tinkered with the mechanism as Audra looked over his shoulder. After a moment, the clasp let go and Galen opened the box.

They both gasped at the beauty of the item in the center of the box. The box was lined with velvet, and an object about the size of a tennis ball sat inside. It was clear, like glass, with hundreds of tiny v-shaped grooves cut into it, leaving its surface covered with little pyramid shapes. For lack of a better comparison, it made Galen think of the Epcott Center sphere at Disney World.

"What is it?" Galen asked.

"I don't know. Whatever it is, it sure is beaut...."

Audra cut her statement short as the object began to glow.

"What the Hell?" Galen said in amazement.

Within seconds, the object glowed very brightly. Audra and Galen instinctively backed away a step.

The box itself began to vibrate and slowly turn before it once again became motionless. The object began to rise slowly above the box. Its glow became less intense, diminishing to about the same brightness as a candle flame. They noticed the object was slowly turning, reflecting the sunlight from the windows like a miniature disco ball. It began to turn faster. They could hear it hum softly as its facets cut the air. Galen held his arm in front of Audra and began to back up. "What is it?" he asked again, not expecting an answer.

Galen continued to back away as the object began to move toward them. It moved directly toward Galen, about chest high off the floor.

Galen and Audra were too confused to know what to do. They stopped in the middle of the room and stared. The object moved closer. Galen instinctively held out his hand to keep it away.

Audra stood behind him, clinging to his arm. She began to tug him back, away from the mysterious ball.

The glowing sphere began to move faster, covering the few feet between it and Galen in a couple of seconds. Audra began to pull him toward the door. She looked up when she heard Galen yell. Blood was pouring down his arm and he almost fell backward trying to make his way to the door. She caught him, and they both fled the room.

They bolted down the wide stairs, hearts pounding.

"What the Hell is that thing?" Galen screamed, his voice cracking with fear and confusion.

He was clutching one hand in the other. Blood covered them both.

"Let me see your hand," Audra said nervously.

Galen stopped and looked up the stairs. Seeing nothing, he held out his hand.

Before Audra could look, a queer noise caused them to look up. The noise was similar to that of a dentists drill, only deeper and louder. They both looked around, searching for the source of the noise. They noticed plaster dust falling from the ceiling. They watched in amazement as the object came through the ceiling, boring a hole as it went.

Before Galen turned to run, and in that instant of total confusion and disbelief, he could have sworn, he saw small flames licking at the hole in the ceiling.

Audra, also staring in astonishment, thought she saw two small, red eyes looking at her through the same hole. Unsure of what was happening, neither said anything about what they saw. "Out the back door!" Galen yelled.

They ran through the kitchen and out into the back yard. They turned toward the car and Audra felt her pockets searching for her keys. She panicked when she could not find them.

They jumped into the car. Audra was relieved to find the keys still in the ignition. She started the car, slammed it into reverse, and turned it around as quickly as she could. Galen was watching the house. Audra shifted into first gear. Galen was slammed back into the seat when she tromped the gas. He continued to watch the house and saw the glass in a front window shatter as they skidded onto the road.

"What was that thing, Galen?" Audra cried. "It scared the Hell out of me!"

Galen was stripping off his t-shirt. "I have no idea what that was. It scared me, too!" Galen began to wrap his hand in the t-shirt.

Audra wiped at her eyes, making a total mess of the mascara she had so carefully applied.

She backed off the gas slightly as they entered town.

"Where are we going?" she asked, with a tremble still in her voice.

"Do you have a med-kit in the car?" he asked.

"In the trunk," Audra replied.

"Swing by my place then," he said. "I'll wash up my hand and see what kind of damage that thing did to it."

"What happened? What did you do to that thing?" Audra asked.

"It was coming at me and I tried to push it away," he said. "It just kind of... tore into my hand."

Galen clenched his teeth together in a grimace of pain as they pulled into his driveway. He lived in the lower half of an older two story home on the southeast side of town. Audra parked the car and ran to the trunk for her first-aid kit.

Audra met Galen at the back door where Galen was fumbling with the keys.

"Let me do it," she said. She sat the first-aid kit on the porch and took the keys from Galen. She pushed the door open in a few seconds.

Galen headed for the kitchen sink.

The t-shirt was about half-soaked with blood, resembling some morbid tie-dyed job of the sixties. He ran cold water over the injury for a minute before taking a better look.

Audra came to the sink.

They both looked at Galen's hand.

The wound nearly covered the palm of his hand. The flesh and skin hung in ragged flaps around the edges of the wound.

"Damn," Galen said. "Looks like the thing just ground its way into it." He stared at the wound for another moment, grimacing as he examined it more closely. "Looks pretty nasty, too," he said as he turned off the water.

"We better get you to the ER and have it looked at," Audra suggested.

"Yeah," Galen said as he piled gauze pads onto the wound. He walked a few feet to the utility room. He opened the clothes dryer and retrieved another t-shirt.

"What are we going to tell the doc," Audra asked, "that you were attacked by a spinning ball and it chewed up your hand?"

"Good question," Galen responded. "We'll have to think of something."

Galen pulled a chair away from the kitchen table and sat down. He was thankful he had done up the dishes the last time he was off. He glanced around the apartment, thinking it really did not look that bad for a bachelor's pad. He had never kept his place neat, but at least it was clean. His sole attempt at decorating was Miss August, held neatly to the refrigerator door with a magnet. She displayed her wares on a white-sand beach somewhere. He snatched a quick peek at Audra, hoping she had not noticed it. He decided to keep his hand as the topic of discussion.

"I can't think of anything that would make a wound like this," he said.

"Well, we can try to think of something on the way to…"

Galen lifted his good hand in a motion of silence and they both heard a loud grinding noise on the west side of the house.

"Shit!" Galen proclaimed as the orb began digging through the kitchen wall. "Back outside!" he yelled, grabbing the first-aid kit and the t-shirt. The object came through the west wall of the kitchen cutting them off from the kitchen door. Galen grabbed Audra by the arm and shuffled her into the living room. They exited the front door, just as the ball was boring its way through the living room wall. They ran to the car.

Tires smoking, Audra took the first turn so fast that Galen had to struggle to keep his head from banging into the doorframe.

"What the Hell!" Galen screamed. Beads of sweat had appeared almost instantly over his brow.

"Where to now?" Audra asked, a tremble returning to her voice.

"I don't know," Galen said. "Just drive. Keep driving."

Chapter 6

The pouch vibrated wildly at Tobias' side as the snarling dog left the ground, leaping directly at his face. Tobias lifted his left arm to ward off the attack and caught the dog by the throat. The momentum of the dog's weight carried them both backward, knocking them to the ground.

Tobias held tight, gasping for the breath that had been knocked from him. He was amazed he still had the grip on the dog after they landed. Tobias sensed that the strength he now possessed came from a supernatural source. Whatever was in that pouch was feeding his body with energy from the gods. He squeezed with all of his might, having a firm grasp on the dogs windpipe. The dog thrashed wildly, snarling and growling, trying to shake his opponent's grip. Tobias felt the animal's warm blood spill over his fingers as they tore into the dogs flesh. His grip now completely encircled the windpipe and Tobias squeezed with a newfound strength. The animal, its windpipe crushed, could not move enough air to whimper.

Tobias was lying on his side and felt relief when the dog finally stopped struggling. He lay there for a moment longer; staring at the animal, wanting to make sure the dog was dead.

Tobias slowly released his grip on the dog. He pulled his fingers out of the bloody mess of its throat and stared in amazement. The pouch at his side began to cool and Tobias could feel the sudden burst of energy ebbing away.

"Hey! Duke!" the foreman shouted from nearby. He had rode into this field, in hopes the dog may flush out a deer. Having not heard any barking for a moment or two, he now called for the dog to return. "C'mon boy, Duke!" The foreman stopped his horse and listened for a sound from the dog.

Tobias lay perfectly still.

The foreman turned around to look and listened in the other direction.

Tobias slowly and quietly pulled the limp beast's body behind a tree. He then turned, crawling on his stomach, and made his way to a shallow ravine. He lay still, listening for a sound that would indicate the position of the foreman. He hoped he would not spot the dog's body from the field.

"Duke!" the foreman shouted, followed by a loud whistle.

Tobias was slightly relieved to hear the foreman mutter something about that *damned dog*. He then heard the sound of the horse and rider making their way back toward the road.

Tobias took this opportunity to put as much distance between him and the foreman as possible. The small stretch of woods carried a ways to the east and Tobias made his way in that direction. After going about a mile, a narrow span of trees turned to the north along the backside of a tobacco field.

Tobias stopped in this corner for a while to catch his breath. He sat down and leaned back against a tree. The scent of wildflowers hung in the still air and Tobias sucked deeply to fill his lungs. The pouch hung quietly at his side

The foreman and the slaves were still too close to satisfy Tobias. He would go as far as luck and good sense would permit, and then hold up for a while.

After resting for a few minutes, Tobias began to move again. Now traveling north, he hoped he could find a safe place to hide out until nightfall. His left hand was still covered with the dog's blood and hair. Bits of leaves, grass and dirt also stuck to the viscous gore.

Tobias traveled slowly north for about twenty minutes until he came upon a small stream that crossed his path. He sat on the bank and looked both up and down stream.

The banks of the creek were steep, and the surface of the water was about six feet below the level of the surrounding fields. He slipped over the rim of the creek bank and shambled down to the water. If he traveled upstream, it would take him east, away from the foreman. The high banks would also offer him ample cover for a while.

He dropped to his knees allowing the cool water to swirl between his legs as he washed off the blood. He thought about having done this two days in a row and hoped this would be the last time. At least this time it was not *his* blood.

Tobias walked in the water, slightly hunched over to keep his head low. He wondered if this had been such a good idea. The stream offered sufficient cover, but also blocked his view of the surrounding area. He could possibly walk within yards of a cabin or house and not even know it was there.

The stream offered him safe travel for a couple of hours until the banks began to lose their height. Tobias noticed the gradual change, but could spot no cover to hide him. He hunched further over and maintained slow progress. The stream had made dozens of turns but continued to meander toward the east.

Tobias stopped after a sharp turn in the creek and peeked over the bank. The fields around him were covered with tall, dry grass and wildflowers. They went on for as far as he could see. There was a hill to the north and a cluster of dense trees and brush lay in that direction.

He could see no signs of civilization—no buildings or grazing animals. He decided to head for the trees and hide there until nightfall.

He cautiously approached the trees, trying to avoid another encounter with a briar bush. He walked the perimeter of the brush looking for an easy opening. Finding a spot void of the clutching greens, he walked into the thicket. The shade was welcome relief to his back and neck. He searched for anything edible, but found nothing. He then sat against the base of a tree. With a glance in all directions, Tobias felt it would be safe to sleep for a while. He nestled himself into the brush and made himself as comfortable as possible.

He went to sleep rather quickly, but dreams of the past few days haunted him, causing his sleep to be shallow and restless. He dreamed about Gabriel and Titus.

How proud he had been at their birth. Twin sons, on his first try. The sons he loved with all his heart. The sons he would probably never see again.

Even when Master Richards had given them these names out of the *good book*, Tobias had still been proud. The white man's names would not daunt the spirits of those two boys. They had grown up so big, so strong. Master Richards had even been proud. He would show them off to all of his gentleman visitors as if they were a pair of show horses. *Fine couple of darkies you've got there, Richards*, the visitors would say. A few of them had offered to buy the twins, but Master Richards had declined, stating he had *special plans* for those two. That had not only made Tobias thankful, but even more proud. They had *special plans*; maybe they would be field bosses some day.

Master Richards had two children of his own, a boy named Raymond and an older daughter, Mary.

Raymond, sixteen years old this summer, had taken over many duties at his father's plantation. Raymond was the boss, directed by Master Richards. Four hired hands acted as field bosses and Raymond never let them forget who was in charge. They dared not cross him, for whoever did would have to answer to Richards himself.

Raymond was a scrawny kid with a sloped-back forehead and a big nose. He could often be found following his father and shouting orders like, "Get those slaves into the fields!" That had been one of his favorite commands since he was big enough to shout. It seemed to be the only order he could give without checking with his father first. He barked it often, always getting a nod of consent from the bosses. Raymond would strut away, like the biggest rooster in the barnyard after shouting out orders. Someday he would own the plantation and Tobias hoped the kid would change before then.

Mary, a lackluster girl of nineteen, had recently acquired a gentleman caller, Ralph Watson III, a handsome man of twenty-five. He had been seeing Mary for only a few weeks before they announced their wedding plans. Master Richards had been happy about the news, having taken an instant liking to the young man. An elaborate wedding was planned for late summer, on the front lawn of the plantation house.

People from all around the area came to the summer wedding and stuffed themselves on roast pork and all the trimmings.

Not all of the slaves worked in the field that day, for it took many of them to cater to the guests. There were wagons to park, horses to care for, and water to haul. Some of the women slaves helped prepare the food. They were under the direct supervision of Richards' wife, Helen. They had spent many hours chopping vegetables, making butter, and preparing the pigs for roasting.

The wedding had gone well. The guests were happy. Food and drink had been plentiful.

The newlyweds began opening gifts from their guests. They thanked each one for their generosity. After the couple had opened their last gift, Ralph's father made an announcement.

He had purchased a house and a parcel of land in the next county for the newlyweds. A cheer went up from the crowd. Ralph appeared to be surprised, but clearly, it was an act.

Master Richards *had* been surprised. Being one of the wealthiest men in the state, he wished he had offered such a gift. He had clearly been outdone.

He scrambled within his mind to think of a gift as suitable as that of Ralph's father. "I think the father of the bride should fill the new house with the best of furniture!" Richards said.

Another cheer went up, along with a considerable amount of subdued chatter.

The look on Benjamin Richards' face said he was still not satisfied. The senior Watson had outdone him with the gifts, but he would certainly show that his generosity was endless. He told the guests he would also supply the young couple with a fine team of horses. Richards was beginning to look smug. After all, he was getting in the last word but one more gift flashed across his mind. "What good will the team be with no one to work them?" he said, indicating that he had an answer. "I will also give the newlyweds their first two slaves. They are as strong as the horses themselves—Gabriel and Titus!"

Tobias' wife, Martha, had been serving roast pork at a long table. She immediately fell to the ground upon hearing the news and began to crawl toward Master Richards.

"Ooh, no, no Masta Richards! Please, please, PLEASE!

Martha continued to crawl, the crowd falling silent.

"Masta Richards, please, don't give my babies away! Please Masta Richards."

Martha continued to grovel, and Richards tried to reason with her.

"Martha! You stop that! Those boys are nearing their thirteenth birthday! They don't need to hang onto your apron strings anymore!"

He began to talk softer, as if in comforting her. He sounded sincere, but Martha could see a spark of hate in his eyes.

"Your babies are men now, Martha. It's time for them to move along."

The crowd listened intently, amazed at Richards' compassion for the slave.

Martha bawled openly, still on her knees, hands clasped before her, begging for retraction of the last gift. Tears streamed down her face as she begged for her boys.

"They're going to be with Miss Mary," Richards continued, "and you *know* she'll treat them well."

This, Martha knew to be true, for Miss Mary had always been fond of the twins, calling them her "baby dolls". Martha reached out for Richards' hand, which he tried to pull away.

"Masta, please, them boys is all I got in this world! Please don't be takin' 'em away from me, please!"

Gabriel and Titus had been serving coffee and tea. They were placed at each end of the long main table, like matching bookends to balance the scene. Tears swelled in their eyes, but they maintained their posts. They had been specially dressed for the occasion.

Martha had never thought she would see her boys look so handsome.

Richards was getting fed up with trying to reason with her.

"Well then, you and Tobias need to make some more babies!" he said, smiling. The crowd chuckled quietly. "Go now! Go on!" He waved his hand, motioning her to leave. He nodded to the pair of field bosses who came to drag her away, kicking and screaming.

"Mamma!" Gabriel uttered, then stepped back into his position. He looked to Titus, his eyes brimming with tears. A quick glance from Master Richards assured them both that to make a scene would truly be a mistake.

"She'll get over it," Richards said to no one in particular. The crowd nodded in agreement and began the chatter again, as if nothing had happened.

Tobias had missed the ordeal. He had been ordered to the stables to care for the guest's horses and carriages. He heard someone wailing as he went about his work, and then looked out the stable doors. He saw the bosses dragging Martha. She was putting up substantial resistance. One of the bosses, Frederick, stopped and slapped the wailing slave across the face.

Martha quieted for a moment, but soon began the wailing again. Tobias sprinted from the stable to intercept the slow-moving group. He still had no idea of what was going on, but knew something bad had happened. Martha, unlike Tobias, had always been a well behaved slave. She had been punished only a few times, usually when Master Richards was in a bad mood and looking for things to complain about.

"Martha!" Tobias yelled.

The bosses stopped and looked toward him.

"Get back to the stable!" Frederick shouted.

"But, what's goin' on?" Tobias asked.

"Nothing we can't handle," the other boss said.

"Master Richards gave away our babies!" Martha sobbed. She looked at him with pleading eyes, knowing there was nothing Tobias could do.

58

"What?" Tobias asked quietly, looking at the bosses.

"He gave 'em away, Tobias!" Martha cried again. "They're goin' to live with Miss Mary!"

Tobias reached down to comfort his wife, still not fully comprehending her claims.

Frederick, now worked up from dragging Martha from the front yard, struck Tobias across the jaw. Tobias had not expected the blow and his head pivoted back, blood swelling immediately from his busted lips.

"I said, get back to the stable!" Frederick shouted. They began to drag Martha again, who now sobbed steadily but no longer had the strength to resist.

Tobias walked back to the stable, thinking there must be some mistake. *Master Richards would never give away Titus or Gabriel,* he thought. Richards, although capable of temporary fits, was generally good to the slaves. Richards did not tolerate misconduct from the slaves, and had stopped the bosses from dealing out unjust punishment.

Several of the previous bosses had severely beaten some of the slaves. Master Richards had been quick to discover these actions and handed out his own punishment to the offending bosses. More than once, Richards had discovered a slave had been beaten so severely that he or she had been unable to work. His intent was to keep the slaves working and able to work, as long as they were well behaved.

. . .

Tobias paced nervously about the stables for the rest of the afternoon, contemplating what to do. He shoveled the stalls to keep busy. Slaves were bought and sold regularly on the Richards plantation, but Tobias had never considered the possibility of his boys being moved away. He heard no more on the subject until after all of the guests had gone home that evening.

Master Richards came into the stable with the last of the guests, Raymond at his side. Tobias was fetching carriages as Richards and his son said their farewells to the departing visitors.

59

After the guests were out of hearing range, the smile that had adorned the master's face melted into a look of rage.

"Tobias!" he shouted.

He walked toward the slave, pointing at him with his index finger. "You better talk with that woman of yours!" He began to tap the finger steadily on Tobias' chest, a sudden rage building up inside of him. "She has embarrassed me in front of all of my guests!" He began to pace back and forth in front of Tobias, while rubbing his chin.

Raymond, seeing his father was angry, decided to fuel the fire. "Embarrassed the entire family!" he said, looking smugly at Tobias.

Master Richards nodded.

"She will have to be dealt with," he said. "I will have no slave conduct herself in a manner such as that while on this plantation."

Tobias interpreted this as meaning that Martha was in for a beating. He sensed Richards was in a mood that would prove dangerous to any disobedient slaves.

"Master," Tobias said, "she was jus' upset about what you said." He looked at Richards, pleading on his wife's behalf. "You done give away our boys."

"And justly so!" Richards countered. "I have every right to do with the twins as I see fit!" He began to pace again, his face reddening as his anger increased.

"They're our *property*," Raymond said, backing up his father.

"Master, them boys mean the world to Martha and me, and we've been good workers for y'all for a long time. Couldn't ya' give Miss Mary somebody else?"

"And give in to Martha?" he shouted. "Absolutely not! I will not give in to her just because it causes her grief! I would be a laughing stock if I let my slaves tell *me* what to do! Miss Mary has grown fond of the twins and they shall be hers!"

Tobias began to feel he was doing more harm to Martha than good, so he turned the attention to himself.

"Masta Richards, please, don't take my boys from me. I loves 'em too much to see 'em go. Please Masta, have mercy on me."

"That has nothing to do with anything!" Richards screamed. Raymond found a place to sit down, not wanting to miss anything should his father get *really* angry.

"Tobias, you're a *slave!* Do you know what that means?"

His face was reddening more and the veins at his temples pulsated with anger.

"You will do as I say," Richards shouted. "You will do as I say and you will not question me about my decisions. If you do, you will suffer the consequences!"

Tobias' heart sank as Master Richards lifted a whip off the wall of the stable. He felt his muscles tighten, and then quiver with fear.

He looked at Tobias. "You, come with me!" he shouted.

Raymond almost tripped over himself as he scurried behind them, staying close to the action.

Tobias braced himself for a beating. He had not seen Master Richards this worked up for a long time.

They walked silently to a small group of shacks. There were four slave camps set up on the plantation and Tobias lived in the one closest to the big house. After the twins had been born, Tobias and Martha had gotten a shack of their own.

Tobias followed Richards to his shack where they found Martha, eyes swollen from the crying, hunkered down in a corner on a straw bed.

Raymond hung back a bit, not wanting to get into his father's way. He walked over to the shack, and peeked into the window.

The inside of the shack contained no furniture of any kind, save a small table, and was dimly lit by the glow of an oil lamp.

Richards ignored Tobias and looked directly at Martha. "Get your dress off," he told her in no uncertain terms. She looked at him, surprised, and began to crawl into the corner. "Masta, please, no," she muttered.

"Now!" Richards screamed.

61

Raymond readied himself to see some action and the shapely nude body of the slave. He often peeked in on the slave women, and had had several serve him sexually in the past. They dared not say a word to anyone about it and they all cringed at the sight of him.

Martha jumped to her feet when Richards shouted at her, understanding he was in no mood to be talked to. "Please Masta," she pleaded. "I'm sorry for what I did!"

"Too late," Richards shouted. "Lift it off and put your hands on the wall"

Sobbing uncontrollably in anticipation of the forthcoming licks, Martha struggled with the simple dress she had worn to the wedding. She lifted it up over her head and dropped it to the floor. She continued to beg for mercy but to no avail. Richards' jaw was locked in determination. He swept a strand of hair from his face.

"Masta, please, beat me instead," Tobias said, tears swelling in his eyes. "I'll make sure she don't do no more wrong," he said.

"I'm quite capable of that myself!" Richards screamed. "Now you shut up," he told Tobias. He then turned back to Martha. "And you get against the wall. Now!"

Tobias watched in horror as the wickedly thin end of the whip slashed a whelp across her back. Richards ignored Tobias as he continued to plead for mercy.

Martha screamed with the landing of each blow.

"Do you understand what you are?" Richards screamed. "You're a *slave*, and you *will* show respect for me when I address you."

He laid on another lick and Martha shrieked. Richards acted like a crazy man. His eyes were wild in the frenzy of handing out pain. He drew back again and let the whip fly.

"*I* am the master, *you* are the slave!" he howled.

Tobias, openly crying for his wife, watched as the last crack of the whip opened a bloodless gash from the small of her back to the top of her buttocks. As if in slow motion, he watched as the blood began to ooze into the gaping wound.

"I *own* you and will do with you as I see fit," he yelled as he gathered the whip for another lick.

Richards drew back, ready to release the leather beast again.

Tobias, his love for his wife overriding his fear of his Master, grabbed Richards' upheld hand. He held it steady in his powerful grip.

Raymond was still watching from the window. Rather than confront the slave himself, he ran for the house.

Richards looked at Tobias with astonishment. "How dare you!" he screamed, sweat running down his brow. He drooled from the corner of his mouth. "You take your filthy hands off of me at once." Richards struggled hopelessly against the strength of the slave. His anger grew into full fury as he grappled for release.

Tobias held fast, not knowing what else to do now that he had gone this far. He hoped Richards would cool off and regain his temperament if held for a moment.

It would prove to be a fatal mistake.

Frederick stormed into the shack, with Raymond close behind. He had his pistol in one hand and grabbed Tobias around the neck from behind. Frederick put the business end of the pistol to Tobias' head.

"Are you alright?" he asked Richards.

Richards ignored the question. "You bastard!" he shrieked. He stared unbelievingly at Tobias.

Richards had gone mad. Tobias could see the flames of Hell in his eyes. His hair was strewn about his face and spit flew from his lips as he screamed.

"You dirty, disgusting, *nigger*!" he howled.

Martha had since collapsed to the floor, moaning and rolling slowly about.

Richards looked back at Tobias, held fast from behind by Frederick. An evil grin spread across Richards' face.

"You will learn," he shouted. "If it's the last thing I do, you will regret having ever touched me. I own you. You belong to me. If I want to beat you, I can. If I want you to eat pig shit, you will, or you will deal with the punishment!"

His eyes bulged with fury as he took the pistol from Frederick.

Richards looked into Tobias' eyes, their noses almost touching. "The punishment is for me to decide," he said in a low, deliberate voice. His lowered voice was even scarier than his shouting. The grin widened as he motioned Frederick to let the slave go. Tobias stood still as Richards placed the muzzle of the pistol against his forehead. "For me to decide." He chuckled wildly.

Martha lay face-down on the floor, whimpering, barely conscious.

Richards cocked the single shot pistol.

Frederick and Raymond, their faces drained of color, backed against the wall near the door.

Tobias closed his eyes and held his breath.

Tobias felt the barrel of the gun leave his head and he opened his eyes. Richards held the gun down, toward the floor, where Martha lay, still face down.

"Nooooo!" Tobias screamed, as the shot rang in his ears.

Chapter 7

Audra drove north on Willow River Road. Galen sat quietly holding the blood-soaked bandages around his injured hand. At the intersection of route 72, Audra stopped the car.

"Where to?" she asked.

"Hell, I don't know," Galen responded.

"We're going to have to get that hand looked at sooner or later."

Audra looked at him and he shrugged.

"Hey, I'm not real keen on having that thing show up at the hospital while I'm sitting there waiting," Galen said. He looked to Audra for a response.

She nodded affirmation, a tight-lipped resolution of reality - if you could call this reality.

"I mean, I don't know what the Hell that thing is, or what it'll do, or why the Hell it's pissed off at us!" Galen said. "What if we get to the hospital and the damned thing comes rippin' its way into the ER?"

Audra considered this then turned right toward Rockford anyway. "We have to do something; we can't just drive all night." She looked toward Galen, whose face was a study of concentration, his brows almost touching in the center of his forehead. His light-brown hair was disheveled and his face was paler than usual. "Do you think that thing could get all the way to Rockford?" she asked.

"How should I know," he exclaimed. "It got all the way to my house from Al's...." Galen became quiet, his thoughts turning in a different direction. He asked Audra, "how long would you say we were at my house?"

"About twenty minutes or so. Why?"

"I was just thinkin', he said. "I live about six miles from Al's place...." Galen did a quick calculation in his head, "which means the ball-thing was moving at about 18 miles per hour."

"You mean you think it's following us?" she asked.

"I don't know!" he shouted. "How the Hell am I supposed to know?"

Audra became silent and tears welled up in her eyes. Galen had yelled more out of frustration than anything else but had not meant to take it out on her. He sensed her fear and pain and quickly apologized.

"I'm sorry, Audra. I just don't know what to think." He hit himself lightly in the center of his forehead with the heel of his right hand. She caught the movement out of the corner of her eye and looked at him.

"I don't either, Galen. What should we do?"

He thought for a moment.

"Take the next road going north," he said. "I've got an idea, if you're game."

She hung a left at the next intersection. "What are you thinking," she asked.

"I'd like to know if it's following us," he said. "And we should try to find out if it is. Maybe we should get out into the open and just watch for it."

"Don't you think that's a little risky?" she asked with concern heavy in her voice.

"Well, yeah, but we could find a place where we could have advanced warning. Someplace where we could see it coming, or hear it, or something. What do ya' think?"

"That's one idea, assuming that it *does* travel. What if it just...."

Galen looked at her, trying to understand.

She was making motions with her free hand as if looking for a word. "Poof," she said. "What if it just kind of 'poofs', and it's there?"

Galen chuckled, then hesitated a second. "Then at least we'd know that it 'poofs' here and there instead of hopping or flying or taking a bus."

Hearing Galen say it made it sound funny. He was being so serious, but she laughed despite his seriousness.

"What's so funny?" he asked, cracking a smile.

She shook her head and the laugh dwindled to a snicker.

"Poof," she said, and laughed again. "Just sounds so funny hearing two adults talk like this."

He eyed her suspiciously, but continued to smile. "What if it does just 'poof', like you suggest?"

"Like you said, then we'd know."

They drove north for a while and Galen spotted something.

"Hey, hold it," he said, pointing out the window. "Pull in there."

Audra turned the car into a large parking lot. A few semi-truck trailers lined one side and at the far end, a small metal building sat darkly, showing no signs of activity. The sun had set below the horizon but there was adequate light to see.

"What is this place?" Audra asked.

"A trucking company owns it," Galen said. "They park their rigs and stuff here on weekends."

A tall chain-link fence surrounded the lot, with a gate at each end. The gates were open, only locked on the weekends when the lot was full to help prevent vandalism.

"Just park in the middle," Galen said, "but leave the motor running."

Audra shifted the Mustang into neutral and coasted to a stop. She turned off the radio that neither of them had noticed was on, and then turned to Galen.

"Should we stay in the car, or get out?" she asked.

"I guess we could just open the doors and stand outside," he said.

He opened his door and stepped into the evening air. Audra also got out and they looked at each other over the top of the car.

Galen laid his injured hand on the hood and began to fiddle with the bandages.

Corn and soybean fields surrounded them. A farmer's co-op market was across the road from them, but there were no cars in the parking lot. A dairy farm lay about a half-mile north of them and Audra watched the peaceful Holsteins graze in the pasture. She looked back to Galen.

"How is it?" she asked.

"The pain's easing up a little," he said as he reached into the back seat for Audra's med kit.

He opened it up on the hood and retrieved a roll of tape. He began trying to tape the bandages into place - a struggle with only one hand.

Audra walked to the other side of the car and took the tape from him.

"Here, let me do it," she said as she stripped off some of the tape. The hand had stopped bleeding, but may still need stitches.

"Hurry up," Galen said. "I want to be able to get out of here quick if that thing shows up."

Audra finished the wrap and placed the tape and the med kit back into the car.

"Thanks," Galen said, as he looked around. He glanced at his watch. He then began counting on the fingers of his good hand, touching the tip of each finger to his thumb as he counted silently.

"What are you doing?" Audra asked.

"Just trying to figure out how far we came and how long it will take that thing to get here. If it travels at the same speed it did in town—and if it doesn't just 'poof' itself here."

It was not as funny this time, sitting here in the open waiting to see if the thing showed up and hoping it would not.

"How long do you figure?" Audra asked, consulting her own watch.

"Well, we came about fifteen miles from The Willows," he said. "And at 18 miles per hour it should take a little less than an hour for the thing to travel this far. It also took us about fifteen minutes to get here, so deduct that and I'd say about... a half-hour or so."

Local people called the Village of Willow River, 'The Willows.' Audra looked over the roof of the car at Galen. His face looked worried and his eyes kept a keen watch on their surroundings.

Audra caught herself mindlessly staring at him, wondering what he was like after you got to know him better. So many people were so much different than you thought they were after you got to know them.

Audra's older sister, Sharon, had found out all about that. Her husband had changed dramatically after they got married. Audra had been a senior in high school when they had started dating. She had envied her sister at the time, so in love with a boy named Jack. They had dated for three years before being married and seemed to be happy the whole time. Now, after five years of marriage, Sharon was married to a monster. Yes, people do change.

Audra pictured Galen as being a little shy, but fun to be around. She wondered if he liked kids and pictured herself and Galen as a couple. They could go to movies together, visit friends, and attend local functions arm in arm. Her eyes glazed over in a daydream. What would Galen be like after, say, three years? Galen's voice snapped her out of the trance when he spoke.

"You got a staring problem?" he asked, looking at her, seemingly embarrassed.

"Oh...no," she said. "I was just thinking about what that thing might be," she lied. "Did Al ever mention anything like this in any of your conversations?"

He reached into his shirt pocket, and pulled out a cigarette. "No, we talked about a lot of weird things, but a ticked-off-glowing-ball that chases people and chews through walls, wasn't one of them."

He lit the cigarette and the sudden flicker of light caused her to realize how dark it was getting. She was just about to say

69

something about his smoking and how bad it was for him, but decided he already knew that and now wasn't the appropriate time. She would work on that some other time.

"Keep an eye out in all directions," he said, as he exhaled the blue-gray smoke. After a moment of silence, Galen said, "Al was into a lot of different stuff. Not 'into', like he did it as a hobby, but he studied all kinds of things. People from all over the world would send him stuff and he would try to tell them what it was, or where it came from, or what kind of people made it."

He took another drag on the cigarette, exhaling the smoke through his nose. Audra watched him and her nose began to tickle, thinking how the smoke must feel coming through his nose like that. She began to rub her nose, unaware that she was even doing it.

"The thing could be from anywhere," he said, "and could be *anything*, knowing Al."

"If the thing shows up, we should call the guy that Al wanted us to send it to," Audra said. "Maybe he knows something about it, or maybe he sent it to Al in the first place."

Galen nodded his head then looked at his watch. He dropped the cigarette to the ground and crushed it out with the heel of his Nike.

"Keep your eyes and ears open," he said as he glanced around.

A street light at the corner of the lot began flickering to life, casting a cold, blue-white light onto the oil-spotted asphalt. The other lights, one in each corner of the lot, followed suit. They could hear the hum of electricity.

"Whether that thing shows up or not," Galen said, "I'll have to get in touch with this guy and tell him what happened. If he wants the damned thing, he's gonna have to catch it himself!" A chuckle escaped him and he looked at Audra. "That should be some conversation, huh?"

"Yeah, I want to be around when you-" Audra's words were cut short by a hollow metallic sound. It sounded like someone was rubbing a coarse file on the side of a coffee can. Galen twirled around, searching for the cause of the noise. They both looked toward the southwest corner of the lot in time to see sparks flying from the corner fence post. The ball-thing had sheared the metal post about halfway up. The sparks only lasted a second, sending a spray of hot metal off to one side like a tiny meteor shower. The top half of the fence fell inward, caught before hitting the ground by the next post on either side. The ball-thing glowed faintly as it came steadily toward them.

As Galen turned to get into the car, he again thought he saw flames in the direction of the ball. A faint, almost ghostly orange light surrounded it and flickered with movement.

Audra looked across the parking lot as the ball approached and saw white, moving shapes below the ball itself. The asphalt below the ball seemed alive, shimmering, like the heat rising off a highway on a hot, sunny day.

"Let's go!" Galen shouted, not realizing Audra had already climbed into the car. Galen spun around in his seat, trying to keep an eye on the orb while Audra steered the car toward the nearest gate. The ball changed directions to intercept the car. Audra turned to the south and Galen watched as the ball again changed course, coming directly at them. Its speed was evidently no match for the Mustang. Galen watched it fade from sight through the rear window, still shrouded in the orange, flickering light.

"Darn that thing!" Audra yelled, "What's it after?"

Galen shook his head. Seeing the damage the thing had done to a metal fence post had caused his pulse to quicken. He began to realize the thing had incredible power.

"I don't know," he said, "but let's get in touch with this Paxon guy and tell him to come get his damned ball! I'm tired of playing with it!"

Deep in thought, Galen toyed with his mustache. They were putting some distance between themselves and the ball, which made both of them feel a little better.

"Well, we know a couple of things about it that we didn't know before," Galen said.

71

Audra looked at him. "Like what?"

"I doesn't just "poof", he said, "and it is definitely following us. It also seems to change direction, depending on where we are, always on a direct-intercept course."

"It looks like it can go through anything," Audra added. "It seemed to come through that fence post like it was nothing!"

"What do we do now?" Galen muttered more to himself than to Audra.

Audra was staring at the road, both hands on the wheel, looking like the model drivers education student - except for her speed. She was doing nearly eighty as she approached the intersection at route 72. She made a quick stop, then turned left; back on course to Rockford.

"Do you have any idea of where we're going?" Galen asked.

"To the hospital," She replied.

"Are you crazy?" Galen said, not quite shouting.

"We've got to get your hand taken care of," she said.

"Right," Galen responded, "we're just going to sit in the ER and wait for the killer ball to come and get us."

"I'm not exactly that stupid!" she shrieked.

She tried to calm herself down and Galen did the same. They sat in silence for a moment, both taking deep breaths before either of them could think of what to say. Audra's hands trembled.

"I'm sorry, again," Galen said. "Of course you're not stupid.

It's just hard to think with all of this going on." He looked out the window and noticed a full moon just above the horizon. That seemed appropriate, he thought.

"What did you have in mind?" Galen asked, again nervously twisting his moustache.

Audra wiped at her eyes. She was not normally so easy to cry. She just hated it when people yelled at her, especially someone like Galen, whom she admired. She thought perhaps Galen liked her, but was beginning to have doubts. Maybe she was already getting to know him better and did not like what she was finding out about him.

"I thought I would go into the ER and try to swipe a stitch kit."

"You don't look like the stealing type," Galen said.

"I would replace it or something. Maybe donate a little money to the auxiliary."

Galen laughed to himself. Audra was special. She was one of those special people, the kind God did not create enough of.

"Do you think you can get away with it?" he asked.

She gave him a little disgusted look, still mad at him for yelling at her.

"If I didn't think I could, I wouldn't try." There was a definite note of hostility in Audra's voice.

"Okay, okay, I just don't want you to get into trouble," Galen said, now on the defensive.

"I'm already in trouble, in case you hadn't noticed. I'd say that thing that's following us could definitely be called *trouble*."

"Jees, lighten up, will ya'? You know what I mean. We'd be in worse shape if we had to get you out of jail."

Audra felt sorry for acting like this, but Galen deserved it. He certainly did not like the taste of his own medicine.

There was an uncomfortable silence in the car for the next minute, and then Audra offered her plan. "Do you know Suzy? Suzy Halverson, who works in the ER?"

Galen nodded, "Not very well, but yeah, I know her."

"Well, she's getting married in a couple of months and she loves to talk about her wedding. I know she's working tonight, and maybe I can go in and get the nurses to talking about it..." She paused, because she was really just hoping she could get into the supply room for a minute and really did not have a plan.

"You can stay in the car," she said. "If I can't get into the supply room right away, I'll come back out. Then we can try plan B."

"Plan B?" Galen asked. "What's plan B?"

"That's the plan you're going to come up with if mine doesn't work," she said.

73

Galen laughed a nervous little titter. "I'm terrible at coming up with plans," he said. "I can't even plan a meal."

The drive to the hospital took about twenty minutes from the truck lot. The hospital parking lot was well lit and Galen caught himself looking for escape routes should the ball-thing show up while they were here. There were plenty of cars in the parking lot, but Audra found an empty slot close to the ER entrance.

Audra opened her door and stepped out. "Why don't you get into the drivers seat in case the thing comes while I'm in there," she said.

Galen nodded and got out of the car. He walked around to the driver's side and she handed him the keys.

"What should I do if it does come?" he asked. "Just leave you here?"

"If it does come, I'll be running out the nearest set of doors," Audra said.

"I figure we've got less than an hour so I want you out in twenty minutes. If you can't get the stuff in that amount of time, just come back to the car and we'll try plan B."

Audra nodded. "Twenty minutes."

Galen watched as Audra entered the brightly lit ER. He admired the graceful way she moved across the parking lot. Yep, she sure was a cute gal, damned cute.

He began to think of the ball-thing. Maybe it was not such a good idea to have come here. He certainly did not like being separated from Audra. He wondered who it would come for first, and why. He had the feeling it would come for him first. He did not know why, perhaps because he had opened the stupid box. Why hadn't Al warned him that it could be dangerous? He must not have known. Al would never have knowingly placed Galen—or anyone else for that matter—into any kind of jeopardy.

A sickening thought occurred to him as he thought about the whole situation. *Where was the damned thing now?* Was it chewing its way through some one's living room wall? What if it killed somebody on its way to get them? What if it chewed its way

74

through a fuel tank, or a city bus, or the hospital? People could *die*. But what was he expected to do? Just sit and let it come and get him? What would it do to him, if, or *when*, it caught up with him? The numerous thoughts sent chills down his spine. He had to get in touch with Paxon. Maybe he would have some answers. Galen absentmindedly watched moths flutter crazily around the parking lot lights as he contemplated the many questions.

Audra entered the Emergency Room through the public doors. She pulled her hospital ID from her purse and tagged it to a belt-loop on her jeans. She walked down a corridor and went through a set of double doors that lead to the ER nurses station.

The ER was a tangle of motion. People were moving quickly from here to there, carrying clipboards and pushing carts and wheelchairs. *Good*, Audra thought, *it's a busy night*.

She made her way to the nurse's station and walked behind the counter. A couple of the nurses sat reading patient files. They did not even look up to see who she was.

Audra knew most of the people who worked in the ER. She often had to X-ray the trauma cases that came in and had plenty of contact with the ER personnel. She glanced around to see if she could locate Suzy.

They had gone to high school together in Willow River. They did not get together very often and their brief encounters at the hospital were about their only time together.

Audra was hoping she could use Suzy's wedding as the reason for her visit, even if it was an odd time. It was a Friday night, about nine-thirty and the ER would only get busier as the night wore on.

Audra walked to the end of the counter and looked around the ER in search of Suzy. One of the other nurses walked up to her, although Audra could not remember her name.

"Hi," the nurse said, forcing the smile of acquaintance and evidently not remembering Audra's name either. "Are you looking for someone?"

Audra's face flushed with the redness of dishonesty. "I was wondering if Suzy was working tonight," she responded.

The nurse was bending over looking for a file. She did not look back at Audra but responded over her shoulder. "Yeah, she's around, but I'm not sure where right now." She turned around, a file clasped in one hand. "If I see her, I'll tell her you're here."

"Thanks," Audra said as she watched the nurse disappear into the confusing busyness. She walked over to the water fountain. It was right across from the supply room and it would offer her the opportunity to see if anyone was in there. She bent over to get a drink and peeked up and down the hall. No one was paying her any attention. She pretended to read the notices on the bulletin board above the fountain when a hand clasped onto her shoulder.

Audra turned with a start.

"Hi, Audy!" Suzy smiled. "What are you doing here?"

Audra had been caught off guard and she fumbled for her words.

"Well...I...uh," she stumbled. "I think I may have left a blanket here after our last ambulance call.

"It'd be in the supply room closet," Suzy said. "Take a look in there and let me know if you don't find it. Did you hear about Bill's new job?"

"Uh, no, I didn't," Audra answered.

Suzy began to babble about her fiancée's new job. Audra was beginning to think she may pull this off. She hoped that when she got to the supply room she could quickly locate the suture kits. Since the ambulance crews never used them, she was not sure where they were stored.

"...and then his boss said, 'Bill, we need a good man to run the accounting department,' and that was that," Suzy continued.

Audra had not been listening to her friend's story. "That's great," she said, hoping it was an appropriate response.

"Yeah," Suzy said, "I think he'll like it."

"You know, we're just going to have to get together soon," Audra said, pretending to be interested.

76

"Yes, let's," Suzy continued. "We never get to talk anymore." Suzy quickly left, explaining how busy they were in the ER.

Audra had meant to ask Suzy about the wedding but the blanket story seemed to work fine. Blankets were an item frequently left behind. The hospital would launder it, and then place it in the supply room to be picked up the next time the ambulance came in. She walked into the supply room where another nurse was gathering supplies for one of her patients.

Audra casually walked over to the closet, hoping the nurse would not be long. It may look suspicious if Audra spent too much time checking out the closet.

The nurse was only a minute and nodded a greeting to Audra as she left the room. Audra looked into the closet searching for anything marked "Willow River Fire and Rescue." She peeked out the door and saw nobody. She began reading the contents of the many drawers the supplies were stored in. After only a moment, Audra spotted what she was searching for and pulled opened the drawer. She stuffed two of the cellophane packets into her purse. She also discovered a supply of topical anesthetic pads and took a few of those.

Nervous, Audra quickly zipped her purse closed and trotted over to the closet. She riffled through a stack of blankets and to her amusement found one of theirs. She retrieved it and exited the room.

Walking back through the ER, she hoped she wouldn't run into Suzy. She headed for the door to the outside corridor. The ER was still busy and no one noticed her as she left the building.

Galen saw her as she exited the ER. She carried a bulky, unknown object under one arm and her purse in the other. He got out of the car and walked to the other side as she approached.

"Get it?" he asked over the top of the car.

Audra let out a deep breath. "Got two," she said as she tossed the blanket into the small back seat.

They both got into the car.

"I was also able to get a topical anesthetic," she said as she unzipped her purse. "It won't be as good as a shot of Novocain, but it'll be better than nothing."

The thought of her stitching up his hand suddenly became frightening to Galen, but it had to be done. Galen had never stitched any one up but had seen it done many times. Part of their training had required many hours of emergency room duty, working with the ER docs and nurses, assisting in any way they could. He did not know if Audra had seen it done before, but hoped that she had.

"Where to?" she asked.

"Well, don't take this wrong, but I was thinking of a motel."

Audra flushed at the thought but Galen did not notice in the car's dark interior.

"I was thinking," Galen continued, "that we could drive to Madison. I figure that would give us about five-and-a-half hours before the thing could get there."

Audra was nodding her head, thinking it sounded like a reasonable idea.

They headed for the toll way, which was the quickest way to Madison. Traffic was light at this time of night and they made it to Madison in an hour-and-a-half.

Several motel signs were visible from the highway. Audra pulled the car onto the next exit ramp. She steered the car into a Red Roof Inn and parked near the office. The sudden brightness from the lights caused them both to squint their eyes.

"I better check us in," Audra said. "You shouldn't go walking in there with those bloody bandages on your hand. They'll think we're a couple of escaped convicts or something."

Galen nodded and smiled. "Just like Bonnie and Clyde," he said.

He watched her through the plate-glass window as she requested a room for the night. After a few moments, she reappeared and tossed Galen a key.

"Two-twelve," she said and backed the car out of its stall. "I almost made a big mistake," Audra continued. "I was going to check us in as Mr. and Mrs. Smith, and then I decided to put it on my credit card. I thought that might look pretty stupid since my real name is on the card."

Galen looked at her, feeling guilty for having made her pay for the room.

"I'll pay you back for the room and for the gas and stuff," Galen told her.

"Why?" she asked.

"I'm the one who's hurt. I'm the one who needed the room," Galen said.

"I'll split it with you, fifty fifty," she responded.

Galen nodded and they pulled into the stall closest to their room. Audra retrieved the med kit from the back seat and handed it to Galen. She grabbed her purse and they climbed the stairs looking for two-twelve. The room was fairly small but adequate. A large window covered the far wall. The curtains were opened all the way, revealing a shadow-filled view of the night beyond.

Galen walked into the bathroom, unwrapped a plastic cup and took a long drink of water. "I guess we better get right down to business," he said, setting the cup on the vanity.

Audra reached into her purse and pulled out the suturing kits. She laid them on the small round table at the far end of the room and pulled the curtains shut. She dug into her purse again and pulled out the packets of topical anesthetic, tossing them onto the table also.

"What else are we going to need?" she asked.

"A fifth of Jack Daniels and a doctor," he replied.

She gave him a strange look and then asked, "anything else?"

Galen was speaking to her from the bathroom as he carefully removed the dressings on his hand. The gauze stuck to the wound, sending sharp quirks of pain through his hand as he gently pulled them loose. Audra stood in the bathroom doorway watched.

"Need help?"

"Nope. Last one," Galen said as he put his injured hand under the running water to loosen the last layer of gauze.

"Do you think I could I have the bathroom for a minute?" she asked.

Galen looked at her funny, gently pulling the soaked gauze away from his injury.

"I have to go... bad," she said. "It's been a long drive."

"Oh, yeah, sure," he muttered, reaching for a hand towel.

Galen wrapped the hand in the towel and exited the bathroom. Audra stepped in and closed the door. Galen walked over and sat on the corner of the king-sized bed. He could hear the faint "tinkling" through the door and the sound of toilet paper rolling off the reel, punctuated by a roaring flush.

They both took a seat at the small round table and flipped on the hanging lamp above it. Audra pushed their supplies to one side and covered the table with a bath towel.

"Not exactly an operating room," she claimed.

"Just as long as you can see what you're doing," Galen replied.

Eyes widening, Audra's face flushed white.

"What do you mean, 'as long as *I* can see'? I'm not going to stitch you up!"

"Well, I sure can't do it!" Galen exclaimed. "I'd need both hands to tie a knot."

"Yeah, but you're the Paramedic and I'm just an EMT," Audra pleaded. "They didn't teach us how to stitch people up. We only got to watch."

Then you got as much training as I did on this subject," Galen responded. He paused a moment. He looked Audra sternly in the eyes. "But now *you're* going to play doctor and I'll be your *patient*."

Audra shook her head, sending her ponytail swinging from side to side. "I *can't*, Galen. I told you. I've never done this before."

"It was your idea, Audra. You've got to do it!"

Audra stood up and placed her hands behind her head. "Okay, hang on a minute," she said. "It's got to be done, and we don't have time to argue."

Galen looked up at her and saw how nervous she was. "Listen," he said, "what if I do the needle work and you tie the knots?"

Audra cut her eyes toward Galen, nodding her head. "I think I could handle that," she said as she resumed her seat.

Audra got the supplies together and set to work cleaning and disinfecting the wound.

The cleaning was clearly painful. Galen flinched each time Audra touched a tender spot.

After Audra finished cleaning the wound, she opened a packet of the topical anesthetic. "This should help a little," she said, gently wiping the area.

The stitch kit came in a small cellophane bag and consisted of a small curved needle that was pre-tied to suturing thread. It resembled a tiny fishing hook with black line attached to it. Audra dug through her med-kit and retrieved a pair of forceps. She handed them to Galen.

They hesitated for a few moments, waiting for the anesthetic to begin working. Galen picked up the needle with the forceps. He poked the skin with the tip of the needle to test the anesthetic. His skin only felt slightly numb, but that is what he expected.

"Here goes nothing," he said as he poked the needle slowly into a loose flap of skin. He felt a pinch, and then the point of the needle was through. He repositioned the forceps, gripping the needle near the point. He pulled the needle the rest of the way through the skin. He was surprised that the smooth thread tickled more than hurt as he pulled it through the tiny hole the needle had made. He then poked the needle into the firm skin surrounding the wound, which hurt considerably more, but again pulled the thread through. He carefully handed the forceps, with the needle, to Audra. She nervously accepted the tools and grimaced in anticipation of the pain she would cause Galen.

"Pull it tight," he instructed, "and leave a little slack to tie the knot with."

Audra worked slow and did as Galen asked.

"Okay, now take the long end and wrap it around the needle to make the knot." Audra had a little difficulty with this but managed. "Now tighten the knot by pulling both ends of the thread."

Again, Audra did as she was instructed and watched as the knot slid down the thread, cinching the flap of skin to the firmer skin at the point of the stitch.

"Good," Galen said, "now, again, tie another knot on top of that one, then snip the thread above the knot."

Audra seemed pleased with her work and they both gained confidence and speed as they continued the process. They finished almost an hour later, having lost count of how many stitches they had put in.

Galen's hand looked like something you might have expected on Frankenstein's monster. A series of ragged-shaped lacerations radiated from the center of his palm, looking somewhat like a gruesome asterisk. They spent a few more minutes wrapping the hand with bandages before calling the job complete. It was now a little after two a.m., Saturday morning.

"How long do you think it will be until that *thing* gets here?" Audra asked.

"Another couple of hours," Galen responded amidst a yawn.

"Do you think we should get going?" she asked.

Galen shook his head. "Not yet," he said. "We can't go back the way we came or we'll be headed toward it."

Audra nodded. "What's your plan?"

Galen got up from the table and inspected the new bandages on his hand. He moved over to the bed and stretched his tall frame out to its full length.

"We still don't know if its speed is consistent. It could show up here at any time." He began to rub his tired eyes with his good right hand. "If its speed does remain consistent, we should go east or west from Madison. That should cause it to follow us.

After we lead it east or west for a while we could cut to the south, toward Willow River. That would give us more time to find out where this Paxon guy is."

Audra looked at him and knew he was very tired. She was tired herself but far too nervous to sleep.

Galen looked at his watch again. "Let's hang out here for another hour and hope like Hell it doesn't show up before then.

Audra thought for a moment, and then said, "What do you think that thing is?" I mean, I know that you don't *know* what it is, but what do you *think* it is?"

Galen stared at the wall twirling one side of his moustache between his thumb and index finger.

"You know," he said, shaking his head, "I have no idea. I can't even begin to imagine *what* it is, but I think Al must have been studying it. Somebody probably dug it up somewhere then sent it to him, asking the same thing. *What is it?*"

Galen stopped twirling his moustache and began unconsciously tugging at his earlobe. "That means it could be anything, from anywhere."

Audra looked at him with the appearance of someone who has lost her last bit of faith. Her bottom lip began to tremble and tears slowly spilled from her eyes. She dropped her face into her hands and began to sob. Audra was good at handling a crisis. As a member of the fire department, she was trained to do so. In those moments, Audra could call upon her many hours of training and experience to deal with whatever the circumstances might throw at her. However, this was something different. This situation was one she had no control over. It scared her badly.

Galen got up and knelt beside her chair. "It's going to be alright," he said. "We'll figure out a way to get away from it." He put his hand on her shoulder and gave a gentle squeeze. "I should have never asked you to go with me," he said. "I'm sorry that I got you mixed up in this."

She looked up, her eyes meeting his. "It's not your fault," she said. "How could you have known?" She took his hand into hers. "I was glad you asked me to go with you and I'm still glad."

She was silent for a moment, then added, "Whatever it is, we'll come through it alright." She made a little smile, tears running around the corners of her mouth. "Maybe it'll just 'poof', disappear and leave us alone."

Galen laughed with her, hoping she was right. Maybe they would never see the thing again.

"Let's get our stuff into the car," he said. "We don't want to have to grab all this stuff if that thing comes chewing on the door."

Audra nodded then helped Galen gather all the things they had used during the 'operation.' As they carried it to the car, Galen had a thought. "Maybe we should just wait in the car until time to leave," he said. "Then we can make a quicker getaway if it does show up."

"Okay," she said, "I'll go lock the key in the room."

"I'll go with you," Galen said. "I don't want to be split up if the ball shows up early."

In a few moments, they were back in the car, Audra behind the wheel. She reached over to turn on the radio but Galen stopped her. "I want to be able to hear," he said. She nodded and leaned back in the seat.

After a few long, silent moments passed, Audra said, "Being chased by magic balls can be boring." She sighed, then looked at Galen. "But after a night like this, I can use a little boredom."

Audra then asked, "What was Al like? It's obvious you two were close, so what was he like?"

Galen let out a long breath. "He was just one of the coolest guys I've ever known. I've always said I hope I have half the energy he did when I get to be his age. You know, he had that big house but he spend most of his time in his study and his bedroom. He had a housekeeper come in twice a week to dust and vacuum and stuff. He was very wrapped up in his work and that's what he loved."

"But I thought he was retired," Audra said.

"Oh, he was *officially* retired, but he never stopped working. He told me one night he had spent many years traveling and

84

studying people all over the world. He wrote many books on his studies, but they were all academic stuff. He told me that after he retired, he started writing novels, telling *stories*. He said he had an endless supply of novel ideas, many of them based on stories he had heard from all over the world. He told me lots of stories and said most of them were based in truth, but could never be proven or documented. Those are the stories he turned into novels.

"I see his books all the time in the stores," Audra said.

Galen nodded, "I'm not much of a reader, but I guess his books were pretty popular. You know, that's one of the funny things about Al. Once he was finished writing a book, he couldn't wait to start on the next one. In fact, sometimes he had a couple of books in progress at the same time and worked on whichever one struck his fancy that day." Galen was silent for a moment, then said, "I think he knew his time was short and wanted to tell the world as many of his favorite stories as he could before he died."

Galen checked the time. It was only a half-hour before he expected the thing to arrive, if it arrived as predicted. He decided it was time to head back to The Willows.

"Let's go west," Galen said. "Over to route 51 and take that south."

Audra nodded and started the Mustang.

"Are you okay to drive?" he asked. "Not too tired?"

"I'm okay," Audra said. "I'm tired, but not sleepy."

The Mustang left the hotel's parking lot and turned left. Route 51 was about twelve miles to the west and ran parallel to the highway they had traveled north on. This route was a two-lane highway with stoplights and stop signs at every small town along the way. Galen knew it would be slower trip back to the Willows. He felt they would still have ample time to find Paxon's phone number or address once they reached Gaston's house again.

Audra drove in silence, the heavy thoughts of their predicament weighing on her mind. They reached the junction of route 51 and Audra pointed the car to the south. The traffic was almost non-existent at this time of the morning, but a few cars did share the road.

The Mustang was traveling just a little over the 55 mph speed limit. Audra noticed a pair of headlights coming up fast from behind her. She lightly tapped the brakes to flash her brake lights and warn the driver to slow down. The road was curvy here, winding its way through the rolling hills of southern Wisconsin. Just as the headlights bore down on her rear bumper, a second set emerged from behind the first. The second set swung crazily into the other lane and passed the other car and Audra. It then swung back into the right lane as the first car also began to pass Audra.

"Kids," Galen said, "out partying at this time of the morning."

Audra slowed a bit and gave the kids some room. The car in the rear swung back into the left lane and attempted to pass the first car. Both cars rocked back and forth and Galen and Audra could see that both cars had multiple passengers.

"They're going to kill themselves," Audra said. As if on cue, the cars touched sides.

The two speeding vehicles swerved together in the middle of the road. One of the drivers hit his brakes. The braking car swerved hard to the right, colliding into the rear of the other in a shower of sparks. Both vehicles went out of control. The car on the right swerved to the right, onto the gravel shoulder. The driver over-corrected and swerved back to the left, clipping the front end of the other car. One of them rolled over after it hit a concrete embankment along the side of a small bridge. The car leaped into the air, and at the same time began a slow spin. It landed on its top, a trail of sparks following it into the ditch. The other car hit the guardrail leading into a curve then went out of sight.

Audra shrieked as she slammed on her own brakes. The Mustang quickly skidded to a stop. "We've got to help them, Galen!" she said as she spotted small flames escaping from under the hood of the first car.

"We can't!" Galen shouted. "The thing's not too far behind us. We may have all of twenty or thirty minutes before it'll be here!"

Audra bit her bottom lip, and then spoke. "Galen, we've got to, we're obligated to help them. We can't just ignore this!"

Galen tried to decide what to do. If they stayed, the thing would surely show up. They would be a long time at the scene with this many victims to care for. He wondered how long it would take the local authorities to arrive. His mind seemed to process a dozen thoughts at the same time. The "wall" loomed again before him, creating a hard knot in his stomach. He tried to ignore it and acted on one of his favorite sayings; *indecision gets you nowhere.* In the final analysis, the duty to act overrode his fear of the ball-thing, and the 'wall.'

"Okay," Galen said, "you get to the nearest phone and call an ambulance, but I can't guarantee what the Hell's gonna happen!" He reached into the back seat and withdrew Audra's med kit. It had seen more action in the last few hours than it had since she had put it together.

Galen jumped out of the car. "Go!" he shouted. "And hurry!"

Chapter 8

Tobias awoke from the dream with a start. His breaths came to him in short, dog-like pants. He looked around, trying to discover if he had attracted any attention upon waking. Seeing no apparent onlookers, he tried to calm himself, to slow the pounding pace of his heart.

This had not been the first time since the night of Martha's death that he had replayed the scene in his mind. Each time the pain of the memories tortured him worse than the most severe beatings of the whip. The pain seemed to reach up from within his soul, wrapping its icy fingers around his heart and pulling it unmercifully into the dark realm of suffering.

He tried to fight the rush of horrible memories and concentrate on the mission that would avenge the senseless death of his beloved Martha. The gods had sent him on a quest and Tobias had set his mind to its accomplishment.

He was reminded of his hunger by the clutching pangs in his abdomen. He had not eaten anything since the sour apples of the night before. Finding food would have to be his first objective for the night.

The day was almost to an end. The sun cast the golden light of evening upon the surrounding fields. Tobias hoped to make his way back to the road leading north, back to the plantation where he would once again face the man who had caused him such agony.

He dreaded the confrontation with Richards, but at the same time relished the thought of unleashing the power of the gods upon such an evil man. This ember of revenge within his heart would keep the memories warm until he returned.

Tobias began examining his many wounds. Although most of the wounds were superficial, the sweat caused them to burn like the flames of Hell. He touched the deeper cuts across his forehead, discovering them to be the most painful. His right arm still throbbed. The pain seemed more subdued now and parts of his arm felt numb.

Tobias lay quietly for a while longer, awaiting the approach of twilight. Then, like some nocturnal animal, he left the safety of the trees to begin another night of running.

He first went to the stream where he drank of the cool water. The moon reflected brightly upon it, broken into shimmering shards of light by the rippling surface. He could see no detail of his own reflection, only the silhouette of his shape like a quivering dark shadow on the fluid surface of the stream. He recognized the sight as a reflection of how he felt, like a shadow, his spirit dark and formless. Tobias realized he was living his last few days upon the earth. He would soon join the spirits of his ancestors and his wife in the land of the dead. He had no fear of this knowledge. When he finished his duty here, he would reap the rewards of the life beyond this world. Tobias placed his fingertips into the cool mud at the edge of the stream. He wiped the mud into a pattern of shapes on his face, something he had not done since he left Africa. These mud lines on his face were the markings of a warrior from his tribe. If he were to die in this awful land, he would die as a warrior of his people. He would die as Karmanna, not Tobias.

Darkness fell swiftly upon the land of the white man. Tobias made his way north. He crossed open fields where he made good time. By the time the moon was high overhead, Tobias had spotted a long row of trees. He cautiously approached them, listening for any sounds. The road was there and it appeared to be free of travelers. He walked silently along, the moon casting a blue glow upon the landscape around him. He held the pouch, still at his side, now like a part of his anatomy.

He walked the road for hours. The sounds of his feet on the road were as steady as the beating of his heart. It became a tolerable rhythm.

The faint glow of a distant fire caught his eye. He stopped for a moment, the rhythm broken, and trained his eyes on the tiny flicker. It was only a pinpoint of light, slightly off the road to the right. Tobias knew the fire meant men—white men. He decided to go west from the road and to skirt the fire at a safe distance.

He climbed through the brush along the side of the road and peered into the woods beyond it. They seemed unnaturally dark, the glow of the moon unable to reach the forest floor through the boughs of the great pine trees. The ground was covered with fallen needles that had accumulated over the years. It made for quiet travel, except for the occasional dry twig that would crack under the weight of the slave. He turned north, parallel to the road, and walked quietly in that direction.

Tobias moved as silently as possible and kept a steady pace. As he approached the area where the fire was, he stopped and looked to his right. He could make out the flames quite well through the sparse trees. In the dark, he had not realized he had drifted back toward the road and was now only about fifty yards from the fire.

He slowly crept ever closer, until he was just beyond the circle of light. He tucked himself behind a tree for cover and watched for movement. He heard the slight breathing sounds of a sleeping horse. The horse was behind the fire, the glow almost hiding it from his sight. He could also make out the shape of a man, covered by a blanket, asleep on the ground near the fire. Just as Tobias decided to move on, he spotted two leather pouches hanging on a branch of the tree to keep animals from dragging them off in the night. They hung about fifteen yards from where the man was quietly sleeping. The hunger pangs, which he had tried to ignore, flourished wildly as he thought of what lay inside the pouches.

No! he thought. It was too risky. He should keep going, leave this man behind.

Food.

Perhaps he could quietly sneak over and pluck the bags from the branch as if they were ripe fruit, he argued in his mind.

Hunger won out over common sense.

His thoughts were now controlled by the need for food. He pictured himself gnawing at a length of jerky as he plodded along the road. The mental picture gave him hope as he quietly approached the sleeping man's camp. His mouth watered as he thought about the food. He was now only twenty feet away. He again looked around the camp.

The man was still lying alongside the fire, apparently asleep. The only sound Tobias could hear was his own breathing and the subtle snapping from the small fire. He approached the pouches, keeping to the dark shadows of the night as best he could.

When Tobias reached the tree where the bags were hanging, he noticed something that caused his blood to run cold. A second horse stood a few feet behind the first. The horse was black as coal, hardly noticeable in the dark woods. Before he could move away, Tobias heard the distinct *click* of a gun's hammer locking into position.

"Well now, what've we got here?" a voice from somewhere in the darkness asked. A man walked toward Tobias, gun held at waist level and pointed at the slave. "Down on the ground, darkie," he said, "and don't move 'til I tell ya' to move."

Tobias froze, considering his chances of survival if he were to bolt into the dark woods.

"Belly in the dirt, boy!" the voice belted out.

Tobias hit the ground, his years of slavery causing him to instinctively act upon the order. He heard shuffling sounds from the area of the fire as the sleeping man awoke.

"What in the name of God's goin' on, Vince?" the waking man asked as he jumped to his feet.

"Got us a darkie tryin' to steal our horses," Vince said as he approached Tobias. "Prob'ly would'a cut our throats if we was *both* sleepin'. I told ya' one of us ought to keep watch."

Tobias kept his head down and heard the steps of the other man coming toward him.

"Here Lukey, hold the gun on 'im," Vince said. "If he moves, put a hole in his hide."

Tobias felt the pouch begin to grow warm again and relished the now familiar energy that flowed through him. He lay quietly in the semi-darkness, keeping his mind alert for a chance to escape.

He had just raised his eyes to look toward the feet of his captors when pain exploded in his left side, sending his breath rushing out in one harsh blast. The force of the kick from Vince's heavy boot caused Tobias to lose his grip on the pouch and it was flung, unnoticed, under a nearby bush.

"Is that what you was goin' to do boy? Was you goin' to cut ol' Luke's throat and steal his horse?" Vince asked, expecting no reply.

Tobias rolled on the ground, still unable to utter a sound from the lack of air in his lungs. He fought desperately for a breath. He could feel himself slipping into darkness, unable to breathe. Tobias blacked out.

Vince walked around Tobias then kicked him again. This time the blow landed on his buttocks. Unconscious, Tobias did not flinch.

"Good Lord, Vince, I think ya' killed him," Luke said. Luke was a short, heavy man with dark beard stubble covering his face. He held the gun unsteadily, pointed in the general direction of the slave.

Vince was a big man, nearly six-foot-four. A large brimmed hat cast shadows across his face. He knelt down beside Tobias, watching and listening. "Prob'ly should'a killed 'im," Vince said, "but he's still breathin'."

The two men dragged Tobias towards the fire and rolled him onto his back. Tobias' chest moved slightly, drawing quick shallow breaths. His clothes were now just tattered rags and hung loosely about him. The deep cuts on his face from the encounter with the briar patch were swollen but had scabbed over. The rags that were wrapped around his stump arm were caked with mud, dirt and dried blood.

"This boy looks like he's been drug through a knothole," Vince said, looking over the slave.

"Look, he ain't got no hand!" Luke exclaimed. His face grew pale. "Whadda ya' think happened to 'im?"

"Maybe a 'gator bit it off," Vince said, grimacing at the thought. "Let's tie him up," he said. "He ought to be worth a little silver to somebody if we can keep him alive."

They drug Tobias by the ankles to the nearest tree. They leaned him back against it and lashed a rope around him pulling him snugly against the trunk of the tree, until they were satisfied that he would not get away. Then, the two of them began looking for more wood to put on the dying fire.

After they got the fire built back up, Vince walked over to look at Tobias. In the better light, Tobias looked worse than he did the first time Vince had seen him. His head hung limply to one side, but his breathing had become smoother and steadier. Luke took a canteen from his saddlebags and poured some water over Tobias' face. Tobias twitched and his mouth opened slightly. His tongue began to lick at the water. His eyelids trembled slightly before opening to dull yellow slits.

"See there, I told ya' he was still alive," Vince said as he watched the slave begin to move.

Luke was about to slap Tobias gently on the cheeks to help bring him around but then thought better of it, considering the ugly cuts that criss-crossed the slave's face. He decided to try talking to him instead.

"Hey, boy, can ya' hear me?" Luke asked.

Tobias' eyes opened a little more, but the look was unfocused and confused. Luke poured a little more water over Tobias' face and the two men watched as awareness grew on the slave's features.

Tobias jerked back. He shrank away from the two, cowering against the tree. His breathing became harsh once again and he gasped for air. The pain in his side was brutal.

"Ease up now, boy. We ain't goin' to hurt ya'," Luke said.

Tobias struggled hopelessly against the rope.

"Here, drink a little of this water," Luke said as he poured a little more into Tobias' mouth. He smiled at the slave, showing a row of black, rotted teeth. He was careful not to touch the canteen to Tobias' mouth and poured from a couple of inches away.

Tobias allowed the sweet water to run into his mouth, swallowing between labored breaths. He remained very suspicious of the two who now seemed eager to help him.

"Who do you belong to, boy?" Vince asked as he looked into Tobias' eyes. He turned his head to one side and spit out a wad of chewing tobacco.

Tobias let the last mouthful of water run down his chin and considered whether he should answer.

"Speak up, boy," Vince said, "or I'll plant this boot on the side of your head."

"Richards," Tobias croaked. "Masta Richards."

Vince sat back on his heels. "Richards?" he asked. "Benjamin Richards?"

Tobias nodded.

"Are you the slave that killed a field boss when you took to runnin'?"

Tobias looked at Vince suspiciously, his eyes again narrowing to slits. "I ain't killed no field boss."

"You lie!" Vince shouted. "Lukey! I think this here's the slave that killed that field boss on Richards' place a few days back. I'll bet it is!"

Luke began to eye Tobias like a lynching mob might have. "What's your name, boy?" he asked.

Tobias thought a moment; he did not want to answer. Yes, he had gotten into a fight with Frederick, but he had not *killed* him.

94

Had he? Tobias' mind drifted back to the start of his run.

.   .   .

After he shot Martha, Richards went pale. He had not meant to pull the trigger; he had just wanted to make a point. He had lost control in front of his son and Frederick. "Raymond," he said, barely above a whisper, "please go inside." Raymond did not hesitate to comply.

Tobias was on his knees, next to Martha's body, sobbing uncontrollably. "Frederick," Richards said, "find Tobias another place to sleep tonight and take him there. See to it that the body is buried properly."

Frederick approached Tobias and was trying to coax him onto his feet when Richards left the shack.

Richards went to the stable and sat on a stool in the tack room. He felt terrible for having lost control as he had. He had always tried to lead by example, and wanted Raymond to learn that there were times when you had to be stern in order to maintain control. If your slaves and hired hands thought you were soft, they would walk all over you.

Richards was deep in thought about how he would explain this, as he left the tack room and went to find Raymond.

The next day, Master Richards had ordered Frederick to keep Tobias away from the twins. Richards was intent on playing the whole thing down. He wanted the twins to leave with Mary and Ralph before Tobias could say goodbye. He knew Tobias would make a scene and the twins would only be worse off having to see their father and learning of their mother's death.

Richards had also ordered Frederick to keep quiet and not to tell anyone what had happened. He wanted the twins to get to their new home and hoped they would never find out about the death of their mother. Soon after the twins settled into their new home, Tobias would be sold off. Richards would tell Mary that the twin's mother had died a natural death. Soon, it would all be behind him and he would forget it had ever happened. It was just a part of the business that made him a wealthy man.

Tobias had been in the stables that morning after Martha's death, tending to the horses as he did every morning before he went to the fields. Ralph, who had heard nothing about the previous night's activities, ordered Tobias to ready a wagon and two horses for the trip to their new home. Tobias hoped the twins would soon come to fetch the wagon.

A few moments after Ralph had left for breakfast in the big house, Frederick walked in and told Tobias to get into the field.

"But Mista Fred, Mista Ralph done told me to ready-up him a wagon."

"I told you to get into the field!" Frederick said, "Master Richards' orders! Now, *move!*"

Tobias pleaded with Frederick to let him stay for a few more minutes but Frederick would not listen.

"You get your ass into the field *now*," he said, "before I have to drag you out there myself."

Frederick untied the leather strap that held the length of whip to his belt and let the wicked length of braided hide unroll onto the floor.

Tobias backed off and began to walk out of the stable. As he turned the corner outside the door, he heard Gabriel call to him.

"Papa! Papa!" he called.

Tobias twirled around and Frederick gave him a shove from behind. Tobias went sprawling onto all fours. He looked up to see Gabriel running toward him and Titus close behind.

Both boys came to their father.

Frederick gave the whip a snap, a sort of warning shot.

"Into the field boy, and I mean now!" Frederick yelled.

Gabriel was already putting his arms around his father who was still on his hands and knees. Titus was running hard but slowed as he approached, watching Frederick cock his arm back, ready to release the whip.

Frederick pushed Gabriel away from Tobias with his foot, sending Gabriel rolling onto his side on the dusty path.

The whip sailed. Tobias howled as it fell across his back, feeling as if his shirt had caught fire.

Both boys leaped up and simultaneously shouted, "Papa!"

The back door of the big house slammed shut and all heads turned toward the sound. Miss Mary was walking steadily toward the group, hefting her long dress up above her ankles to facilitate maneuvering across the still wet grass.

"For land's sake!" she shouted. "What *is* going on here?"

She walked over to Frederick who let the length of whip fall slack at his side.

"Just followin' your daddy's orders, Miss," Frederick said.

"I doubt my daddy told you to come out here and whip this poor negro," she said. "Now you let these boys tell their daddy 'bye, and I'll send him to the field when they're finished and not a minute before!"

"But, Miss—"

"No buts! Go on, and get to work. I'm sure my daddy would want these boys to get a proper good-bye, so I'll see to it myself!"

Frederick walked over to the stable and stood in the doorway. Richards would be angry with him for letting this happen.

"Now, you boys tell your Papa 'bye and then get busy loadin' that wagon," Mary said, turning to walk away. She stopped in the garden, out of hearing range but close enough to stop that brute Fred if he was to try anything.

Tobias crawled over to the grass alongside the path with one of his boys on each arm. He pulled his boys close, putting an arm around each. For the first time, he and Master Richards had the same idea; he could not tell the twins about their mother. Not now.

"Time for you boys to go away now," Tobias said, trying not to cry. "Mista Ralph and Miss Mary will be good to ya', so you listen good," he told them. "Miss Mary has a likin' for ya' and someday, maybe you might be a field boss, or maybe work all the time in the big house." Tobias squeezed them close and could not hold back the tears. The twins were crying steadily, sobbing between breaths. Tears streamed down their cheeks.

"You two has grown into fine young men," he said as the tears ran from his eyes. "And I'll never forget when the two of ya' was born. You was cryin' and squawkin'...."

Tobias couldn't tell them the stories of their youth; it was too hard. He wanted to let them know he would never forget them and that he loved them. He wiped at the tears in his eyes and remembered how he and many other slaves kept from feeling so sad; they sang.

"It's a long row to be hoein',
It's a long row to be plowin'."

Tobias fought back the choking sobs in his throat and the twins joined their father in the song.

"It's a long way to the Big-House,
but that's where I'll be a goin'.
Them bales are mighty heavy,
Them horses a' mighty strong,
but we'll keep them wagons rollin',
while we be singin' a song."

The twins looked into their fathers eyes and saw the love. They saw, and they understood. That day the twins became men.

Tobias stood up, starting the verse a second time. He felt his legs would not carry him. His grief was like an anchor holding him in place. The boys, still singing, gave their father a hug. Although tears streamed from their eyes, the singing was joyous. Tobias kissed both of them on the forehead and then sent them toward the waiting Miss Mary. He watched them go to her. She put her arms around them and led them to the house. Tobias thought—but was not sure—that she too, was crying.

Frederick still stood in the doorway of the stable. Tobias made his way down the lane. Frederick strode behind him. Tobias could feel Frederick's stare as though it were boring holes through his still-stinging back. Tobias could hear the sound of Frederick's boots on the dusty lane and could tell he was closing the distance between them. Tobias walked steadily and dared not look behind him.

About halfway to the nearest of the fields, Frederick moved close enough that Tobias could hear him breathing. There had been no words spoken and Tobias grew more apprehensive of the man behind him. He expected to feel the crack of the whip, but was very surprised when Frederick looped the whip around his neck, pulling it tight enough to choke him and wrestled him to the ground.

"If you ever do anything like that to me again," the field boss said," I swear I'll beat you like you've never been beat before."

Tobias struggled against the whip, trying to wiggle his fingers between its tight wrap and his throat. Frederick pulled up on the whip, lifting Tobias to his feet. The whip was digging into his flesh and Tobias was desperately struggling for air. In an unconscious attempt to free himself, Tobias swung back with his arms. One of his elbows connected forcefully with Frederick's ribs. Frederick winced and fell backward. Tobias fell to his knees, finally able to breath again.

Tobias was still on his knees when Frederick recovered and again Frederick let loose the whip. It cracked across Tobias' right shoulder and the slave jumped to his feet. He turned to see Frederick loosing the whip again but did not have time to react. The whip landed across the side of his neck. Tobias put his head down and rushed toward the field boss.

Frederick saw him coming and readied himself for the blow. The force of the collision carried them both backward. Tobias fell upon Frederick with the force of a raging bull. Tobias rolled over and quickly stood up.

Frederick was still lying on the ground, moaning softly. Tobias knew he may not survive the punishment for having attacked Frederick and decided immediately, that he must run for his life.

What he had not noticed was the large pool of blood accumulating on the ground behind Frederick's fractured skull.

. . .

"I asked you a question boy. What's your name?" Luke stared into Tobias' eyes, eager to know if this was the slave that killed Richards' field boss.

"Karmanna," the slave said.

Luke looked at Vince. "Is this the one?" he asked.

"I didn't hear the name," Vince said. "But I'd bet my bottom dollar that this here's the slave they're lookin' for."

"Then I'll be guessin' there's a reward out for a renegade slave like him," Luke said as he looked Tobias over again.

Luke walked back toward the fire and dug into one of the bags. He pulled out a bottle and held it up over his head for Vince to see.

"I been savin' the last few swallows for a special occasion," he said as a grin spread across his face. "I guess that this may be the one!"

Luke pulled out the cork and put the bottle to his lips.

He had just begun to rub his ample belly when Tobias heard a thin sound from the woods. Luke dropped the bottle and yelled out, spraying liquor as he fell to the ground. It happened so fast that Tobias did not see the arrow sticking out of Luke's side until Vince ran over to see what the yelling was about.

Vince also did not see the arrow in Luke's side until it was too late. Just as he saw it, another arrow pierced his own back, just to one side of the spine. He also screamed and reached frantically behind himself. His hands searched for the cause of the pain, but could not reach it. Another arrow pierced Vince's side, this one causing him to fall to his knees. Before Vince could fall over, a third and fourth arrow also found their marks. Vince was dead when he landed facedown in the dirt.

Luke was still alive. He squirmed around on the ground, blood beginning to flow from his mouth. He was reaching for Vince's gun as another arrow flew into the light. This one ended what little fight Luke had left in him.

Tobias looked around, frantically, hearing noises from near the horses. He watched as several dark shapes lead the horses deeper into the woods. Three young Indians entered the circle of light from the campfire and began rummaging through Luke and Vince's things. They gathered the bags, took the guns, and looked around for anything else that might be useful. One of them found a hatchet and hefted it a couple of times to get the feel of it. The other two Indians headed back into the woods, carrying their booty. The one with the hatchet took a couple of practice swings, cleanly cutting the air.

Tobias sat quietly, afraid to utter a sound and thought he may go unnoticed. He was then horrified as the young Indian with the hatchet made a quick run toward him, drawing the hatchet back behind him, as if readying a blow. Tobias closed his eyes and screamed.

Chapter 9

Galen cautiously approached the ditch where the first car had come to rest, flipped onto its top. Two teenagers were struggling to free themselves from the wreck. Cries of pain reached out from someone still in the vehicle.

Galen helped the two kids crawl out of the shattered windows and instructed them to move away from the wreck and to lie still. He looked into the car and saw the shapes of two other passengers. Quickly opening the med kit, he withdrew the small flashlight used to check pupil reaction. The tiny light threw just enough of a beam to see the other occupants of the car.

The driver, a young boy, was hopelessly crushed behind the steering wheel, his chest visibly collapsed by the impact with the concrete wall. Galen checked for a pulse and other signs of life. Finding nothing, he moved to the other side of the car. The person on the passenger's side was a girl. She was conscious and in a lot of pain. She moaned loudly, then screamed as if reliving the moment of the crash. Her head was cut badly, but Galen could not remove her from the wreck without risking further injuries. He tried talking to her, in an attempt to determine her level of consciousness. She made no coherent replies to his questions but seemed to be breathing steadily. He shined the light into her eyes. The pupil of her left eye reacted. The right eye was fixed and dilated.

"Damn!" Galen shouted. He felt frustrated. He looked at Audra's med kit, which seemed hopelessly inadequate for this situation. He placed a dressing on the girl's head and held pressure on it for a moment while he thought. The best he could do was to triage the patients in order of severity and hope that the emergency crews would get there soon.

He heard the sound of a motor running on the road. A moment later, a man scrambled down into the ditch. "What the heck happened?" he asked as he looked at the wrecked car.

"Lost control," Galen said. "Can you come over here and keep an eye on this one?" He instructed the man to hold pressure on the bandage and to try to talk to the girl. He also instructed the man to call him if the girl stopped breathing.

The man watched as Galen picked up the med kit. "You a doctor or somethin'?" he asked.

"Paramedic," Galen said. "Now keep an eye on her!"

Galen trotted back over to the two kids who had climbed out of the car. A boy and a girl, they sat under a large tree about twenty yards from the wreck.

The girl seemed to be in better shape, physically, but was sobbing uncontrollably. "Are they dead?" she asked as Galen approached. "Are they?"

Galen told her he did not know yet and asked her to sit back down. He had personally seen many accident victims walk away from the wreck only to die later of spinal, internal, or other critical conditions. The flow of adrenalin would keep them going for a while, but eventually, the injuries would manifest themselves causing a worsening condition or death. They called them the 'walking wounded'.

"Please, just sit still. The ambulance will be here soon," Galen said, as he turned his attention to the boy. "How are you doing?" he asked. The boy was favoring his left leg and complained of a sore neck, but otherwise seemed as if he would make it.

The other car had crashed about fifty yards further down the road, but could not be seen from where Galen was.

Galen shouted to the man who was watching the girl in the car. "How is she?" he asked.

"Still breathin', but actin' kind of out of her head," he replied.

"Keep watching her," Galen shouted as he began to make his way to the other car. He jogged toward the other wreck. He saw headlights coming down the road and hoped it was Audra.

It was.

She saw Galen running toward her and stopped her car. "How are they?" she asked, concern covering her face.

"Looks like one dead, one pretty bad, and two will be okay."

"The ambulance and fire department are on their way," Audra said as she followed Galen into the ditch.

The second car had flipped end-over-end, evident from the shape of the wreck. Audra had grabbed a regular flashlight from her car and they looked inside.

There were three kids in the car, all boys, and none of them seemed to be conscious. Galen began checking for a pulse on the driver and Audra ran to the passenger's side. Most of the windows had been shattered by the impact, the broken glass covering the ground like tiny gemstones.

Galen again found no pulse on the driver. He slumped over in the front seat, his legs a twisted mess crushed beneath the dash. "What've you got over there?" Galen asked as Audra surveyed the other front-seat passenger.

"I don't think this one made it," she said as the horrible look of the knowledge spread across her face.

"What about the one in the back?"

Audra looked into the back seat. The passenger back there was moving slightly, lifting his hands.

"He's moving," Audra said.

Galen tried to gain access to the patient through the twisted metal of the wreck.

"Can you reach him from your side?" he asked Audra.

Audra attempted to wriggle a little further into the wreck, being careful not to injure herself in the process of reaching the victim.

"I can only get a hand on him," she said. "The roof's going have to come off to get to him."

Galen nodded his head in agreement. "Damn," he muttered in frustration. Galen was not accustomed to being on the scene of an accident without the aid of the fire department and their rescue equipment.

The man who had been keeping an eye on the girl in the other car began to yell.

"Hey! This girls startin' to spit up blood!"

Galen looked at Audra and told her to stay with the patient in the back seat.

He began to run back to the other vehicle. The man was waving his arm wildly, calling for Galen to hurry. Galen could hear the wail of a siren in the distance, noting that it sounded like a police squad car.

He reached the other car and took a place beside the girl. A trickle of blood spilled over her bottom lip, mixed with saliva.

Galen took a close look, and realized that the inside of her mouth was cut, probably by her teeth.

"She's still breathing okay," Galen said, wishing he had a portable suction unit. "You're doing a great job," he told the man. "Has she said anything to you?"

The man shook his head. "She just started to spit up that blood and I thought she was gonna die or somethin'."

Galen glanced over at the other two kids still sitting beneath the tree.

"You guys still okay?" Galen asked them. The boy had his arms around the girl as he cried into his shoulder. He nodded to Galen that they were okay.

Galen began to walk over to them, but was distracted by a strange buzzing sound. He stopped and listened, having almost forgotten about the ball in all of the excitement. He strained to hear the strange sound. It was difficult to hear anything over the sound of the many sirens in the distance. He looked intently toward the woods, the dark silhouette of the trees visible below the star speckled night sky.

He saw a small branch quiver then fall from the tree as if it had been clipped of by a pair of shears. Just before he turned to run, he saw the faint light of the ball moving steadily toward him. He turned and scrambled up the ditch to the road. Reaching the road, he turned toward the other wreck. He noticed flashing lights cresting a hill about a half-mile away. He began to yell as he ran toward the other wreck.

"Audra! It's here! Now!" he shouted as he ran.

Audra nearly cracked her head on the wrecked car as she pulled out to listen to him. A feeling of dread quickly crossed over her. She realized that she had also nearly forgotten the thing during the excitement.

Galen looked over his shoulder as he ran toward the car. The thing angled toward him. It was still glowing faintly, an orange aura beginning to grow around it. It moved at a steady rate. He got to the car and yelled again, hoping that Audra was coming - fast.

Galen jumped into the driver's seat of the Mustang and groped desperately for the ignition switch. He cursed beneath his breath when he realized the keys were not in it. In the rear view mirror, Galen could see the ball approaching directly from behind him now. He glanced around to look for Audra, who was just scrambling out of the ditch and onto the road.

She saw the thing when she reached the road, merely a few feet in front of her. Fear grabbed her. She came to a stop, not knowing what to do. The ball continued on a path toward the car and she could see Galen opening the door. She tried to yell, but the sound that left her was no more than a tiny squeak. She was frozen in place. Her mind screamed for her to run, but her body was paralyzed. Galen leaped out of the car. Their eyes met for an instant. She stared in amazement as she saw what appeared to be ghostly-white snakes slithering beneath the ball. The ball was now between the two of them and continued to move on a course directly toward Galen.

Galen turned and began to run. He could see the fire trucks coming down the hill ahead of him. He ran up the road about a hundred yards and turned left onto a dark road that went into the woods.

Audra's paralyzing fear finally turned her loose. She ran for her car realizing she had habitually pulled the keys from the ignition when she parked it along side the road.

106

She saw Galen turn off the road and disappear from sight. The faint glow of the ball was barely visible. The white, snake-things were just a slight glow on the black road. She started the car as the fire trucks began to slow down, approaching the scene of the accident. She sped past them, driving on the shoulder of the road, hoping to catch up with Galen.

Both sides of the road Galen had turned onto were lined with trees, casting darkness over most of the route. In this rural area, the few streetlights were a considerable distance apart.

Galen's pulse was racing and his breaths came in deep pulls. He ran directly down the side of the road, glancing over his shoulder every few seconds trying to locate the ball. This was all like a dream, he thought. One of those dreams where no matter how hard and fast you run, you never seem to make any progress.

The ball disappeared from sight when he turned the corner as it angled on an intercept course through the woods. After about a quarter mile, Galen saw it directly behind him again. He stepped up his pace a bit, knowing he could not hold it there for long. The ball never wavered from its path. Galen lost sight of the ball's faint glow as it was washed out by the more powerful street light. The road ahead of him was clear of traffic and seemed to cut through farmland. A cornfield flanked his left and pastures to his right. He looked over his shoulder again and noticed the ball cutting the corner and coming across the pasture toward him. His pace was wearing down and a stitch in his side was a painful reminder of how exhausted he was.

The sun, still below the horizon, was turning the sky pink in the distant east. He slowed his pace, physically unable to maintain it. Soon, his pace had slowed to no more than a brisk walk. He turned again, and watched the orb as he moved along. It was gaining on him and had closed the distance between them to about thirty yards.

Galen kept his eye on the glowing sphere as he walked backward. Breathing deeply, he hoped to capture a little more energy with which to run.

The ball began to flicker and the strange, orange halo again appeared around it. It shone brightly in those last minutes of morning darkness and the halo began to change shapes. Galen scanned the road before him hoping to see the Mustang.

He turned back to the ball again. Less than fifteen yards behind him, he saw a sight that stole his remaining breath.

A wall of bright orange flames was creeping silently toward him. Its many tendrils seemed alive with fury, reaching into the air, swirling feverishly. Galen felt no heat from the flames, but was mesmerized by their beauty, while at the same time, terrified of their approach. He watched the wall of fire come nearer, the flames licking out at him, trying to draw him in. The wall of flames was wider than the road, engulfing the ditches on both sides. Galen noticed shapes in the flames. Only slightly darker than the flames themselves, the shapes flowed within them, moving, writhing, churning about. He continued to walk slowly backward, eyes locked on the vision before him. He tried to identify the shapes within the churning fire. The wall grew closer, the shapes moved more vigorously.

Galen stopped.

One of the shapes moved forward from deep within the flames. Galen recognized the shape as that of a person whose body was burning violently. He instantly realized the other shapes were also those of people. He could see them more clearly as the wall approached. As they grew closer, he could make out hideously deformed faces enshrouded in the flames. The mouths were gaping holes and the flames were pulled in and blown out as they breathed. The eyes were a pair of dark spots in the flames, the fire rushing over them in hot streams.

The faces could see him, Galen was sure of it. They silently begged him to deliver them from the flames, to save them, to stop the incredible pain. They reached out to him, pleading. Their mouths sucked in and spit out the flames as they cried for his help.

Galen was totally unaware of his surroundings. He could only focus his attention on the shapes within the flames. They were close now, very close. He continued to walk slowly backward, unaware that he was doing so. His chest had tightened to a point that he could scarcely breathe. The sweat that poured over him turned instantly cold.

He peered into the flames. Another shape moved to the front of the flames, a smaller shape. He watched as it became evident that it was the shape of a child. Galen could not tell the sex of the child, but it was clutching the burning, blackened shape of a teddy bear. His heart ached to help this child. He wanted to dive into the flames and pull this child from its clutches. Instead, he cried. Galen had just smacked the "wall," head-on. Too much had happened. His warm, loving heart could not withstand any more pain. The vision of the child was simply the final blow.

His attention was pulled from the burning child by a light so intense that it could not be ignored. Its brightness was such that the flames seemed drab in comparison. It was about chest high, and merely a few feet away. It moved toward him, slowly but steadily, and Galen had to squint his eyes to see it.

Galen stood his ground, unmoving.

A hand grasped Galen from behind, nearly pulling him from his feet. He spun around, his nerves at their ends. He was momentarily blinded from looking into the bright light in the flames.

"C'mon, Galen, run!"

Audra dragged him backwards. He seemed lethargic, almost in a stupor, hardly moving on his own. Half running, half stumbling, she managed to push him into the car. Galen fell across the passenger side bucket seat with his legs still hanging out the door. Audra leaped across to the driver's side and stepped on the gas. Gravel spun from the rear tires sending a spray of rocks and dust into the air as the Mustang shot forward.

Galen had enough presence of mind to grab onto the console between the seats and drag himself fully into the car. He reached for the door handle and pulled it shut. He sat staring through the windshield but saw nothing but the burned-in images of those horrible blazing faces.

Even in the dim light of early morning, Audra could see Galen's face was nearly white. Sweat beaded on his forehead and ran down the sides of his face. His dark t-shirt had a wet v-shape down the front, soaked with perspiration. He breathed in heavy sighs.

Audra was breathing heavily herself. The snakes, translucent and white, were nearly at Galen's feet when she had gotten to him. Their beady red eyes glowed fiercely as they slithered toward him. She had to fight with herself to approach them, even to rescue Galen. Her fear of snakes went back as far as she could remember. There was nothing she could think of that scared her as much.

"You...alright?" she asked.

Galen didn't answer.

"Galen?" she asked again, placing her hand over his.

Galen still did not respond. Audra grabbed his shoulder and began shaking him. "Galen! Answer me! Are you alright?"

Galen looked at her now and she almost wished he hadn't. A gasp escaped her when she saw the look in his eyes. They were so saturated with fear that her own fear nearly doubled.

She had left the accident and tried to follow him, losing him just after the first turn. Searching the adjoining roads, she knew he could not have gotten far. She had come upon him from behind. Slowing, she honked the horn. He acted as if he never heard it. She saw the orb steadily approaching him. That is when she stopped the car and jumped out.

He continued to look at her, eyes still dripping with fear but said nothing. Audra continued to drive ahead, having no idea of where she was, or where she was going.

"Galen," she said. "Where should we go?"

He continued to stare, but said nothing. Audra felt he wasn't even looking *at* her, but *through* her.

"Galen!" she yelled.

His eyes seemed to focus and she could tell that he heard her. She could see the transformation in his face as if he had been sleeping with his eyes open, then suddenly waking up. He shook

110

his head and placed his hands at his temples as if nursing a severe headache.

"Oh, God..." he mumbled.

It was all coming to him now; the accident, the dead and the injured. He remembered the orb appearing. He remembered running. More than anything, he remembered those faces; those horrible, pathetic, suffering faces. Galen shuddered and began to weep.

"Oh, my God," he cried.

"Galen, what's wrong? What's the matter with you?"

"All those poor people!" he cried. "I...I couldn't do a thing! They kept calling me, but I was too afraid. I couldn't go in there. Damn, Damn, DAMN!"

He buried his face in his hands and wept.

Audra, totally confused and scared, tried to get him to talk. "What people, Galen? What people are you talking about?"

"The people in the fire!" he cried. "They needed me but I was too damned scared to help them!"

"What fire? Galen, what are you talking about?" She began to cry herself. "Galen, you're scaring the Hell out of me!"

Galen began to realize he was talking nonsense. He felt as if he had just awoken from a horrible dream, realizing the horrors had not really happened—except in his head.

He remembered a fire in Chicago where he had gotten his first full-time firefighting job. An apartment building had caught fire and Galen had gone into the building on a search and rescue mission. The air-pack he wore had felt tremendously heavy. The bottled air had been dry and heavy in his lungs. He climbed the stairs of the smoke-filled building with the other two members of his team, crawling on their hands and knees, lugging a fire hose along with them. Galen had felt the level surface of a landing and the team spread down the smoky hall. He had breathed so hard he thought he would drain his air supply and not make it back out. The team had come to a door and pushed it open.

Flames had been clinging to the walls of the room. Through the heavy smoke, Galen had seen a faint light where the windows were. The fire had swept toward the broken windows, searching for the air it needed to survive. The leader of Galen's team had trained the hose on the rioting flames, sending the fire into retreat. Galen had spotted the burned bodies of three victims on the floor.

The bodies had been burned beyond recognition and Galen could not tell if they had been male or female, young or old. The team had battled the flames for control of the room. They had made their way toward the bodies. Upon reaching them, Galen had turned one over. The back of the body had been scorched, the hair burned off, the skin a dry, bubbly black. The body had been lying face down, and when he rolled it over, he could make out the face, unburned where it lay against the floor. Parts of the clothing had been sheltered from the flames by the body and the bright colors had looked odd in the colorless black and gray of the rest of the room.

The team, knowing the people were dead, had forced the flames back; back until they were just smoldering wisps of steam and smoke.

Galen had been unsure of his career as a firefighter after that day. It took hours of counseling before he realized he could continue being a firefighter. He *had* decided to leave Chicago and soon afterwards found his way to Willow River Fire and Rescue.

The nightmares of that day in Chicago still haunted him on occasion and Galen's worst fear was that he may someday relive such a devastating scenario.

"You didn't see the fire?" he asked Audra, trying to reassure himself it really *had* been some kind of dream.

"Galen, for God's sake, what are you talking about?"

"The fire… I was running from the ball and when I looked back there was this horrible wall of fire creeping along behind me." He took a deep breath. "I know this sounds crazy. It even does to me now. But then, *then*, when it was happening, it was so real, so damned *real!*"

Audra looked at him, her eyes swollen from crying. Tears caused her cheeks to shine slickly and her mouth hung open with a string of saliva stretching from her top lip to her bottom lip.

"There were people in the fire, Audra. They were burning up. They were still alive, but their bodies were ablaze. They called to me to help them, but I... I couldn't do anything."

Galen looked away from her and gazed at the farmland passing by his window. He felt somewhat ashamed that he had not helped the people in the fire, even though he knew now it could not have been real. Maybe it had not been real, but the feeling of terror remained in his gut, way down deep.

"Take me home, Audra. Please, take me home."

"I don't even know where we are," she said.

The sun was now well above the horizon and they were driving straight toward it.

"We're heading east," Galen said. "We can find out where we are at the next little town." He glanced at the gas gauge, which read less than a quarter of a tank. "We need gas and something to eat. Then we can head back to The Willows and call this guy Paxon."

Audra nodded and began looking for a road that went south. She wiped the wet remnants of the tears from her eyes and concentrated on her driving. All that crazy talk about the fire and the people had scared her badly. She had only seen the white snakes and the ball, glowing as bright as a headlight. That had been bad enough. She had certainly seen no fire and no burning bodies. She wanted to tell Galen about the snakes, but waited. Maybe, she thought, they were suffering some kind of hallucinations. He, like herself, hadn't had any sleep. Maybe it was a combination of stress, exhaustion, and the absurdity of the ball that had caused them to see whatever it had been. She had no sooner thought these things when she noticed Galen had leaned against the car door and had closed his eyes.

The next town to the south had turned out to be Oakton. The town bustled in its small town, early morning way.

A rotund little man swept the sidewalk in front of the local grocery, clad in his white apron. The donut shop on the corner had a steady stream of customers going in empty-handed and coming out eating rolls and drinking coffee. A telephone truck was parked on the wrong side of the road preparing to get the day started. Shops were beginning to open their doors along the main street." Sorry, we're CLOSED" signs were being flipped over to read "Come in, we're OPEN."

Audra drove along, searching for gas and food. She spotted two cafes, directly across the street from each other. The town was too small for fast food chains to have moved in yet. She hoped to grab something quick, and eat it on the road. Instead, it looked like they would to have to sit in a cafe and wait for the food to be prepared. She had no idea how far behind the ball-thing was or how much time they had before it would find them again.

She spotted a convenience store and gas station combination and decided to get gas first. She pulled the Mustang up to pump #4. As she moved around the car she noticed Galen waking up in the front seat. He stretched his arms out behind his head and yawned deeply. Audra removed the gas cap and began filling the tank.

"Where are we?" he asked.

"Oakton," she replied. "There are a couple of cafes in town if you're hungry."

He nodded and shuffled toward the building.

When Audra entered after filling the car, she found Galen at the checkout counter paying for the gas, along with a diet soda and a pack of Salems.

"Anything you need?" he asked her as she walked over.

"A toothbrush and a tube of toothpaste would be nice," she said, opening and closing her mouth, indicating how sticky it was.

"Good thinking," he said. "See if you can find two."

The cashier patiently waited as Audra browsed through the aisles. After a moment, she appeared with the required items plus a bottle of Listerine. She placed two toothbrushes on the counter, (pink for her and blue for Galen, so as not to get them mixed up) and pushed them, the mouthwash and the toothpaste toward the cashier. She rang up their purchase and they headed back toward the car.

"Want me to drive for awhile?" Galen asked as they approached the Mustang.

"Think you're up to it?" she asked.

"Sure, no problem," he said, flexing the fingers of his bandaged hand. "It feels a lot better this morning."

Galen sat in the driver's seat, his knees hitting on the steering wheel.

"I didn't realize you were so short," he said as he searched for the lever to slide the seat back.

"I'm not short," she said. "You're just taller than me, that's all."

Galen managed to get comfortable and drove back toward downtown. He parked in front of one of the cafes and looked into the window.

"Looks kind of busy in there," he said. He turned to look at Audra who was looking across the street at the other cafe. She was wondering if it was any less crowded and if so, why?

"How long did it take us to get here?" Galen asked.

"About thirty minutes, I guess."

Galen did some quick calculations in his head, wondering how accurate they would be.

"Let's not spend more than thirty minutes in here," he said. "We should be safe with that."

They got out of the car and walked to the cafe across the street. They entered and Galen lead them to the only unoccupied booth.

They ordered breakfast from a young girl named Jennifer and ate as they discussed their next move. They spoke quietly, not wanting to be overheard by the locals who sat all around them. Within the half-hour limit they were back on the road. Their stomachs were satisfied and their minds more relaxed after the meal.

Galen was driving as Audra looked at a map, searching out the shortest route to Willow River. Galen was watching the road, deep in thought.

"Did you see the ball while we were at the accident scene?" he asked.

"Yea. After you yelled, I climbed out of the ditch. It passed by me while you were running for the car."

Galen nodded. "The car with no keys in it, I might add," he said, heavily laced with sarcasm.

"Excuuuuse me!" Audra said. "I have a habit of removing the keys from my car when I park it. It deters auto theft!"

"Yea?" Galen said. "Well, it damn well could have gotten us killed in this case!"

"What do you mean, *us?* You were about to save your own skin and leave me there with that thing!"

"It was after *me!* What did you want me to do?"

"It would've been nice for you to have thought of me. What would I have done if you'd taken the car and the thing turned on me?"

"The same damn thing that I did. Run your ass off! And then I would have..." Galen realized she had done the same thing he would have done. "... come and found you. Like you did for me," he said, now sorry he had gotten so upset.

Galen looked at Audra who had turned away from him. He could not tell if she was hurt or angry, without seeing her face.

"Audra, I'm sorry. I didn't mean to get upset with you. It's just that—"

Audra looked at him and Galen still could not tell if she was mad or hurt that he had yelled at her.

Maybe that's why his first marriage had bombed. He just could not seem to read a woman's face. He also seemed to be able to get into an argument with a woman over the stupidest things. He hadn't meant to bring up the thing about the keys. It just came out.

"It's okay, Galen," she said. "We're both under a lot of stress right now. Who wouldn't be? Let's just drop it and get

116

back to The Willows. I'm tired and I'd like to sleep for a few minutes on the way back. Okay?"

Galen nodded. *Yep, she's pissed,* he thought as she turned back around and leaned against the door. He couldn't blame her. If he had a nickel for every time he had done the same thing to his first wife, Laurie, he would be a rich man.

He remembered having a nice pleasant conversation with Laurie that would suddenly become hostile. He would say something that made her feel stupid or inadequate in some way. He did not mean to do it and was always sorry for it afterward. But a woman could only accept so many 'sorrys.'

He liked Audra a lot and really thought she was a bright, intelligent woman. He had thought the same thing about Laurie or he wouldn't have married her. *If I can't learn to keep my foot out of my mouth, I'll never be able to keep a good woman around,* he thought.

They drove the rest of the way to Willow River in silence. Audra leaned against the door and slept. They entered The Willows at mid-morning. Galen drove straight to his house and woke Audra.

"I'm gonna take a quick shower and change clothes," he told her. "If you want to do the same, why don't you just meet me back here when you're done?"

Audra got out of the car and walked to the driver's side.

"We can go over to Al's and try to call this Paxon guy," Galen continued.

Audra reached for the door handle and hesitated.

"I've been thinking," she started, "I might just take my chances alone. I don't want to slow you down, Galen." She pulled the door open.

"Don't..." Galen bit his tongue before blurting out the rest of what he was about to say. *Don't be stupid, Audra!* He had almost done it again.

"Don't go, Audra," he managed to say instead. "I'm sorry for what I said back there. I really am."

Audra was drawing little lines in the gravel driveway with the toe of her shoe while leaning against the open door.

117

"I don't know, Galen. Maybe it would be better if we—"

Her words were cut short when Galen slowly, but firmly, grabbed her arms and pulled her close to him.

"I want you with me," he said.

Their chests were touching, sending a certain excitement through them both. Audra looked at him uncertainly and started to pull away. Galen gently pulled her closer and could feel her resistance fade away.

"I can't think of anybody I would rather face this thing with," he said, "except... maybe, Superman."

Audra giggled and they looked into each others eyes. A moment of uncertainty passed between them, just before Galen kissed her. She wrapped her arms around him and laid her head against his chest, squeezing him tight.

"I changed my mind," Galen said.

Audra looked at him, uncertain of what he meant.

"Not even Superman," he said, and kissed her again.

Chapter 10

Tobias shrieked as the young Indian swung the hatchet. He heard the hatchet bite into the tree and shuddered as he felt the bindings around him loosen.

When he opened his eyes, he saw the young brave grinning wide and nodding at him as he backed away. His body was dark in the light of the fire. His long, black hair was riding on his shoulders. Within seconds, all of the warriors were gone. Tobias could hardly believe they had actually been there, except the bodies of Vince and Luke were still lying near the fire. He could hear the horses in the distance as the Indians led them through the woods.

The Creeks, Tobias thought. The tribe lived in and around the great swamps of the southeast where their ancestors had built a way of life they still knew. He had heard stories of the Creek Indians. They had been known to help runaway slaves. Sometimes, they had even taken the slaves into their camps and protected them. One story told of a Creek Chief who had taken a slave girl as his wife. He had found her as a runaway. She had become a Creek, living with them as one of their own.

The Creeks were also enemies of the white men. The whites were stealing their land. The native tribes and the slaves had a common bond; their battles against the overpowering white men. The same white men who sought to steal the way of life from those who had a different colored skin.

Tobias sat for a few moments; wanting to be sure he wasn't dreaming. He pushed away the loose ropes and stood up. The pain in his side caused him to slump. He was unable to stand fully erect without the pain becoming too intense. He palpated his aching side, certain his ribs had been broken.

The slave hobbled over to where he had dropped the pouch. Sinking to his hand and knees, he felt about for it. When his probing fingers brushed against it, he felt a shock travel the length of his arm. Picking up the pouch, he placed it in its now accustomed resting spot; nestled between his right arm and his side. The energy coursed through Tobias as he rolled over onto his back. He basked himself in its warmth and felt the power of the gods pumping through his veins.

He limped back to the fire and looked at the bodies of Vince and Luke. The Indians had taken anything of value from their pockets, but both men still wore their clothing. Tobias struggled to one-handedly remove Luke's heavy shirt from his dead body. He would have taken the pants as well, except that his attention was caught by the sight of an overturned pan lying at the edge of the fire. It must have been knocked over during the struggle. Tobias raked it from the heat with a stick.

The pan was still a quarter full of beans and pork fat. The perimeter of the food had grown crusty from the heat, but the center was still moist. Tobias dragged the hot pan over to a large rock and used Luke's shirt to set the pan on top of it. He discarded the rag, which had been his old shirt, and put on Luke's as he waited for the cool rock to draw some of the heat from the pan.

It seemed it would take forever for the pan to cool. Tobias used the tail of the shirt and carried it into the woods. He did not expect anyone to be traveling the road this late at night but wanted to take no chances.

He traveled carefully through the dark woods, walking parallel to the road. He stopped to check the pan. His mouth watered in anticipation of devouring every bean.

The pouch had slowly stopped giving off the strange, but wonderful, energy that kept Tobias going.

He found a short, stubby stick and drug it through the food. He gently blew on the steaming beans and cautiously touched them to his lips. Soon, he was scraping as much of the dried, burned food from the sides of the pan as he could.

He began to move again discarding the pan for the forest creatures to have their try at it. He approached the road. Seeing nothing, he emerged from the woods. The night was unusually cool for this time of year and Tobias was glad to have the newly acquired shirt.

He began to put distance between himself and the bodies, which lay beside the fire. He wondered if Frederick had really died. If he had, there was no way Tobias would live. The punishment for a slave who killed a white man was public hanging. If a black killed another black, he would most likely be beaten. Though Frederick was poor, he was still white.

Tobias plodded along the lonely road keeping a steady rhythm. He was in considerable pain. He eagerly awaited another dose of the warmth from the pouch. He had begun to realize that whatever was in the pouch cared for him. Whenever he felt like he could not go on or needed a sudden burst of energy, the pouch grew warm. Sometimes it grew hot, and beyond that, it would begin to vibrate. Usually, when he was traveling, it would give him small doses of the warmth. It would gently feed him, a little at a time, like a mother nursing her young.

He traveled a considerable distance before the sun rose for that day, causing him to seek refuge in the woods. Before he left the road, Tobias looked at the land around him. He recognized some of the features here and if he recalled correctly, a small town lay ahead.

Tobias would rest awhile after looking for some water. He would travel as far as the woods would allow before stopping for the day. He figured he had roughly a days travel back to the plantation. It may take a little longer, due to his present physical condition, but Tobias could feel its closeness.

He found a trickle of water running in a small stream about a mile from where he entered the woods. He drank deeply. He then pulled together a mattress of pine needles. As he lay down to rest, he had a bout of the recurring ghost-pains from his missing right hand. He imagined flexing his fingers as the pain shot up his arm. He would never become accustomed to not having the hand. He still reached for things with the stump before realizing his mistake. The missing hand also itched. It was so strange to have these sensations.

He began to inspect the rags wrapping the stump of his arm. They were constantly working themselves loose. He moved his right arm away from his body, letting the pouch slip gently to the ground. He held the stump across his lap and attempted to tighten the rags. He loosened a knot and unwrapped one of the rags, intending to re-wrap it more tightly.

As he unfolded the rag, small wriggling maggots fell from between the wraps. Horrified, he stripped the remainder of the rags from the stump in a panic and jumped to his feet.

A thick, yellowish liquid oozed from the wound and Tobias began to feel sick. He had not seen the wound until now, for Wilbur had wrapped it before he awoke that first morning. His nostrils flared at the repulsive smell of the infection. He leaned against a tree and fought the sudden urge to vomit. The wound immediately became more painful, as if seeing it triggered in his mind a more severe condition than he had imagined. He managed to escape the urge to vomit with just a few dry heaves then regained his composure.

Tobias stripped off his new shirt and attempted to tear it into bandages. He tried desperately, but the material was too tough. He took a few deep breaths to help settle himself, then walked over to pick up the rags he had just taken off. He carried them along the small stream, looking for a pool in which to rinse them out.

After rinsing the rags as best he could, he returned to his pine-needle mattress. He covered the sickening stump and began to tie the rags back into place. Once finished, he lay back on the makeshift bed.

He managed to sleep for over four hours before waking to the sound of a nearby flock of crows. Tobias sat up. The woods were dark for midday, storm clouds moving in from the west. He drank again from the small stream and decided to put on more miles. He picked a route that was as northward bound as the terrain would allow. He walked for several hours until he heard the sound of a blacksmiths hammer ringing in the distance.

Nearing the town, he would now wait until nightfall before moving further. Again, he made a comfortable place to lie down, but this time sleep would elude him.

He tried to imagine his confrontation with Master Richards. He must get Richards alone. He contemplated various plans, knowing Richards' daily routine. The morning ride would be a good time, but Tobias was certain that another slave would have taken over his old job in the stables. Tobias had readied Master Richards' horse for him almost everyday for the last three years. He had inherited the job from old Jake, who had gotten too sick to work. He had eventually died and Tobias had filled the position permanently. Tobias thought he could sneak into the big house, perhaps into Master Richards' study. Richards always stayed up after the rest were in bed to look at his books.

Tobias would think of something; some how, some way, he had to get the pouch into Richards' hands. He could feel he was going to make it. The gods had blessed him so far and he felt they would guide him to the plantation.

He lay awake, looking at the sky. He watched the storm clouds drift across it in varying shades of gray. Before nightfall, the rains began to seep from the clouds. The rain was gentle at first, washing the last of the day's light away. It became violent toward nightfall, almost abrasive as it hammered the land.

Tobias began to move again keeping to the woods to shelter him from the heavy rain. The lightning blazed across the sky and thunder rolled in waves. Tobias could feel the thunder pounding in his bones. He came to open fields as he neared the town, dashing across them as quickly as he could.

He skirted the backside of a farm and thought of entering the barn. He looked at it from the field, thinking of its warmth and dryness. The pouch began to warm his side, as if in warning. *Just move on, Tobias*, it seemed to say. *Just keep going, and I'll give you strength.*

123

The wind began to howl, sending the rain into Tobias' face in sheets. He bent into the wind, leaning against its strength. Chilled on the outside, the pouch warmed him from within.

He made slow progress during the storm but soon after the rain had stopped, he was able to get back onto the road. He had by-passed the town and now made much better progress.

By the time morning came, Tobias was beginning to recognize more and more familiar landmarks. He had traveled this far occasionally, running errands for Master Richards. He crossed the road that lead to the Reynolds farm, where Master Richards sometimes sent him to fetch a pig or two. Just ahead a couple of miles, was the big river. After he reached it, he would go west and eventually cross it. There was a bridge to the east but it was two or three miles out of his way.

When he had escaped, he had floated down the river hanging onto a large branch that he had pushed into the water. He had hoped it would throw off the dogs for a while, giving him a chance to get a lead on them. They would eventually find his trail and the hounds would pursue him relentlessly. He was thankful, though surprised, that they had not caught up to him yet.

Unknown to Tobias, the hounds had led the slave catchers to Wilbur's camp and were now on their way back toward him. The slaves in Wilbur's camp had pleaded ignorance. The lie had worked well enough to avoid a beating but the slave catchers left with a suspicious look on their faces. They were now only hours behind him, but the rains of the night before would make the scent harder to follow.

Tobias made his way through the woods to the banks of the river. He was exhausted from the night's travel. His body ached like never before. The ghost-hand feelings had returned, along with the excruciating pain of the stump. The cuts on his face and back were becoming infected. His ribs ached with each breath. His buttock sported a large bruise where Vince had kicked him while he lay on the ground.

He looked around for some edible plants and found enough to satisfy his raging hunger for a while. He decided to set some snare traps before resting. Tobias had shown his sons, as his father had shown him, how to set the traps. Their meager meals had often been supplemented by the capture of a rabbit or a squirrel. He could remember clearly when he caught his first dik-dik, a tiny deer-like creature slightly larger than a rabbit, native to his homeland. He had been so proud. His father had shown him how to clean his catch and how to build a smokeless fire to cook it over.

He set three of the snares across the small paths he found among the undergrowth. An untrained eye would never have noticed the slight paths made by the small animals but Tobias knew where and what to look for. He grew hungrier as he thought about a meal of cooked rabbit or squirrel.

After completing the traps Tobias looked for a place to rest. He chose a spot beneath a large, fallen tree. The runner immediately fell into a deep, dreamless sleep.

When he awoke, he discovered he had slept the entire day away. The sun indicated it was late afternoon. He had almost forgotten he had set the snares. The first and second traps he set were empty, but the last one contained a good-sized swamp rabbit. The rabbit kicked wildly as Tobias approached, but the snare held him fast.

He reached out to grab the swamper by the hind legs when he heard the sound of several hounds, hot on the trail of something; probably him.

Chapter 11

Galen quickly finished his shower and put on a clean change of clothes. He calculated they had about two hours (including a safety factor) before the ball-thing would reappear in Willow River.

His attention was captured momentarily by the hole in the outside wall of his kitchen where the ball-thing had entered the house the last time he was there. It was a perfectly round hole. Slightly smaller than a tennis ball, it allowed Galen a view of the morning sunshine outside. He inspected the hole in the interior wall between the kitchen and the living room. He noticed by the angle of the hole, that the ball had altered its course to match his when he had fled through the front door.

Galen sat heavily on his couch. He felt nervousness in his stomach, as if he were about to be forced to speak to a large crowd. Galen wondered if he were about to have a nervous breakdown. He fought with these thoughts, trying to push them back. He thought of his Dad, quietly working his life away as an accountant in Chicago. His father had approached Galen about taking over the family business several times. "Make a lot more money," he would say. "Use your head instead of your back, Galen," was another favorite.

Now, for the first time, Galen gave it a serious consideration. No more accident scenes. No more heart attack victims. No more house fires that put families on the street. He wanted a quiet job in an office building. It did not look so bad from where Galen sat right now, but he had to deal with the situation at hand.

Audra had gone to her apartment to freshen up and change clothes. She had agreed to meet Galen back at his place before going to look for Paxon's phone number.

She thought about calling her mother who also lived in The Willows. Audra was sure her mother had called her apartment looking for her and was probably wondering where she was. Talking on the phone was a Saturday morning ritual for Audra and her mother. They would talk for about an hour, usually about Sharon and Jack's latest marital problems. Her mother would usually cry, and then Audra would go over to visit her in the afternoon. She would be asked to stay for dinner. She knew if she called her mom now she would never be able to explain what was happening. She decided to call her later, from the road.

She slipped into a clean pair of jeans and took a few minutes to put on some makeup. She did not care what was after her. If she had to be out in public, she was going to look presentable. She sacrificed the few minutes it would take to blow-dry her hair and went out the door.

She passed her mailbox on the way out of the building intending to leave her mail until later. She hesitated when she saw a picture of a family friend, Mr. Carter, on the front page of the paper. She picked it up and read the headlines on the way to her car.

Audra pulled into Galen's driveway a few minutes later and honked the horn. Galen closed his back door and hurried down the steps. Audra had acquired a pair of sunglasses since Galen last saw her. He did not like not being unable to see her eyes, but the glasses gave her a mysterious look, somehow making her seem more elegant.

"What's in the bag?" she asked as Galen tossed it into the back seat.

"Just some extra clothes, a razor, junk like that," he answered. "I don't know how long we will have to run from this thing," he said. "It's not like we can just call time-out or something."

Audra looked behind her as she backed out of the drive. "Maybe I should have done the same." She noticed the newspaper on the back seat. "Grab that newspaper," she said, tossing her head toward the rear of the car. "Read the front page."

Galen turned in his seat and located the paper. He looked at the photograph and began to read the words below it.

"Ball lightning?" he asked.

"Yeah, only we know better," Audra said.

Galen began to read the story aloud.

"Ball lightning is the only explanation anyone can think of for the unusual happenings that occurred at the Walter P. Carter residence last night. Carter, 63, resides on the village's north-west side. At about eight-thirty P.M., he and his wife, Maggie, were interrupted while watching television. 'All heck broke loose,' Carter said. 'We were just sitting in the living room, when we heard this funny noise.' Carter describes the noise as a high-pitched, raspy sound. 'That's when we saw the little ball of light. It just kind of floated through the kitchen and then went into one of the bedrooms. It made a hole right through the wall,' says Carter. The unknown object continued on a path of destruction through the house. 'It hit some wires in the wall and the whole place lost power,' Carter says. The Willow River Fire Department was dispatched to investigate. 'We have no explanation,' says Fire Chief, Roy Atley, 56. 'We checked the house for any signs of fire, and called the electric company to restore power,' says Atley. Damage to the home is estimated at $1,200, and the Carters say they will begin repairs 'as soon as we can find someone to do the work.' A neighbor's house narrowly missed being damaged, as the Carters said they saw the 'ball of light' turn suddenly and cross an open field. 'We're just glad it's over,' says Carter."

"Someone could have been hurt, or killed," said Audra

"I know," Galen said, obviously troubled by the story.

"Let's get in touch with Paxon and try to stop this thing."

Galen just about yelled, wanting to ask, *what the Hell do you think we're doing?* Instead, he nodded and bit his tongue.

As they approached Gaston's house, Galen immediately noticed a sheet of plywood covering the shattered front window. He began to wonder who may have done this, but was glad that someone had.

They parked near the back door. Galen saw it had been fitted with a metal hasp and padlock. He walked around to check the front door. It had also been fitted with a new padlock.

"Damn," he said as he rattled the lock. "Who's been out here?"

Audra shrugged. "Maybe his lawyer," she suggested.

"We gotta get in there," Galen said as he began to check the windows. He then had an idea. Galen led Audra to the back of the house and stopped at a pair of old-fashioned cellar doors. A padlock also held the doors shut but it was older, showing signs of light rust.

"There's a hidden key for this one," Galen said. He walked over to a nearby flowerbed and lifted a stone, retrieving a key. He slipped the key into the padlock and struggled with it slightly before it fell open. The heavy door groaned as Galen pulled it up.

"Galen, I don't think we're supposed to be in here," Audra said. "Someone put those locks on the doors for a reason."

"Yeah, well, this is the only place we're going find that number," Galen said. "And without that, we've got nobody else to call for help."

"If we get caught in here, we could go to jail," Audra said nervously.

"It's better than the morgue," Galen replied, putting an end to the question of whether or not they should go in. He braced the door open with a metal rod and they went down the steps.

"Kinda spooky down here," Audra mentioned, brushing cobwebs from her path as they approached another door. Galen pushed it open. They walked through the basement, the only light coming from the small windows along the top of the wall. The house was amazingly quiet and Audra felt like a burglar as they prowled. They worked their way upstairs, and eventually entered Al's study.

"My guess would be it's in here somewhere," Galen said. "Let's look for a phone list and anything we might find about that ball." He checked his watch. "We've got a little over an hour," he said. "Let's get busy."

Audra walked over to the cluttered desk and Galen to the table where he had opened the box and let the crazy ball out in the first place. The box lay overturned on the table. He cautiously turned it over with a wooden ruler. Seeing nothing unusual, Galen removed the velvet the ball had sat on, along with the wooden insert that held the ball in place. He found nothing else in the box.

Audra was shuffling things around on the desk searching for a personal phone book. She searched the drawers and the surrounding bookshelves but could not locate a list of phone numbers. She glanced up and looked around the room. Galen was searching a table below a window, sorting through the various piles of stuff. She noticed the personal computer on the small desk along one wall.

"Did Al use his computer much?" she asked.

"All the time," Galen answered. A smile crossed his face as he realized what she was thinking. The smile turned to a frown as he approached the computer desk.

"Do you know how to work a computer?" he asked Audra. "I haven't the foggiest idea."

"Sure," she said, walking toward him. "We use them all the time at the hospital."

"Well, what are you waiting for?" he asked as she approached.

"Hey, just keep your pants on, Buster," she said as she pulled out the chair.

Galen watched over her shoulder as she turned on the machine. "Al used to say these things were the greatest tools in the world, once you got used to it."

After the machine warmed up a moment, the screen displayed a menu. "Word processor, spread sheet, checkbook manager," Audra said, reading the list of programs. "Recipes?" she said, and looked at Galen.

"The man had to eat," Galen chuckled.

"PC maps, a disk manager, and a telecommunications program," she continued. "Ah! Electronic Phone Book," she said and pushed a couple of keys.

The screen blanked for a moment then reappeared with a list of names and phone numbers. They were in alphabetical order and Audra stopped the scrolling when she reached the P's.

"Paxon, John," she said. "555-403-5621."

Galen grabbed a pen from the desk and wrote the number on the back of an envelope.

"Good," he said. "Can you find out if there's anything about the ball in there somewhere?"

"We can look around," she said. "He probably kept written notes in the word processor."

She exited the phone-listing program and entered the word processor. Another menu appeared and Audra chose "List Files". The screen filled with the names of the files Al had stored there. At the bottom of the screen, a message appeared saying, "press any key to continue".

Each time Audra pressed a key, the screen filled with the names of more files.

"There are hundreds of files in here, Galen," Audra said, reaching the end of the list. "He must have written an awful lot of things."

"Is there any way to tell if any of that stuff is about the ball?"

Audra thought for a moment. "We could look through the file names and see if any of them say anything about a ball. But since we don't know what he called it, it'll be a long shot."

Galen scratched his chin. "Why don't you keep looking through the computer and I'll see if I can get Paxon on the phone." He walked over to the desk and sat in the big leather chair.

Audra continued to search through the hundreds of files, looking for anything related to the ball. Audra knew that on this type of computer, a file name was limited to eight characters. She had herself experienced the meaning of this limitation. For instance: if you wrote a letter to your mother every week you

131

couldn't name it "letter to Mom, March 13, 1991", so you might shorten it to "LTM31391". Like a personal code, filenames could be hard to decipher. Audra searched for clues to the meaning of the filenames. She heard Galen as he began to speak into the phone.

"Yes, Mr. Paxon. My name is Galen Morris, from Willow River, Illinois. I'm calling because a good friend of mine, Professor Albert Gaston has passed away. Before he died, he instructed me to send you something. The *something* is what I'm calling about. It's very urgent that I talk to you. Actually, it's a matter of life and death. I'll be leaving soon, but will try to call you again later. Thank you." He hung up the phone and looked at Audra. "I hate answering machines," he said as he folded the envelope with the number on it. He stuffed it into his pocket. "Having any luck over there?"

"Not really," she answered. "There's just too many files to go through and without having a clue as to what he named them..." She shrugged. "It'll just take time."

"Something we don't have a lot of," Galen said. He leaned back in his chair and let out a long breath. He reached across the desk and retrieved an ashtray. "I don't know what to do next," he said after lighting up. He blew a cloud of smoke toward the ceiling. "I guess we're gonna have to go somewhere and call Paxon again later." He took a long draw on the cigarette. "I hope like Hell he's not on vacation or something."

Audra looked around the room as if searching for something.

"What are you looking for?" he asked, bellowing out another cloud of smoke.

"Where's the printer?" she asked.

Galen took his feet off the top of the desk and sat up. "Beats me," he said, looking around.

"Maybe it broke down or something," she said, still scanning the room. "If he did this much writing, he must have had a printer."

Galen shrugged again. "He didn't mention anything about it to me," he said.

"Let's take it with us," Audra said, still tapping at the computer's keyboard.

"Take what with us?" Galen asked.

"The computer," she said, turning to face him.

"Can you plug it into the cigarette lighter in your car or something?" Galen asked.

"No, silly," Audra responded. "You can't plug it in to a cigarette lighter, but you can plug it in to a motel room's electrical outlet."

"Hey, give me a break. I told you I didn't know anything about computers." He crushed out the cigarette. "Let's get rolling and put some time between us and that thing."

They unplugged Al's computer. Galen carried it while Audra carried the monitor. They placed it carefully on the back seat, which was now becoming cluttered with supplies. They drove quickly back to Audra's.

Galen was amazed at how quickly she returned with extra clothes. He had pictured her going through her closet, making sure everything matched. He visualized her neatly folding all of the clothes as she placed them into an overnight bag.

"Your turn to drive," she said, as she motioned Galen to take the driver's seat.

She felt as though she were going on some great adventure. Although the fear of the ball remained with her, she couldn't help being excited by the thought of traveling with Galen. Maybe it was just that she was breaking out of the boring routine she had fallen into. Work, read a book, sleep; sometimes a movie. Of course, there was always laundry.

This was different, it was *exciting*. It meant facing the unknown in a world where everything was the same all of the time. She wanted to find out what the ball was, even if it meant risking her life.

Galen, on the other hand, was truly frightened. He had thought a lot about the night before when he had been running from the horrible wall of flames. That had scared him badly. He did not want to know what it was, or how it had come into Al's possession. He wanted to be rid of it. He wanted to feel the freedom of his mundane, regular life again.

It had been less than twenty-four hours since he had first set eyes on the thing, but it seemed as if it were years. Now his entire life depended upon staying ahead of the ball, which meant constant running. What if this guy, Paxon, had never heard of it? What if he offered no help at all? He could not run for the rest of his life.

Galen was also feeling a tremendous responsibility for Audra. He had been the one who had invited her to Al's last night. She had been generous in her offer to help. Now she was in danger because of her generosity and for no other reason. It was his fault. He must find a way to set them both free, to enable them to return to normality. Galen, once again, considered life as an accountant.

Galen drove west on route 20 toward route 39 south. Audra slept for a while, leaning uncomfortably against the door. She stirred only once and had asked Galen if she could use his bag of clothes for a pillow. He had told her she was welcome to it and she seemed to drift back to sleep within seconds.

Audra had fallen asleep thinking about Galen. She could smell his scent on the bag. She had never felt this way about a man before. She felt different about him now than she did when she had first gone to Al's with him. At that time she felt he was so confident, so strong. Since then she had seen him cry. She had witnessed his uncertainty, his vulnerability. She felt now that he had leaned on her in his time of need. It felt warm. She wanted to be needed by someone like him.

Of course, there were things she disliked about him. She did not care for his temper or his harsh use of words. She also did not like his smoking. However, she felt something for him on a different level of her consciousness; something that she could not describe, but liked. She felt that by spending a little more time with him she would learn what drew her to him. She would learn if the qualities she envisioned him to have were really there.

She hoped he did not show her that he could be like her sister's worthless husband, Jack. She did not want to find herself in the same trap that Sharon was in. She would be very careful. She fell asleep with these thoughts hanging like cobwebs in her mind.

She was still sleeping soundly when Galen pulled the car into the parking lot of the Pinewood motel, just outside of Bloomington. Galen woke her by gently rubbing her shoulder.

She awoke with a yawn and looked around. She had a large mark across her cheek from lying so long on the handle-strap of his bag.

"I'll get us a room," he said. "Sit tight. I'll be right back."

She nodded her sleepy head.

A few minutes later Galen carried the computer from the back seat of the car to the motel room.

The room was small and dim. The dark brown carpet seemed to absorb what little light there was. The bed was the main attraction in the room, as with most cheap motels. On the nightstand, a small sign with a coin-slot promised a luxurious massage in exchange for twenty-five cents. The room could not be described as *dirty*, but *well-worn* seemed to fit fine.

Audra cleared a place for the computer on the small desk. She plugged it in. After seeing that it was working, she told Galen that he might as well sleep for a while.

Galen looked at his watch. He calculated in his head how far they had come. He figured it would be about a ten-hour trip for the ball and subtracted the three hours it had taken them to get here. He subtracted another hour for a safety factor.

"About six hours and we'll have to go again," he said. "I'll call Paxon from here before we leave."

Audra nodded, already pounding the keys. "Sweet dreams," she said before turning back to the computer.

"Yeah, right," Galen said. "I'll try to sneak them in between the nightmares."

Audra ignored the sarcasm. She turned back to her work on the computer.

She noticed many of the file names started with common groups of letters. She considered that they were somehow related. She pulled up a file called "RFP.001", and began to read. It was a piece titled 'Rain Forest Peoples'. It was also chapter one. *This makes some sense*, she thought. She could cut the time to reading just one file out of a group.

She searched the files for almost four hours. She was amazed at the diversity of Gaston's writings. There were stories, articles and letters to other educators and friends. There were notes from his many studies and an unfinished novel. Finally, after all of the searching, she found what she was looking for.

It was in a group of files starting with the letters *EOH*. She pulled up the first file in this series, *EOH.001*, and began to read. It told of Gaston's studies of a legend from the south called the "Eater of Hearts." It described how and where Gaston had found an object, shaped like a ball and made of crystal.

"Galen! Galen, wake up!" Audra said.

Galen leaped from the bed. He looked as if he were ready to do battle—or run. The sleepiness drained from his face in an instant leaving the look of stark terror.

Audra clasped a hand over her mouth, quickly identifying her mistake. "Galen," she said. "I'm so sorry. I didn't mean to scare you like that. It's just that I... I found the files."

Galen dropped backward onto the bed. He slapped his right hand over his heart and his bandaged left hand across his forehead. He really wanted to yell now but again fought the urge.

"I'll be alright," he said, looking at the ceiling. "Really, I will. Just give me a minute." He took a deep breath and let it out slowly. Sitting up on the bed, he said, "I hope you have some kind of really good news."

"I've found the files describing the ball," Audra said. "It's called the *Eater of Hearts*."

Galen grimaced, and then a look of surprise sprang upon him. "That's what Al was saying before he died! 'Eater of Hearts,' that's it!"

Audra nodded. "You're right," she said. "That's what it sounded like."

"What does it say?" Galen asked.

Audra began to read. Galen sat against the headboard of the bed and listened.

She read to him about how Al had heard of the legend on a trip to the south. It said in the entry; "*I have become totally fascinated by the legend and want to study it in more detail. It looks like this legend would make for an outstanding novel.*" She began to skip over paragraphs trying to quickly locate more substantial information.

"Does it say anything about how to stop it?" Galen asked, looking over her shoulder.

"I don't know yet," she said, scrolling through a file. "There are dozens of files in here concerning that thing. We'll have to read through them."

"How long will that take?" Galen asked, obviously anxious for any information that might help them stop the ball.

"I don't know," she said. "Could be awhile; seems like there's enough information in here to fill a good-sized book."

"Shit!" Galen said, and then slapped a hand over his mouth. Galen tried not to swear in front of women, although it happened quite often. Even in the nineties, it still seemed a little *wrong*. His face flushed red as he turned to her. "Sorry," he said. "I didn't mean to swear. It's just that we don't have time to read a whole book!"

"Gee, Galen, lighten up," she said. "We'll do our best. Just try to mellow out a little."

Galen looked at his watch and saw that it was after four o'clock, after five in Georgia. "I'll have to call Paxon again in a little while," he said. "You want a soda or something?"

"Yeah, that'd be great," she said, beginning to read through the files again.

Galen left the motel room and walked to the soda machine at the end of the long, one-story building. He took a quick glance around just in case there was a chance the ball arrived a little early. Realizing he had no change, he walked to the office.

137

The same woman that checked him in was still behind the counter. A few pounds overweight and her face heavy with makeup, Galen thought she was at one time an attractive woman. She was reading a romance novel with the typical half-dressed man and woman on the cover entwined in a heated embrace. She looked up when she heard the bell over the door ring. She removed a pair of old-fashioned black framed glasses and laid them on her desk. She looked much better without them.

"Checking out so soon?" she asked, as a "you-devil-you" smile crossed her face.

Galen knew what she was thinking as she smiled. *You read too many of those damned romance books*, Galen thought. "Actually, I wondered if you had any change for the soda machine."

She looked disappointed and turned to retrieve some change from the cash drawer.

He dropped a dollar onto the counter.

"Did you get a listing of our closed circuit movies?" the woman asked. She handed him a listing.

"Uh, no, I...I didn't," Galen responded.

"Well, it's a little early yet. The really good ones come on a little later," she said, showing a lot of teeth.

"Thanks," Galen said, just wanting to get away from her.

She waved to him in what he guessed was supposed to be a seductive way. He glanced at the X-rated movie listing then tossed it into the trashcan next to the soda machine.

He carried the cold sodas back to the room.

Audra was still plugging away on the computer. "Thanks," she said. He set the can of Coke on the desktop next to her. She did not even look up, focused only on reading the computer files.

Galen sat on the bed. He dug for Paxon's phone number in his shirt pocket. "Find anything interesting yet?" Galen asked, rubbing his eyes.

Audra held up one hand. "Just a second," she said. She then turned her seat to face Galen. "It's incredible," she said. "What I know so far is that the thing was a part of some religious ceremony a hundred-and-somethin' years ago."

Galen lifted an eyebrow.

"Yeah, really, by some runaway slave down south. He was captured in Africa and brought here as a slave. He and other slaves from the same tribe still practiced their African religion after being brought here. They cast a spell on the slave's master."

"Get out of town!" Galen said.

Audra saw the disbelief on his face. "I'm serious. The ball was supposed to have been created during this ceremony and was supposed to go after this runaway slave's master." She crossed her heart with her right hand and then held it up as if taking an oath of truth. "Come over here and read it for yourself if you don't believe me!"

A look of dread had flickered through his face when he began to believe her. "Are you sure this is the right thing?" Galen asked.

"It describes the same kind of crystal ball with little spikes all over it. Sure sounds like the same thing to me," Audra said.

Galen looked at the computer screen. Audra pointed out where she had read the things she was telling him.

"See if it says in there what the magic words are that will turn it off," Galen said. "I've got to call Paxon."

Magic spells? Galen thought. It sounded so crazy, but the thing itself defied any reasonable explanation. *African religion and runaway slaves.* Galen wasn't sure what to think. It sure sounded like something that Al would have been interested in.

Galen dialed Paxon's number. It rang three times.

"Hi, this is Paxon. I'm not here right now..."

Galen hung up the phone. "I still hate answering machines," he said, stuffing the phone number back into his pocket. "By the time we get something to eat it'll be time to get rolling again," he said.

Audra looked up. "Okay," she said. "I'm starved."

They grudgingly loaded the computer into the back seat, both wanting to continue reading but not having the time. There was a row of fast food chains and a mini-mall just up the road. They pulled into a Wendy's.

139

Audra went in for some food while Galen looked at a map. He tried to imagine where the cursed ball might be. He again calculated its course and figured it was still an hour north. He did not want to leave here too soon. If they took off now it would just veer off in whatever direction they chose to go, shortening the distance between them. It would be better to let it almost catch up then speed away again. He thought about what it would be like to try to run from this thing without the aid of the Mustang's V-8 and realized that running on foot from this thing would be futile.

Audra returned to the car carrying a white bag and two drinks.

Galen put away the map. He glanced at the mini-mall as Audra got herself adjusted in the seat. A Radio Shack store caught his attention.

"Is a printer all you would need to get those files on paper?" he asked.

Her eyes followed his to the Radio Shack sign on the front of the store. "Worth a try," she said. "It would give us a chance to read them as we drive."

"My thoughts exactly," Galen replied

A teen-aged boy greeted them immediately. He looked like the typical egghead who would know about all the stuff in the store.

"Can I help you folks?" he asked in an unstable voice.

"Do you sell computer printers?" Galen asked as he glanced around the store.

"Sure," the kid said, "Right over here."

He led them to one side of the store where several computer systems were on display.

"This is a nice model," he said, stopping in front of a $1,400 price tag. "Laser printer," he said. He began a technology-laden sales pitch.

"We were looking for something a little less expensive," Audra said. "Just a simple dot-matrix printer would do fine."

"Actually," Galen said, "I don't want to buy a printer at all. I just need to have something printed."

The kid pushed his glasses back up on his nose.

"We've got a computer in the car and it has some very important information on it," Galen started. "We just need to print the files so we can read them without the computer."

"I don't think we can do that," the kid said. "I mean, yeah, it can be done, I just don't think that I'm supposed to."

Galen looked around the store. It was empty. "Listen, uh..."

"Randy," the kid said, pushing his glasses up again.

"Okay, Randy. We're from out of town and we've got these important files on this computer. You could say that this is a matter of life and death," Galen said, looking at Audra to back up his story. "We need to get them printed because we're leaving town right now." Galen leaned over and cupped his hand around his mouth. "It's worth an easy twenty bucks," he whispered into the kid's ear.

"I don't know," Randy said. "My boss went across the street to get some supper..." The kid thought about it for a moment, and then asked, "how much do you have to print?"

"Not much," Audra exaggerated, "just a few files."

"Well, okay, if we hurry."

Galen slapped him gently on the back and headed for the car.

By the time he returned with the computer, the kid had arranged a place for it. "Don't need the screen," he said, "I'll just hook up one of these," and waved to a row of monitors.

It was only a few minutes before Randy was reading the list of files.

"Which files do you want printed?" he asked.

Twenty minutes and twenty dollars later, Galen and Audra left the Radio Shack with a stack of paper.

Audra quickly ate her burger. She grabbed the stack of papers and began sorting through them. "You know," she said, "I'm convinced that Al was a totally un-organized person. There's no order to any of this stuff." She continued to sort through the printed files, separating them into groups.

141

"He probably just wrote the stuff down as he received it," Galen said, defending his old friend. He had wolfed down his burger much quicker than Audra had. He still had a small smear of mustard at the corner of his mouth. "At least he wrote it all down."

Audra grunted and shrugged her shoulders. "I'm amazed he could make heads or tails out of any of this," she said, using the fingers on her left hand to separate the groups of paper.

They drove on a while and Audra began to read some of the information.

"The runaway slave's name was Tobias," she said. "And guess what?" she asked, but did not await an answer. "They chopped off his hand during the ceremony." She shifted nervously in her seat. "That's pretty gruesome, don't ya' think?"

Galen nodded, but kept quiet.

"It says after the ball-thing was created, this slave gave it to his Master as a gift. It was a part of the ritual."

She read on for a while, gathering other tidbits of information.

She read to him about the African religion and how they believed not in one God, but many demigods. Gaston had gone into great detail in describing this information. They had believed there were many demigods living in the 'above,' and many more living in the 'below.' The gods of the 'above' were generous and good. The gods of the 'below' were evil. The Africans believed they could persuade the good gods to help them battle the evil gods by offering sacrifices.

Galen and Audra drove steadily to Moline, Illinois. It was eight-thirty in the evening. They drove through town and found a park along the banks of the Mississippi.

Galen parked the car. His eyes were burning with weariness and his back and legs were stiff from all the driving.

Audra was also very tired. She handed Galen a portion of the papers. "You can help me read for a while," she said. "I'm so tired that the words are starting to swim around on the page."

Galen placed his stack on the dash. "I'm gonna try to call Paxon first," he said. "Feel like a walk?"

"No thanks," she said. "I'll just sit here for a while."

Galen nodded and began to walk toward the park entrance. He had noticed a Stop-N-Go just before they pulled into the park. Galen spotted a lighted "phone" sign in the store's parking lot. Moths spun dizzily around it. Several teen-aged boys had gathered at one end of the building and were speaking loudly. They quieted as he passed. Galen guessed they were telling dirty jokes. He dug out his wallet and searched for the credit card he had received from AT&T. He quickly read the instructions on the back and dialed Paxon's number, followed by several more from the credit card.

The phone rang only once before a smooth, deep voice answered.

"Hello," the voice said.

"Mister Paxon?" Galen responded, shocked that someone had actually answered.

"Yes," the voice answered. "This is John Paxon."

Galen covered the phone as he cleared his throat. "Mister Paxon, this is Galen Morris. I left a message for you earlier today."

"Yes," he said. "I'm so sorry to hear about Professor Gaston."

"Yeah, we all are," Galen said, not knowing exactly who he referred to as 'we'. "The reason I'm calling, is that before Al died, he asked me to send something to you."

"And what might that be Mr. Morris?" the voice asked.

"Well," Galen started, "I'm not sure what it is, but I think Al referred to it as the 'Eater of Hearts.'"

The phone went quiet, but Galen could still hear breathing at the other end. "Mister Paxon?" Galen said.

"Yes, I'm here," Paxon said, his voice not as smooth as before. "The only 'Eater of Hearts' I know of is an old southern legend, folklore."

"Yes," Galen said. "I think we're talking about the same thing."

"How do you intend to send me a legend, Mr. Morris? Is it written material?"

Galen did not know how to describe what happened, so decided to just say it like it was.

"No, it's not written material, although I have some of that too." Galen paused for a moment before going on, fearing he was sounding like a raving idiot. "Actually, it's a ball, made of crystal."

"Are you saying Gaston actually *found* the 'Eater of Hearts?'" Paxon asked.

"Yes. We're trying to learn more about how and where Al got it," Galen said. He paused and then said what he had to say. "It's after me."

"Excuse me?" Paxon returned.

"It's after me, Mister Paxon. I was hoping you would know something about it."

Paxon hesitated a moment, then said, "Mr. Morris, if this is some kind of joke, it's in poor taste. I haven't got the time for this sort of thing."

"Mister Paxon, this is no joke. It's after me and a lady friend, and it's scaring the Hell out of us," Galen said.

His tone of voice convinced Paxon that Galen was telling the truth, or what he believed was the truth.

"Mr. Paxon, could you tell me everything you know about the Eater of Hearts? My life may depend on it."

Galen and Paxon exchanged information for the next forty minutes. Paxon was unsure how to take Galen's request for help. He certainly sounded convincing. The details he told about the legend were enough to convince Paxon he had gotten Gaston's information on the subject.

"We need your help," Galen said.

Another moment of silence passed before the conversation resumed. "I don't know what I can do for you," Paxon replied.

"I'm sure Gaston's information is more complete than anything I can find here."

Galen began to get the feeling that Paxon was not going to be much help. After a few seconds of silence, the course of the conversation changed for the better.

"Let me go to my office and dig up some records," Paxon said. "Then we can get in touch again and compare notes."

"How soon could you do this?" Galen asked.

"I can go now, but I'm not sure how long it will take," Paxon replied.

Galen explained they had about four hours before they would have to leave again. Paxon gave Galen his office number and they agreed that Galen would call his office and his home as often as he could from the road.

Audra sat in the car reading and decided to turn on the radio for a little background noise. She adjusted the tuner until she received a clear signal. After a few minutes, she closed her eyes to give them a rest.

The music paused and a steely-voiced reporter began describing the day's local events. Included was an account of a driver who had been involved in a multi-car accident. The broadcast described how one of the drivers had hit something that shattered his windshield, causing him to lose control of his car. Three people were reported dead and several others hospitalized. The radio also reported that the object had not been identified and that the police were investigating. A State Trooper was interviewed, stating that "some solid object had penetrated both front and rear windows of the car, possibly a stone or debris from the highway."

Audra tensed at the thought it may have been the ball. If it had been, people were dead because of it. She wanted to find Galen. He had been gone for nearly an hour.

Galen returned with a couple of sodas. Audra got out of the car and took a seat on a nearby picnic table. She decided not to tell him about the news just yet. There was nothing that could be done right now. The news would worry him as much as she was now worried.

"He was in," Galen said as he unscrewed the bottle-cap. "He's going to look up any information he may have about the Eater of Hearts." He took a long swallow.

"Good," she said. "What did he know about it?"

"Not much, but he had discussed it with Al several times. He had also met Al in Georgia to interview people about it."

They discussed what the other had found out in the last hour and got back into the car. They needed gas again. Galen didn't want to be surprised by the ball with an empty tank.

They drove through town looking for a northbound highway. Audra drove while Galen consulted the map. They picked up highway 26 and drove to the edge of town. After filling the car with gas they drove to a small rest stop and parked the car. Galen volunteered for watch duty, while Audra tried to get whatever sleep she could.

Galen leaned on the hood of the car and lit a cigarette. Traffic moved by on the highway, headlights approaching from the left, and receding taillights to the right. The rest-stop was no more than a blacktop loop coming off the main highway with a few picnic tables and restrooms. A couple of semi-trucks, engines still idling, were pulled off the road as their drivers caught some sleep.

Galen looked at his watch, keeping track of how much time before the ball might appear again.

It was ten o'clock. Another two hours and they would drive north to Freeport and wait again.

The time went by agonizingly slow. Galen divided it up by alternately reading Al's files, smoking cigarettes and walking around the car.

At eleven-thirty, Galen decided they should drive to the next phone and call Paxon.

About ten minutes up the road Galen spotted a bar just off the highway and asked Audra to pull in and see if they had a phone. It was a small place with a neon sign in each of the four front windows, each advertising a different brew. The building looked old and cheap, constructed mostly of cement blocks.

About six men sat at the bar and a few people were scattered among the booths along the far wall. Country music played on a jukebox and a couple boogied on the small dance floor.

Galen noticed a pay phone on the dark paneled wall between two beer signs. He picked up the receiver.

Audra sat at a nearby table.

A man sat alone in a booth opposite Audra. He stared at her through drunken eyes, singing loudly along with the blaring jukebox. He lifted a beer bottle to his lips but kept his eyes on the well-built woman who had just walked in.

Galen could not reach Paxon at home so he tried the other number. Paxon answered on the first ring.

"Mr. Morris?" he asked.

"Yeah, please call me Galen."

"Okay, Galen. I've found some records, mostly dealing with the religious aspects of the legend. I was just gathering up some of these papers to take home with me, so I can continue my research there."

As he listened to Paxon talk, Galen noticed the singing drunk wobble across the room to where Audra sat. The man began to talk to her, and he saw her smile nervously as she shook her head.

The man took her by the arm. He was trying to coax her onto the dance floor.

Audra resisted, but started talking to him. "I don't want to dance right now. Maybe later," she said, knowing she would soon be gone.

"Aw, c'mon!" the man said, "jus' one little dance." He grabbed her by the arm again and tried lifting her from the booth. The people sitting at the bar turned to watch the man. A couple of them smiled and began to talk amongst themselves.

A Willie Nelson song began to play on the jukebox.

"Now you jus' gotta dance when Willie sings!" the drunk said. He forcefully pulled Audra from her seat and dragged her onto the floor.

Audra drug her feet, but was no match for the drunk's strength.

Galen quickly asked Paxon to hang on and dropped the phone. He ran to the dance floor, grabbing the man by the shoulder and spinning him around. "She doesn't want to dance," Galen shouted over the music as he placed himself between the drunk and Audra.

The lean, muscular drunk glared at Galen with glassy eyes. He wore faded jeans and a sleeveless t-shirt. His tan-colored leather work boots were covered with blotches of dried cement. He had a short growth of beard and a tattoo of a skull on his upper arm. The drunk backed off a step.

"Jus' wanna dance with 'er," he said. He tipped back and drained the bottle he was holding.

The men at the bar watched and began to chuckle.

The drunk walked back over to his booth and searched the empty bottles for one with a swallow left in it. He sat there for a moment with a mean look on his face. He continued to glance at Audra.

Audra followed Galen back to the phone.

"Mr. Paxon?"

"What's going on there?" Paxon asked.

"I'm calling from a bar," Galen explained. "Things just got a little crazy for a minute."

Both Galen and Audra's eyes followed the drunk as he walked to the back of the room. He disappeared into what they thought must have been the restroom.

Paxon promised to go back home and read up on the information he had gathered. Galen was to call again, if possible, in a couple of hours.

Galen and Audra left the bar. The Mustang was parked facing a small, dark patch of woods. Audra pulled the keys out of her jeans and unlocked the door.

"Stupid drunks," she said, swinging the door open. Galen stood on the far side of the car looking toward the woods.

"I can't believe some -"

Audra gasped as a hand wrapped around her mouth cutting off the rest of her sentence.

The singing drunk had come from the shadows, grabbing her from behind.

Galen froze when he saw the gleam of a steel blade in the sparse light.

"Let her go, pal," Galen said smoothly, not wanting to spook him.

"Screw you!" the man yelled.

He began to rub his stubbly-bearded face against Audra's smooth cheek. He reached the hand that held the knife in front of Audra, crossing her breasts with his arm and pulling her toward him. The knife came to rest at the base of her neck and wildness showed in the drunk's eyes.

Chapter 12

The baying of the hounds was still some distance away. Tobias knew how quickly they could cover ground. He pictured in his mind the men on horses following the running dogs. Tobias leaped to his feet, thinking of entering the river. He looked at the captured rabbit, its eyes wide with fear. He was about to release it, then had an idea.

He pulled at the tattered legs of his britches, pulling off a couple of long strips. Placing one leg over the frightened rabbit to hold it down, he tied the strips securely to its hind legs. It was a challenge to tie the strips with one hand, but by using his stump arm pressed against his thigh, he succeeded in affixing the strips of cloth to the frightened rabbit.

Tobias removed the rabbit from the snare being careful not to injure it. He used his stump arm to hold the terrified creature against his chest and made his way to the river.

He looked around for a log or branch, anything he could hold onto while floating down the river. Seeing nothing nearby, he glanced downstream and spotted a tangle of logs and fallen trees about a hundred yards away. He walked to the bank of the river, still clutching the rabbit. He waded ankle-deep into the cool water.

"Mista Swamper, I guess you better run like you ain't never run before," Tobias said. He carefully released the rabbit onto the bank. He watched as it streaked along the edge of the river before springing into the woods.

Tobias took the pouch into his left hand, wrapping the leather strings around his wrist. He glided out into the current and quietly swam toward the logjam. When he reached it, several turtles entered the water with a *plop!* He scanned the sun-bleached branches and other flotsam for something he could pull loose. A fat water moccasin sat coiled upon one of the branches and began to silently slither toward the shore as Tobias began tugging on a large branch. He settled for a smaller log of about four feet in length. It rolled free with little difficulty. Tobias laid his arms over it, keeping his head above water.

He could hear the sound of the dogs growing closer every minute. Tobias began kicking his feet to speed his progress around the first bend of the river.

The sun had now dropped below the horizon. The woods along the banks cast long shadows across the water. A Great Blue Heron lifted itself from the riverbank, its powerful wings carrying it into the twilight.

Tobias steered himself toward the north bank of the river using the overhanging branches as cover as he drifted along. After about a half hour in the water, he heard the dogs barking wildly. He pictured them in his mind, approaching the bank where he had entered the water, sniffing the mud, then crashing along upstream following the rabbit that carried his scent. He listened intently and heard the sounds of the dogs grow fainter in the distance. He pictured the rabbit leaping over fallen logs, darting through the briars. He hoped the strips of cloth remained attached as the rabbit fled the snarling hounds.

With any luck, the rabbit would remain free until full darkness and the slave catchers would wait until morning to resume the chase. That would give Tobias time to get back to the plantation.

Tobias continued to drift down the river. As the moon began to rise in the clear sky, Tobias climbed ashore.

The Richards' plantation lay to the northeast, about four miles away. He would soon be on Richards' land, crossing the fields he had spent so much of his life in.

Tobias' pulse quickened as thoughts of this land and what had happened here came back to him. He sat for some time just thinking, remembering and grieving.

The sky overhead was deep blue and flecked with stars. He began to make his way across the land. The magical thing in the pouch continued to feed him small amounts of the warm energy. His body was too beaten to have made much progress without it and Tobias continued to pray to the gods, thanking them for it. The nearer he came to the plantation the more his hate for Richards grew. He thought of the many injustices his people had suffered at the hands of rich white men. He remembered how his family had been so tragically broken; erasing the effect of the years of love they had shared. He thought of the suffering of the slaves still being held.

Soon he could make out the familiar shapes of the buildings on the plantation. He planned to skirt the slave camps and to spend the night in the stable's haymow.

He feared meeting up with any of the other slaves, worrying they would hold him and turn him over to Richards. He realized that any slave would want to help him, but to do so would mean a severe beating. He did not want to place any slave in that position.

Nobody would be in the stable at this time of the night, the horses themselves being the only occupants. Tobias felt he could easily slip in during the darkness, and wait there in hopes of meeting Master Richards before his morning ride.

He slipped unseen around the shacks of the many slaves and approached the center of the plantation. The plantation was quiet and Tobias trod from building to building, keeping to the shadows.

When he at last approached the stable, he noticed a glow from within. He could hear voices inside. He shrunk against the outside wall, and listened. He heard two voices. One was definitely Master Richards and the other, Tobias thought, was Raymond. Tobias cautiously peeked around the corner of the stable and peered down the long center hall. The light and voices came from one of the stalls.

Tobias knew immediately that 'Daisy,' Richards' favorite mare, was ready to foal. Richards had been anxiously awaiting this time since having the mare bred by a prize stallion from a neighboring farm.

Richards treated the horses much better than he did his slaves, pampering them to no end. It had been Tobias' job to feed and care for them and he knew that no expense concerning the horses was too great.

He continued to listen to the voices, wondering who else might be in attendance. Tobias knew if he had still been on the plantation, he would be in there now ready to help with the delivery.

He imagined that Chester may be in there. He was sometimes assigned to help Tobias with the horses and seemed to Tobias the only other slave that Richards would put in charge of his precious livestock.

By the sound of the conversation, the foaling was near. Tobias heard Richards shout Chester's name along with a string of orders. It was likely only the three of them were inside, but entering the stables at this point would be out of the question.

Tobias walked around the outside of the stable and sat along the wall. He positioned himself under the window of the stall where the mare was about to give birth and listened.

He listened to Richards give orders to both Raymond and Chester as the mare began delivery. After what seemed to be hours, Richards laughed heartily.

The colt had been born.

Raymond asked to be dismissed, having seen enough of the stables for one night. He did not share his father's passion for the animals, as his father wished he would.

Raymond left the stables and Tobias heard the gate shut with a *clank!*

Richards stayed on, inspecting the new colt. He prided himself on his veterinary knowledge. Satisfied that everything was fine, he also dismissed Chester. He said he would only be a few minutes longer himself.

Tobias quickly jumped to his feet and made his way to the path leading to the big house. He would intercept Richards there and fulfill his mission.

He positioned himself among the bushes along the path and waited. Tobias' stomach swirled with nervousness. After all the struggling, the time of faith was nearly upon him. His head began to pound, the pain centered between his eyes. He said a final prayer to the gracious gods.

Within a few minutes he saw Richards fumbling noisily with the gate Tobias had quietly climbed over. Richards carried a small lantern, which cast a yellowish light upon the path.

Tobias gripped the pouch tightly in his left hand as it began to heat up rapidly. It felt alive in Tobias' grip, vibrating smoothly. The energy pulsed through him, giving him the strength and courage to face Richards.

Tobias did not know what to expect, or how he should approach Richards. He only hoped the gods would again help him to succeed.

When Richards was only a few feet away, Tobias stepped onto the path in front of him. Richards had been looking away from the path and did not see Tobias until he was right in front of him.

He gasped and almost dropped the lantern at the sight of the slave. He held up the light, unsure of who was there.

"Tobias," he gasped.

Richards looked frightened and Tobias thought he might begin calling for help. He wanted Richards to be quiet and not call any attention to the two of them. Tobias decided to give Richards the upper hand for the moment to keep him quiet, make him feel as though he were in control.

Tobias fell to his knees, "Masta, please," he said. "Have mercy on me! Please forgive me, Masta!"

Richards was indeed surprised by Tobias' appearance, but a smirk crossed his face. "Do you think you can just be forgiven for killing a man?" Richards said.

"I...I didn't mean to kill him, Masta. I swear I didn't."

Richards feared Tobias would become violent so he just told the slave what he wanted to hear. "I suppose you want to come back now and that you will behave?"

"Yes! Oh, yes, Masta. You can beat me for runnin'. I know I deserve a terrible beatin' for the wrong I done!"

Richards walked closer with the light. He gasped again when he saw Tobias' condition. The slave's face, normally full and round, was sunken in to a point where it now resembled a skull, covered by thin, leathery skin. His lips were dry and cracked. Several large gouges covered his face, swollen and obviously infected. Pus ran from a few of them leaving yellowish-white trails down his face.

Richards then noticed the missing hand.

"Tobias! What has happened to you, boy? What has happened to your hand?"

Tobias tried to change the subject.

"Masta, I be hurtin' pretty bad, and I'm terrible sorry for what I done." He brought out the pouch and held it before him. "I think I'm gonna die, Masta. I want you to have this. This here is a gift what I got for ya'." He struggled to speak and held the pouch toward Richards.

"What is it, Tobias?" he asked, not really wanting to touch the pouch.

"It's the only one in the world Masta, and I got it for ya'."

Richards took the pouch, mainly just to satisfy the sickly-looking slave. After seeing his condition, Richards felt he could handle him should he become violent like he did with Frederick. He would just pacify Tobias now and then beat him to death for his crime tomorrow, when he could have plenty of help. When Tobias let go of the pouch, he did so reluctantly. Its warmth instantly disappeared. Tobias felt weaker and was in considerably more pain. He gasped as Richards took the pouch, as if someone had stolen his breath.

Richards felt the pouch. Inside he felt something resembling a ball. He could feel points upon its surface. He opened the drawstrings and dropped the object into his hand.

155

Tobias watched, himself having never seen the object.

Richards was amazed at its beauty. It seemed to be made of glass or crystal and reflected the light of the lantern. He noticed the object beginning to glow from within. It became warm to the touch. It frightened Richards and he dropped it as if it were a snake.

The object never hit the ground. It stopped itself and hovered about a foot above the path. It began to glow brightly, lighting the entire area like sunshine.

"What in God's name..." Richards said as he backed away from it.

Tobias sat on his knees, amazed by the sight. He had never imagined such a beautiful thing. He watched as Richards walked backward, the ball of light steadily approaching him.

Richards tripped over a bush and Tobias could see the terror on his face. "Tobias, what have you done?" Richards shouted, scrambling to his feet. He had no time to say more as Richards began to run toward the big house with the ball in steady pursuit.

"Karmanna, Masta Richards. My name is Karmanna," The slave whispered as he watched in amazement.

Chapter 13

John Paxon pushed the opened fifth of whiskey toward the back of his desk. He gathered up the papers concerning the Eater of Hearts and rummaged through the desk drawers for a large paper clip.

He thought about Albert Gaston being dead as he gathered his things to leave. He tossed the stack of books and papers onto the credenza behind his desk. He then screwed the cap back onto the whiskey bottle and stashed it in the bottom drawer.

He wondered if the man who had called was truly serious or if this was some kind of joke. It was not like Gaston to play jokes. He reflected briefly on the memories of Gaston, the old man with the sharp wit. If anyone could have found the Eater of Hearts, it would have been him.

Paxon had a love-hate relationship with Gaston. He admired Gaston, yet he was also resentful. He would not admit to himself that he was actually *jealous* of Gaston's success, but in reality that was closest to the truth. Gaston had been living Paxon's dream for years. Since early in his career, Paxon had dreamed about the kind of success that Gaston enjoyed. He wanted to be recognized by his peers so badly he could taste it. He always figured if he could achieve half of the academic success that Gaston had, it would give him the kind of credibility to move into other areas of interest, like writing novels, just as Gaston had.

He pondered the situation for a moment and realized he truly did believe Morris, which was why he was in his office so late on a Saturday night. He felt somewhat foolish. He wondered how something like the Eater of Hearts could be real. Even though he had seen and experienced things in his life that he could not explain, this seemed to be on an entirely different level.

Paxon had been one of Gaston's associates early in his academic career. Looking back on it, it seemed a lifetime ago. Gaston had taught anthropology and Paxon had been a student teacher. He had accompanied Gaston on several trips to such places as Columbia, West Africa, Australia, and the desert southwest of the United States. They had studied the natives of these lands, lived with them, shared food with them and listened to their stories.

Gaston had gone on to become one of the most noted anthropologists in the world. Paxon had gone to teach at several different schools, the latest this rinky-dink school he was serving now. Nobody ever heard of Baxter College and because of that, nobody ever heard of John Paxon.

Gaston, on the other hand, had written several books concerning his travels and the people he studied. He had even been the focus of a National Geographic special on TV. After retirement, Gaston had gone on to publish a string of bestselling novels as well. Gaston became much more famous because of his novels than from his academic works. Paxon had published two papers a few years ago, neither of which caused much stir in the anthropology circles. He had also accumulated many rejection notices from publishers regarding his first novel, which he had written many years ago. He had not written since then, unable to accept that no publisher wanted his book, after all the hard work he had put into it.

He would never leave this school on his current credentials. He needed a big hit. He needed something that the world would sit up and take notice of.

He gathered up his things and headed for the door. He glanced around the room looking for anything he might have forgotten. He noticed the bottom drawer of his desk was still open. The bottle of whiskey was peeking at him. It silently coaxed him. Paxon sat his armload of things on the chair and pulled the bottle from its hiding place. He quickly unscrewed the cap and took a long swallow. Paxon kissed the cool bottle before he put it away. He gently slid the drawer closed and locked the desk. He locked the door to his tiny office and walked down the hall.

He still felt somewhat foolish as he drove home. Here he was, a college professor, chasing something from a legend. He needed to talk to this guy again, this Mr. Morris from Illinois. Then he would ask him some questions, some *real* questions about the Eater of Hearts. He would figure out if this guy was telling the truth. Nobody was going to make a fool out of John B. Paxon.

He drove to his home, about fifteen minutes from the school. The small house looked depressing to Paxon as he stepped out of his old Toyota. The yard needed mowing, the small hedge out front needed a trim and the whole place needed painting.

The inside was equally depressing. The living room carpet showed a worn path from the recliner to the kitchen. The kitchen counter was piled high with the empty boxes from his frozen dinners. The trash can had overflowed long ago but Paxon hadn't found the time to take it out lately. The same way he had not quite found the time to take the several garbage bags from the garage to the curb on Thursday mornings.

He cleared the desk in the small spare bedroom he called his home office and put all the information he had found on it. He walked back to the kitchen and found his best friend's twin brother—another fifth of whiskey.

Paxon took a swig on the way back to his office. The warmth of the whiskey was the only warmth Paxon knew. He had few friends, and those were just acquaintances. His love life consisted of an occasional hooker, or perhaps a young female student in need of a better grade. The bottle *was* his best friend—and his worst enemy.

He began to read the papers he had brought from his office. Gaston had called him a few months ago requesting the same information. He had said he was interested in the legend and

159

wondered if Paxon had any information on the subject, since the whole thing had taken place in his own geographical backyard. Paxon knew of the legend, but had never investigated it himself. In fact, it was one of those projects he had always intended to get around to, but had not found the time. He had planned to write about the legend, maybe even get it published. The school had some information concerning the story, so Paxon had reluctantly sent copies to Gaston. Paxon felt Gaston was intruding into his territory and taking a project from him. He knew he could not stop him, so decided to cooperate—a little. Perhaps some of Gaston's fame would rub off on him.

Gaston had called him back several days later to thank him and they had discussed the legend in more detail. What he had learned from Gaston was the extent of Paxon's knowledge on the subject. Paxon had to admit then, and again now, that the story was damned interesting, however unlikely it seemed.

If he could only get settled into a good school, he thought, he could really do some good work. It also seemed Paxon was moving too often—six schools in the last fourteen years. The schools would only tolerate him for so long then let him go. *Their loss,* Paxon thought, *John Paxon has yet to do his greatest work.*

That great work was always just around the corner for Paxon. The idea of doing this work was appealing to him but he never got down to the nuts and bolts of getting it done. He always intended to start soon, but it never happened.

Paxon knew he had to get it done soon or he would lose this job too. Even this little school had their reservations about Paxon. He knew the next job would be even harder to find, if he *ever* found one. He could tell by the way the staff acted that he was on his last leg at Baxter. He had seen it too many times at other schools. The coolness toward him, no long range plans for him, not being included in staff meetings; these were warning signals.

Paxon continued to read the papers, taking a slug of the whiskey after each page or so. His eyes began to burn, so he took off his glasses and leaned back in his chair. He took another swig, placed the bottle back on the desk and fell sound asleep.

Chapter 14

Benjamin Richards ran down the lane toward his home. He glanced over his shoulder and saw the glowing orb following him.

He entered the back door of the house and ran to his study. He grabbed the pistol from the rack on the wall.

A harsh rasping sound came from the kitchen.

Richards heard the sound of breaking glass as the ball chewed its way through the wall and then through a china cabinet. The china crashed to the floor, the entire shelf vibrating as the ball bored a hole through the polished cherry-wood.

Richards heard footsteps on the second floor. "Stay up there!" he screamed. The footsteps stopped. He cocked the pistol and stood in the doorway. He glanced up the hall in the direction of the noise. The sound grew louder as the ball began cutting through another wall, seeking its prey.

Richards could feel the boards below his feet vibrating as the ball cut through the house. He spun around, wondering where the thing was. He saw it emerge from the dining room wall and enter the hallway.

The vibrations stopped after it came through the wall. The noise it made was reduced to the sound of the many points on its surface cutting through the air as it spun.

Richards lifted the gun and took aim.

It was too late. The thing was too close.

Richards backed into the parlor as the thing bore down on him. He turned and ran for the front door. Just as he pulled the door open, he felt a searing pain in the middle of his back. The ball had just enough time to touch him, shredding a small patch of shirt and skin, before Richards bolted through the door, screaming.

He stumbled down the front steps and rolled onto the front lawn. He heard his wife and son's voices calling to him. Quickly, he got to his feet, eyes searching for the ball. He spotted it coming for him but this time had more room between it and him.

He lifted the cocked pistol and took aim. His target was small, so Richards waited for it to get closer before he fired. When it was about ten feet away, Richards pulled the trigger.

In a flash of brilliant light, the lead bullet was shredded to invisible particles as it struck its target.

The orb never altered its path. Richards, horrified, screamed again and ran toward the road.

The darkness of the night was near complete. The quarter-moon was partially covered by broken clouds. He ran blindly down the road. Glancing again over his shoulder, he saw the ball of light behind him. He ran, a small amount of blood trickling down his back.

He gained a little distance on the orb as he ran. His wind was leaving him and Richards gasped for breath.

The ball was following about twenty yards behind him. It began to glow fiercely, shedding a stark white light along the road.

Richards' stamina was wearing down and he began to slow. He turned, panting, to look for the ball. He was both surprised and horrified at what he saw.

He saw what appeared to be a band of about two dozen slaves keeping a constant pace behind him. The light from the ball continued to glow from within the crowd of slaves, lighting their faces with cold, white light.

The slaves were carrying tools. Some carried hoes; others carried sickles, scythes, or axes. Some of the slaves carried whips. Long snaking whips they cracked over their heads with a jerk of their arms.

They came toward Richards, their eyes glowing from within. They walked silently toward him.

Richards tried to get his breath while his heart leaped about within the walls of his chest. He could see the hate in their eyes and could feel the hate coming off them in waves. Their mouths worked, as if they were speaking, but Richards could hear nothing.

As they grew closer, Richards could see the slaves had an almost *ghostly* look about them. It was almost as if he could see through them, yet he could not. He recognized many of the faces as *his* slaves, some that now worked on the plantation, and others who had died years ago. They beckoned him to come to them, their arms motioning him to join them.

C'mon, Masta, we've got somethin' for ya'.

Richards turned to run. The pain in his back was hot as coals. The pain in his side slowed him down. He came to a crossroad, and turned right. The road was bordered by woods on both sides, their darkness as black as the bottom of a well.

Richards looked behind him and did not see the ball or the band of evil slaves.

He took a deep breath of relief and stopped in the road. He watched the road behind him and saw no signs of movement.

He then heard a sound in the woods to his left and peered into the darkness. A light came from the woods, escaping the blackness in a multitude of beams, broken by the trees. He gasped as he saw the silhouettes of the dozens of slaves walking through the woods toward him.

He stumbled along, looking back to see the slaves reassemble on the road behind him.

Don't run Masta, take it like a man.

Richards turned from them again, running as hard as he could while still glancing over his shoulder. He only gained a few yards this time as his middle-aged body was unaccustomed to running and he had little stamina.

The slaves had dropped back a bit, but he could still see them clearly. He gazed at them while walking backwards and saw something new in their midst.

A woman now walked among them; a *white* woman.

Richards could not make out the face from this distance, but as the group closed the gap he realized it was Mary—his Mary.

She walked among them and seemed to be terrified. He noticed she had shackles around her ankles and her wrists, connected by a heavy chain.

Looky what we got Masta. Ain't she purty?

Richards gazed in amazement.

Can we have 'er, Masta? Can we?

"No! No! It's not real!" Richards screamed.

The slaves were much closer now. Richards stumbled backwards, trying to move away from them.

One of the slaves grabbed Mary from behind.

I got 'er Masta.

The slave gripped the back of her dress and ripped it off her. Mary seemed to scream, but issued no sound. Her face was distorted with terror.

The slaves drug her along. One of them placed his hand over her breast.

She's so soft, Masta.

Again, Richards turned to run and twisted his ankle. The pain shot up his leg, but he still managed to hobble up the road. He could hear the voice in his head.

Where ya' goin', Masta?

Richards looked back and saw a ghostly Raymond with a slave on either side of him. The slaves had lifted him by the arms, his feet dangling above the road.

The boy was terrified. A slave pulled off Raymond's shirt and cracked the whip across his back. He screamed with the pain, a silent scream of torture. The slave cracked the whip again and Raymond threw his head back and shuddered. Raymond's head then fell forward as if he had passed out. A slave grabbed his hair and lifted his head.

Richards could see the horrified look on Raymond's face, pleading for help. Richards hobbled off the road into the woods, screaming. He was so terrified that he clawed at the underbrush, tearing great gashes across his hands. He was exhausted from the run, but the fear fueled his body to keep moving. He crawled

165

along on his hands and knees trying to stay ahead of the ball and its evil band of slaves.

Richards fell into a shallow ravine, gasping for breath. He crawled to the side and tried to climb up the short bank. His back still burned and his hands were cut and bleeding. His ankle was twisted badly and could barely support any weight.

Instead of running, Richards tried to hide. He lay with his back against the bank, which rose at a slight angle. He began trying to cover himself with dead leaves. He noticed the glow from the light approaching and became still.

The light grew brighter as it approached and Richards peeked toward it with one eye. He could see the group of ghostly slaves, but saw no sign of Mary or Raymond.

The slaves continued to approach him, climbing down the far side of the ravine.

Richards prayed they would pass him, not noticing him under the dry leaves. He could hear nothing of their approach except a faint whirring, humming sound. He lost sight of the slaves as they reached the bottom of the ravine, but soon noticed they were on both sides of him, looking down into his eyes.

Ya' can't hide Masta. We knows where ya' are.

The slaves surrounded him and Richards began to whimper. "Jesus. Oh, God," Richards cried.

They can't help ya' Masta. You're on your own now.

The light grew brighter before Richards' eyes, drowning out the sight of the slaves. The light was so intense that Richards could see nothing else.

A tremendous pain exploded in Richard's chest causing his body to shudder uncontrollably. The pain was so intense that his body could not comprehend it. He gasped his last breath alone, staring up at the dark sky above him. He noticed the light fade as he died, the ball ripping through his chest, shredding his heart before peacefully coming to rest in its place.

.   .   .

Tobias had watched Master Richards as he crashed toward the house. He crawled off the path and was now just inside the cover of the woods.

His pouch was gone, and with it the power that had kept him alive for this long. He was cold now, the pouch's warmth missing from his side. Inside, he was burning, the infection causing a fierce fever to build within him. His vision was blurred, the fever played games within his head.

He had yet another mission while still in this world, one that was not blessed by the gods. He struggled to muster what remaining strength he had and crawled through the woods like some dark animal prowling through the night.

He crawled north a short distance then turned westward toward the next county, where his boys now lived with Miss Mary and Master Ralph.

He prayed to the gods to give him a little more strength, enough to cover the ten miles to the other plantation. Tobias felt the prayers fell upon deaf ears. *You're on your own now, Tobias, we've granted you enough.* He crawled along moving slowly, the fever raging in his skull.

The world contains many wonders, few more impressive than the will of man. Tobias willed himself on, crawling on his hands and knees, head spinning wildly, barely able to see.

The instincts of survival also raged within him. It was these instincts that pumped adrenalin through the veins of his ancestors over the millennia. It was this human quality that granted his distant fathers the strength and the will, to do battle in the face of fear. This instinct provided food and warmth, it provided *life itself*. It provided not courage, but *will*; the will to survive against all odds.

Tobias continued to crawl westward in his three point stance. His right arm hung uselessly at his side as he shuffled along. He found a rhythm. Blocking out all of his surroundings, he continued forward. He was not aware of the pink glow to the east and the birds who bustled noisily about at his approach. His rhythm was finally broken when he came to a swampy area and realized he was crawling in shallow water.

He looked around then gently lowered his head to the water. He sucked up some water, swirled it in his dry mouth and spat it back into the swamp. He then took another mouthful, but this time swallowed. He sat down, the warm water coming up to his waist. He splashed a little water on his face with his left hand and attempted to stand up. The world swooned around him but he fought to keet his balance.

He began to walk along through the swampy land. He disturbed a nest of small black snakes that brought the water around his feet to life in a squirming fury. Like a small explosion in slow motion, the wiggling black fragments of the nest swam in all directions. After Tobias passed, they all came back together, reassembling themselves into the nest.

He made it to firmer ground and in the distance noticed a road running westward. This road would travel west another three miles then terminate into a north-south road. One mile south of this junction, the twins were busying themselves with their daily chores.

Chapter 15

The drunk held Audra with one hand over her mouth and the other hand - holding a knife - across her chest. She stared wide-eyed at Galen, who began to try to talk the guy down.

"C'mon buddy," Galen said. "You don't want to hurt her. Put down the knife and we'll leave."

"Up yours!" he stammered. "And I ain't yer buddy!"

"What's your problem?" Galen asked, keeping his eyes on his adversary.

"The bitch wouldn't dance with me!" he said. "I ought to slit her damn throat." He pulled the knife up close to Audra's slender neck. "What's the matter, bitch? Ain't I good enough for ya'?" he asked. He did not remove his hand to let her answer, but she shook her head. "You want to dance with me now?" he asked. His drunkenness slurred his speech.

Audra nodded, hoping to calm him down. Maybe if she danced with him he would put down the knife.

"Oh, sure," the drunk said. "Now that I got a knife at yer throat, you wanna dance!" He pulled her back and tightened his grip. "Too late bitch!" he shouted. "Yer too late. Should'a danced with me when you had the chance!"

"C'mon," Galen said. "You're only gonna get yourself in a lot of trouble."

"Shuddup, jerk!" the drunk shouted. He was trying to move Audra backward, behind a parked car.

Galen decided the drunk couldn't be reasoned with and risked a different tactic. "You always pick on women?" Galen asked. "Are you afraid to fight with men? Is that it?"

"Screw you, bastard!" the drunk said.

169

"You're a chicken-shit drunk," Galen said. "You're a chicken-shit drunk who's afraid of a real fight."

"Shuddup, you stupid bastard!" the drunk yelled. "I ain't afraid of nothin', especially a skinny runt like you." He shoved Audra toward Galen causing her to fall in the gravel parking lot. She scrambled to her feet and got behind Galen.

"Get to the car," Galen said, keeping a keen eye on the drunk.

"No, Galen, the two of us-."

"I said get to the car, *now!*"

Audra heard something in the tone of his voice, something that clearly said *don't argue with me!* She looked again at the drunk who now wore a maniacal smile across his face. He pitched the knife from hand to hand, beckoning Galen to come. Then she noticed a faint glow coming across the field behind the drunk. She saw Galen switch his glances from the drunk to the ball.

"I said get to the car!" Galen shouted.

"Yeah, little bitch. Get to the car where you'll be safe," the drunk said. He looked at Galen. "Let's rock, asshole," and swung the knife through the air.

Galen saw Audra running to the car from the corner of his eye. The drunk was coming toward him, the knife held ready to strike. The ball maintained its pace across the field, coming straight at Galen. "You really want to do this?" Galen asked, stalling for time.

"What's the matter, you chickening out?" the drunk said.

"No. But I could just leave and you'd never see us again."

"You were callin' *me* a chicken-shit!" the drunk yelled. "You're the chicken-shit!" He laughed loudly, "Now who's the chicken-shit, you *sissy?*"

Galen positioned himself so that the drunk was directly between him and the ball. The ball disappeared behind the drunk's back. Galen continued to stall.

"And what happens after you kill me?" Galen asked.

"I ain't gonna kill ya'," the drunk said in an insane voice. "I'm just gonna carve ya' up a little. Make ya' wish that I'd killed ya'."

Galen could tell the ball was closer now. The glow cast a bright spot on the ground just behind the drunk. He heard the Mustang start in the distance and thought about running to it but the drunk was too close. If Galen turned to run, the drunk could bury the knife in his back. He just began to walk backward, toward the car.

"Where ya' goin'?" the drunk asked, coming steadily toward him. "It's time to rock n' roll. Or, are you gonna try to run?"

"Please man, let's not do this," Galen pleaded. "Let's just call a truce and I'll get out of here."

The drunk took an offensive position, thrusting the knife toward Galen. Galen leaped back, the blade just missing his stomach. "How about it, chicken-"

His sentence was broken off by a scream of pain. The ball had torn into his shoulder pitching him forward. Surprised, he turned to see what had hurt him. The ball tore a path through his skin from his shoulder blade to his chest, digging its way deeper as it moved.

The drunk was just an obstacle in the ball's path. With his back to the ball, the drunk was startled by the sudden burst of pain at the base of his neck. In reaction to the pain, he lost his balance and fell more heavily into the ball, extending the damage to his body, before falling aside. The drunk fell to the ground screaming, a gaping wound at the back of his neck.

Stunned, Galen turned to run and heard the drunk scream a final time. He had no time to see after the man, as his instincts to do so kicked in. He saw the Mustang turning around ahead of him. He looked back to the ball. A wall of fire again appeared and the burning bodies called for him.

Help us Galen, we need you.

He ran into the back of the Mustang while watching the ball and almost fell. He slid around to the open door. Galen had no sooner hit the seat when Audra tromped the gas sending a spray of gravel that bounced off the other cars in the parking lot.

Galen looked out the back window and watched the wall of flame recede into the distance. He kept his eyes on it until Audra turned sharply onto the asphalt with a screech of tortured rubber. He looked straight ahead, white as a sheet.

"Did you see the fire that time?" Galen asked, breathing heavily.

"No, Galen, I didn't see any fire. I saw the ball. Galen it was so close!"

"But you didn't see that wall of flames, those bodies inside, burning up?"

"No!" Audra yelled. "I saw the ball and the drunk! Galen, it *killed* him!" She shuddered, tears beginning to flow down her face. "Galen we've got to stop it. Too many people are dead!"

She had not told him about what she had heard on the radio in the park. She still was not sure it was the ball, but somehow felt that it was. She was almost certain.

"What do you mean, Audra? How many people have died?" Galen asked, looking directly at her. She tried to hide the knowledge of the accident behind a mask of nervousness.

"I just mean that people *could* die. Like that drunk. How many people has it killed along the way?"

Galen could sense she was holding back on him. She knew something she was not telling him about. "You're not a good liar, Audra. What are you trying to tell me?" Galen asked.

She looked nervously around. "Something I heard on the radio," she said. "I... I listened to the news while you went off to call Paxon."

Galen looked at her. "Go on," Galen said, not knowing if he really wanted to hear it.

"They told a story on the news, about an accident on the highway. Three dead," she said, having to force the words out.

"What's that got to do with me?" Galen asked.

"The driver hit something on the road," she said. "He lost control of the car and three people died. More were injured."

172

She became quiet for a moment, then continued. "It happened on highway 39, Galen. The same highway we took to Bloomington." She began to cry, "I... I think he hit the ball, Galen."

She calmed herself down and looked at Galen. "How many other things have happened that we don't know about?" She shook her head, wanting to say no more.

They both sat quietly for a couple of minutes. Audra asked Galen if he would drive.

She stopped the car alongside the two-lane highway. The traffic was very light this time of morning and no cars passed them as they changed places.

After several more minutes of silence, Galen spoke up. "Just what should I do?" he asked. "Should I just stop running and let the thing kill me?"

He knew it was after *him*. It had not made any attempt to single out Audra. Galen could feel it. It wanted *him*.

"No!" Audra shouted, cringing at the thought of losing him. "We just have to find out how to stop it, Galen. That's all I meant. I just... want the thing to stop." She put her hand on top of his, "I just want it to leave us alone."

"Me too," he said. "I just want to go back to the way things were before, when my life was boring. Back to when I had nothing to do when I was off duty except spend a few hours talking with an old man."

"Galen," Audra said, "I know we'll find a way. Don't worry, we will."

She reached across the console and kissed him on the cheek. "Promise me you won't let that thing get you," she said, also sensing it was after him, not her.

"I'll do my best," Galen said. "I want to be around to take you out to a proper dinner when this is over."

Audra smiled and reached into the back seat for the stack of papers. The thought of losing Galen to the ball sparked a new energy in her. She wanted to know everything she could about this thing. Maybe, the answer they searched for was in the files.

Galen drove northward on highway 84. They traveled within a stone's throw of the mighty Mississippi river. Audra turned on the flashlight, shielding Galen from the glare with her hand. She trained the light on the papers and read as much as she could.

As she read, she began to think that somehow the thing had been reactivated by something that they had done. What could it be? She went over the original story, in her mind.

A slave, seeking justice.

A religious ceremony.

The slave giving the thing to his master.

His Master running from the same glowing ball.

Nothing seemed to connect to Galen. She read on, searching for any clues that may connect something that happened almost two-hundred years ago to the present.

They passed through Watertown and Galen spotted a sign for highway 64. He turned west and traveled toward Rochelle seeking the fastest route back to The Willows.

He pictured the ball-thing, altering its path as he turned west and a chill ran down his spine. They could be back in Willow River in about an hour-and-a-half.

They reached The Willows at three-thirty a.m., Sunday morning. The town was very quiet; all its residents sleeping soundly on this cool summer night.

All but two of its residents; those two struggled with where they should go and what they should do.

Audra suggested they go to her place. One of them could get some sleep and the other could read the files.

Galen agreed.

He was so tired he begged for the first sleeping shift. Galen figured they had about a five-and-a-half hour lead on the ball. He wanted to sleep for two hours and let Audra have the rest.

After arriving at her apartment, Audra retrieved an ancient, bell-ringing antique alarm clock from her bedroom. Galen had sprawled out on her couch, a soft, old wonderfully long thing she had gotten from her parents.

174

"Give me two hours," he said, "in case you fall asleep or forget to wake me."

"Don't worry," she said. "If I don't fall asleep, I won't forget to wake you. I'll be counting the minutes 'til my turn." She wound the alarm, and then set it for five-forty-five, giving him his two hours. Audra, nearly exhausted, sat down next to him on the couch and rubbed his shoulders.

Galen moaned with pleasure. He was asleep within moments. He began to snore lightly.

Audra ignored the noise, not wanting to wake him. She moved to her kitchen table and spread the notes on it. Marking the ones she had already read, she set them aside.

She made a pot of coffee, hoping it would keep her awake for a while. She listened to the old alarm clock ticking, a sound that she associated with sleep. She got up and poured herself another cup of coffee.

She looked at Galen, motionless on the couch. She wondered what her mother would think of a guy like Galen. He was a little on the thin side, but muscular. He was tall; but not too tall. She would not approve of him being a smoker, but that could be worked out. He had a steady job and looked neat and clean.

She was sure mother would find something wrong with him. Maybe it would be Galen's first marriage. Maybe the foul language he let slip too often. It would be something. Maybe she would associate him with Jack. Although that would not be fair, she knew how upset her mother was over her sister's situation. Jack was never home, he drank a lot and squandered their money on risky gambles. Galen was about as far unlike Jack as a person could get.

. . .

Audra awoke to the sound of the alarm ringing noisily in the living room.

Galen fell off the couch when the clanging bells started, sounding more like a school recess bell. It only took him seconds to gain his bearings. He was accustomed to coming to full wakefulness quickly from many middle-of-the-night fire alarms. He shook his head, clearing the last of the cobwebs and searched for the button that would kill the hideous bell.

He felt like he had been drinking all night.

Audra was not so quick to wake up. Galen could see she had fallen asleep and really could not blame her. Her eyes were red and swollen, and her right cheek was red from lying on it.

"Couldn't stay awake?" he asked, spotting the coffee.

"Must have just dozed off for a minute," she said. The need for sleep was evident in her voice.

Galen poured a cup of coffee. He smiled at Audra. "Go ahead and lay down for awhile," he said. "It'll be soon enough that we'll have to get rolling again."

She nodded and stumbled toward the couch. She moved the pillows to the other end, (the way she laid down for her naps) and fluffed them before stretching out to sleep. She pulled up the blanket and drew her knees toward her chest.

Galen looked at the papers strewn about the table. He did not feel like reading yet. He wanted a cigarette.

Audra kept no ashtrays sitting around the apartment so Galen walked out onto the balcony for a smoke.

The small second-floor balcony contained a single lawn chair and a small Weber grill. Galen sat upon the railing and lit up. The morning air was moist and cool. The sun was just making its appearance over the horizon. A faint morning haze sat low upon the ground and dewdrops glistened on the hoods of the cars in the parking lot.

Galen watched a robin tug a worm from its hole in the lawn. The newspaper boy pedaled along the street behind the apartments, tossing the papers toward the houses with all the grace of a pro athlete. Lights flickered to life in the gas station down the block, the manager ready for another Sunday morning in The Willows.

Galen wondered how everything could be so normal for everyone else while he and Audra faced such an abnormal day.

Things like this were not supposed to happen. It was just too crazy.

I'm being chased by a killer ball, he thought, *one that goes right through anything and stops at nothing.*

"Tell me," he imagined Oprah Winfrey saying to him, the audience silently awaiting his answer, "what went through your mind as you ran from this thing, this ball that was after you?"

He smiled at his own humor.

He flipped the butt of the cigarette onto the back lawn and walked back into the apartment. After a shower and another cup of coffee, Galen began to read Al's papers. He thought Al's funeral would probably be tomorrow. He wondered if he was going to be able to make it. How could he miss Al's funeral? Galen only expected a handful of people to attend but wanted to be there himself. He was sure Al would understand if he didn't make it, considering the circumstances.

He retrieved Paxon's phone number from the shirt he had changed out of and thought about calling him. It was 7:30 in Georgia. Paxon might be up. He stretched the cord of Audra's phone over to the table and dialed the number.

After five rings and no answer, Galen was ready to hang up when Paxon's voice came over the line.

"Paxon," he said, obviously awakened by the call.

"Mister Paxon, this is Galen Morris. I... I called last night about...."

"Yeah, I know who you are Morris. Call me John; it's too early for formalities."

"I just wanted to know if you found out anything. I mean, about the ball, the Eater of Hearts."

"I might have," Paxon said. "I've been up most of the night studying up on the thing. Are you sure that's what it is?"

"As sure as I can be," Galen said.

"Well, you know it's just a legend, a myth, folklore. As far as my information goes the actual object has never been found."

177

"Al must have found it," Galen said. "I know he made several trips to the area. He tells about them in his files."

"How much is there in his files?" Paxon asked.

Galen surveyed the various stacks of paper. "We've printed about a hundred pages, but there is much more than that still in the computer. Audra has done most of the reading, and she said he has two different books on this thing. One is non-fiction about the legend, and the other is a novel. Audra said that both look pretty much completed, but it appears he was still editing them."

"I see. And does it say anything in his files about where he found it or what it looks like?"

"We're still working on where he got it, but I know what it looks like. I've seen it up close a few times."

"And what *does* it look like Galen?"

"Well, it's a little smaller than a baseball, about the size of a tennis ball. It's made of something like crystal or glass. Al thinks it's a diamond. And it's got these groves-"

"Did you say diamond?" Paxon asked. "You said Gaston thought that it's a diamond?"

"Yeah, I read it in his notes somewhere." Galen began to go through the files searching for that particular passage. "He said he was afraid to take it to have it analyzed because of its size. If it was a real diamond, it'd be worth millions. He didn't want anyone to know he had it. But he analyzed it himself and was convinced it was a diamond."

"Interesting," Paxon said, barely able to control himself. "Do you have all of Gaston's files with you?"

"All that we know of, we've got his whole computer."

"Do Gaston's files have any instructions on how to stop the thing?"

"I wish!" Galen said, "If it did, I'd have told you already."

"Yes, of course. I'm sorry, it's still early."

"I don't think Al ever expected the thing to..." Galen paused, searching for the words, "Come to life, or whatever you'd call it."

"No, he probably didn't," Paxon agreed. "Do you think you can come to Georgia and bring the files with you?"

"Do you mean like, now?"

"Yes, as soon as possible."

"What have you got in mind?" Galen asked.

"I think I might have found a way to stop it, but I'll need a little more time to study. Gaston's notes could be a big help. I think you will have to come to Georgia for it to work."

"I can be there," Galen said. "I'll go as far as I have to if it will stop this thing."

"Good," Paxon said. "How soon can you get started?"

"A couple of hours," Galen said.

"Excellent. Call me from the road. I'll give you directions when you get closer. Just drive to Savannah, Georgia."

"Will do," Galen said. "I hope you're right."

"So do I, Mr. Morris. So do I."

Chapter 16

Paxon was already formulating a plan as he hung up the phone with Galen. He grabbed his best friend from the table and removed the cap. He took a deep slug to calm his nerves. The whiskey instantly warmed his chest, giving him a nice, secure feeling.

Paxon knew the situation was dangerous. He had heard some strange stories on the news over the past couple of days.

While John Paxon seldom found himself claiming the moral high ground, he had never contemplated anything like this before. He could not let this thing continue to endanger innocent people on its path to Morris. He felt he had to stop it, and there was only way sure way to do so. Like most of Paxon's plans, this one was not well developed—yet.

He thought about the possibilities.

Gaston had never written anything that was less than spectacular. Everything he wrote, including the novels, was met with great reviews. Paxon doubted anyone knew about this work of Gaston's except Morris and the girl he was with. If he could get his hands on those files, he would have a couple of books he was sure he could publish.

Of course, he would put his name on the books.

If the thing was truly a giant diamond it would be priceless. Gaston was no fool; if he had studied it and believed it was a diamond, it probably was. Perhaps he could sell it outright. Take the money and run. Go to an island. Live off the money for the rest of his life.

Or maybe just keep it. Publish the books first and then loan the object out for display at museums for awhile. Become famous first, then sell it. He would have offers from all over the world.

Paxon got up to make a pot of coffee. Stopping first in the bathroom, he swallowed a couple of aspirin and washed his face. He looked at himself in the mirror and could not believe he was actually considering his current plan, but felt there was no other choice.

He turned his thoughts to the more pleasant side of his plan. He imagined himself as a famous author. The non-fiction book could wait a while. It was the novel he wanted, along with the object itself. He had always dreamed of the day when he could walk into a corner drugstore and see his name on the cover of a bestseller. It really made no difference to him whether he had actually written it or not, as long as he could see his name on the cover.

Like many alcoholics, Paxon denied that he was one. The bottle had befriended him and had also stolen his career. It was easy to come home after work and drink himself silly while grading papers. He was able to function all these years as an alcoholic, but not to succeed. He had thought about writing many times, but again, it was one of those things he never got around to. It was always just around the corner. Greatness lay just ahead. He would get started next week. Put away the bottle and buckle down. One week turned to the next and the next week turned to another.

Now, in the twilight of his career, he may have a breakthrough. Something worthwhile; *something that mattered.* He would do it up right. Get the thing published and get down the road—that road that led great men to great places.

No longer would he be overlooked. Never again would he be passed by, ignored by his fellow scholars and the publishing world. All of the schools that had foolishly let him go would drown in the sorrow of knowing they had let him slip through their hands. Fools. They should have treated him better. They should have given him more time. They should have recognized him as the accomplished teacher and scholar that he was, published or not. They would be sorry, *very sorry*.

Albert Gaston would make it all possible. They had been close once, working together and had actually become friends. Then, Gaston became so famous, so distinguished, that they had lost touch until a few months ago. He could have helped his ol' buddy John years ago. Now, ol' John would help himself.

Only two things stood in his way—Galen Morris and some woman.

.   .   .

Galen waited a while before waking Audra. She drowsily came around and put her feet on the floor.

"What time is it?" she asked, rubbing her eyes.

"Quarter after seven," Galen said.

Audra looked at him, her face a blank. "You cheated me out of fifteen minutes," she said flatly as she fell back onto the couch.

Galen drug one of the kitchen chairs over to the couch. "I talked to Paxon a little while ago."

Audra turned to face him and opened one eye.

"He thinks he knows how to stop the thing," Galen said with an air of confidence in his voice. "He wants us to go to Georgia."

Audra opened both eyes now and twisted around to put her feet back on the floor. "Georgia?" she asked, thinking she hadn't heard him correctly. "He wants us to go to Georgia?"

Galen nodded.

"What's he gonna do?" she asked.

"I don't know yet," Galen responded." He wants me to call him from the road. He also wants me to bring all of Al's papers so he can compare notes."

Audra considered what he was saying. "When do we leave?"

"As soon as we can get our stuff together," Galen said. "I want to get this thing over with."

"Of course you do," Audra said. "And so do I. But do you think it's wise to just take off?"

"What else can we do?" Galen asked. "I want to stop this thing. The longer I wait, the longer it's around to do damage." Galen rubbed his freshly shaved chin.

"What about work?" Audra asked. "Aren't you on duty at midnight tonight?"

"Yeah, I am," Galen said. "I'll call in and have someone else take my shift for awhile." He saw the concern in Audra's face. "If Paxon thinks he can stop this damned thing, I'm gonna give him a shot."

"I guess I can try to get some time off too," Audra said. "I can call the hospital and try to schedule some vacation time." Galen looked at her knowing what he wanted to say but not how to say it. "Audra," he finally said. "You don't have to go."

Audra's eyes grew wide in disbelief of what Galen said.

"What do you mean?" she asked. "Don't you want me to go?"

"It's not that," Galen said. "It's just that..." Galen fumbled for the words, "I don't want you to get hurt."

"What if it comes after me here?" Audra asked.

"It won't," Galen responded.

"How do you know?"

"Because I just do—it's after *me*."

Audra was quiet for a moment. The look on her face showed that she was already hurt. Hurt by Galen not wanting her at his side during this whole ordeal. She felt betrayed and at the same time happy that he was thinking of her safety.

"I thought we made a pretty good team," she said sadly. "I thought I would be a big help."

"You would Audra," Galen said. "I couldn't have gotten this far without you. But I'm the one that got you into this mess and I don't want you to get hurt."

"But I *want* to go Galen. I want to be with you. Can't you see that?"

Galen looked deeply into her eyes. He saw that she was serious; she really wanted to be with him. A tear rolled from the corner of her eye.

Galen struggled with his thoughts for a moment. He could not bear to hurt Audra. After a long pause, he spoke. "Alright, let's get packing. I want you to come with me," he said. "I want you to be there for the whole thing." Her eyes brightened and Galen pulled her toward him and kissed her on the forehead. "You've been with me so far and I'm glad you were—as long as you *want* to go."

They embraced in a long kiss. Galen tasted the tears that had rolled to her lips.

She looked up to his eyes and hugged him tight. Her lips quivered as she said, "I'm glad you changed your mind."

"And I'm glad you're with me for this. I don't know what I'd do without you right now."

Within thirty minutes, the Mustang was packed for the trip to Georgia. Galen took the first leg of the drive and Audra continued to read the files. The day was sunny and warm, but cool air flowed into the car from the partially opened windows.

They would never know how close the Eater of Hearts was to them when they left The Willows that Sunday morning. While they left the town driving east, the Eater of Hearts was approaching the diesel fuel distribution center on the west side of town. While they drove with the cool breeze caressing their hair, one of the two security workers at the complex was being hideously deformed by raging flames. The other died in the explosion.

The fire roared with intensity, sparked by the ball as it bore through one of the storage tanks. Before the fire department would reach the scene, another tank would explode from the heat, spewing its cloud high enough to be seen more than thirty miles away.

Chapter 17

Tobias struggled along for a couple of miles before resting again. He could no longer focus his eyes. The world was a colorful blur before them. He could make out shapes and the lightness of the road in contrast with the surrounding woods.

He had unknowingly lost the bandaging from his arm stump. The ends of the bones stuck out slightly, covered with dust from the road.

He managed to walk most of the way since the swamp but now dizziness again forced him into his three-point crawl.

Tobias put his head down and crawled along. He took his chances with being captured now, because he did not have the energy to travel through the woods.

The sun had been up just a short while and he hoped that no early-morning travelers were on the road.

He looked up after what seemed hours of crawling and spotted a large white house, set back from the road. Through his feverish eyes, he saw only the general shape, but knew it was the house where Miss Mary now lived. He could smell the fresh cut wood mixed with the smell of paint.

An axe could be heard splitting firewood behind the large house and Tobias began to crawl toward it.

A hound was awakened from his lair under the new house and howled an alarm that an intruder was nearby. The dog came from beneath the house's front porch and cautiously approached Tobias. The smell of sickness was heavy in Tobias' scent and the dog knew he would not have to give chase to this slave.

Tobias lay still, now his only defense. He attempted to cover his head with his arms in case he was attacked. He could hear the dog nearby, still letting loose with an occasional howl. The sound of the axe had stopped. The dog was carefully trying to sort out the various smells emanating from him.

"Jasper!" a young voice yelled out, "you git ova here!"

A sigh of joy escaped Tobias, sounding more like a whimper. He knew the voice belonged to Titus.

"Get on back to the house!" Titus said to the dog.

The dog quieted and Tobias heard cautious footsteps approaching. He attempted to lift his head but weakness had paralyzed him.

"Hey, Mista," Titus said. "Y'all be alright?"

"No," Tobias croaked.

Titus spotted the gruesome looking amputation.

"Good Lawd Mista," he said. "You look like you done been eat up!" He reached over and helped Tobias to roll over.

Tobias saw the shape of his son's face against the sky but could make out no details. It took Titus a few seconds to recognize his own father.

"Papa!" he cried. "What done happened to ya' Papa?" Titus turned toward the house and screamed. "Gabe! Come fast! Papa's here and he's hurtin' real bad!"

Titus began to cry at the sight of his father. The scabs and open sores on his swollen face made him hard to recognize. Titus could not bear to look at the stump of his wrist. His pants were just rags hanging loosely about his waist. The shirt that Tobias had taken from Luke had held up well but was covered with mud, blood and dirt. His feet were cut and blistered and deep cracks opened up on their soles.

Titus looked into his father's glassy eyes and saw all sorts of horrors there. The look was far away and Titus suspected his father was already peeking into the lands of his ancestors, seeking them out for his long journey on earth was nearly over.

The twins sat their father upright and dragged to a tree stump. He leaned back against it still unable to focus his eyes. He heard the slave catcher's hounds howling in the distance but paid them no heed. He turned toward one of the boys and tried to make out which one it was. "I been missin' y'all," he said. "I wanted to see y'all before I go."

The twins were crying and put their heads upon his shoulders. The feel of their arms around him was a much warmer feeling than the pouch could have ever given him. The love that flowed through him was much more powerful than energy from the pouch. "Y'all boys stop yo' cryin' now," Tobias said. "Y'all is all growed up and it's time I told y'all somethin'."

The twins slowed their tears, still sniffling. Tobias told them a story about his childhood in Africa. The boys had always loved to hear these stories and had often begged for them. Tobias realized he could no longer tell stories to his children, because his children were now young, strong men. He needed to tell them one final story, about his amazing journey and the wonder that his gods had sent to Earth in the name of justice. He had to tell them, so they could believe and pass on the story to their children someday. Miss Mary and Ralph quietly ate breakfast in the kitchen and weren't even aware of Tobias' presence.

Tobias finished his story and turned to Titus.

"You gonna make me proud and remember 'bout Africa?"

Titus nodded, "Yes Papa, I'll 'member."

He turned to Gabriel. "You boys gonna tell yo' children 'bout Africa, and 'bout me and yo' Mama?"

Gabriel nodded and began to cry again.

Tobias shook his head as if to clear it. "Y'all are good boys," he said, "and I'll always love ya'." He looked at each one in turn and pulled them close. He kissed the boys again, each on the forehead, as they sat beside him. His dizziness was worse now. The world swam in his view. He closed his eyes, took a deep breath, and began to sing.

"It's a long ol' row to be hoein'
It's a long ol' row to be plowin'
It's a long, long, way to the big house...."

Tobias did not join the twins for the last part of the chorus for his body refused to draw the breath that it required for singing. The boys finished however, a tribute to their fallen father, the father they would never forget. They both looked toward the sky, trying to catch a glimpse of their father's soul as it drifted upward, toward a better place.

The wailing hounds were closing in on him but would not find him alive. They would however, find his body in the embrace of his sons. They would grow up to fight for his people and maybe, if the gods were just, freedom would come to them someday.

Chapter 18

Galen and Audra took turns driving until they reached Louisville, Kentucky. They filled the car with gas and stopped for a couple of sandwiches.

Galen figured they were about twelve hours ahead of the ball, giving them the first chance to get some real sleep since this whole thing started. They checked into a local hotel.

"I better give Paxon another call," Galen said, reaching for the phone.

Audra pulled the blankets back from the large bed and crawled between the sheets.

Galen dialed the number. After five rings, Paxon's deep voice answered.

"Paxon, here," he said.

"John. It's me, Galen."

"Galen, where are you?" he asked.

"We're in Louisville. We had to stop for a while and get some sleep."

"I see," Paxon said. "How long do you think it will take you to get here?"

Galen took the Atlas from the nightstand and looked up the mileage log. "It's about four-hundred miles to Atlanta," Galen said. "That's roughly an eight-hour drive."

"Another three-and-a-half to Savannah," Paxon added. "When do you think you'll be leaving Louisville?"

"I'm not sure yet," Galen said. "We need to sleep for a while." Galen looked at his watch. "We should be there by noon tomorrow."

"How much of a lead will you have on the... thing, by then?" Paxon asked.

"By that time we should have at least..." Galen looked to the ceiling in thought, "sixteen, eighteen hours or so."

"Good," Paxon said. "Give me a call when you get to Atlanta. In the meantime I'll be preparing things here."

"Okay," Galen said, "see ya' tomorrow." Galen had almost hung up the phone when he jerked the handset back to his ear and tried to catch Paxon before he hung up. "Paxon, you still there?" He heard the sound of the receiver on the other end of the connection being placed back into its cradle. "Damn," Galen said as he hung up the phone.

"What's the matter?" Audra asked sleepily, stretching her arms out with a yawn.

"I wanted to ask him what he had planned," Galen said. "I hope we're not making this trip for nothing."

Galen sat on the edge of the bed closest to the nightstand and untied his shoes.

"Galen," Audra said, "You better call the Department and I've got to call the Hospital."

"I completely forgot!" Galen said, slapping the palm of his hand against his forehead.

He let Audra call the Hospital first. He then got an outside line and dialed the Willow River Fire Department number from memory.

"Fire Department," the voice said.

Galen did not recognize the voice. "Hi. Who's this?" he asked, trying to place the voice.

"This is Charlie," a gruff voice answered.

"Oh, Charlie, I didn't recognize your voice," Galen said.

Charlie Boomgarden was a retired volunteer who still occasionally helped out at the station.

"What are you doing there?" Galen asked.

"Big fire," Charlie said. "Who's this?" he asked.

"This is Galen. What's on fire?"

"The fuel depot out there on Martin road," Charlie said. "Big fire, already one guy dead, maybe more. Where are you?"

"I, uh, got called away on a personal emergency," Galen said. "I may be gone for a couple of days and wanted to let the chief know."

"I see," Charlie said. "Well, I'm sure he's pretty busy right now but I can tell him for you."

"Thanks, Charlie. Please let him know." Galen did not feel right about not talking to the chief himself. He was afraid Charlie might forget his message. "You won't forget to give him my message?"

"Nope," Charlie stated. "I'm writin' it down now."

"Good," Galen said. "How long they been out at the fire?"

"Most all the day," Charlie said. "They figure it'll burn for a good while. Got a black cloud driftin' east of town, makes it look like night." Charlie hesitated for a minute then spoke again. "They had to evacuate most of the people east and south of town."

"How many departments are there?" Galen asked, feeling guilty for his absence.

"Let's see," Charlie said. "Got Winnebago, Pecatonica, Seward, German Valley," he paused again as he tried to remember who else was there. "Oh, and Leaf River and Byron are here. Freeport and Rockford are gonna send crews to relieve our guys, and the Haz-Mat guys are here too."

"Sounds like you guys have your hands full," Galen said. "Sorry I'm not there." Audra had propped her head up on her arm and was listening. "I'll let ya' go Charlie. Don't forget my message."

"Yeah, okay Galen," Charlie said. "I better get back and help fill air tanks."

Galen said goodbye and hung up the phone. Audra looked at him, anxious to know what was going on. He explained about the fire.

"My God, that's terrible," she said. She could see Galen felt bad about not being there to help. "They can take care of it," she assured him. "It's not your fault that you can't be there right now."

"I know," Galen said. "But I can't help feeling like I'm letting them down."

She reached over and began to massage his shoulders. "You're not letting them down," she said. "You're facing something here a lot worse than that fire. This is a matter of life and death. I'm sure if they knew what you were up against they wouldn't blame you for what you're doing."

Galen nodded his head and turned to her. She was sitting on the bed with her legs crossed. She wore a yellow t-shirt and a pair of sweat-pants. Her ponytail curved around the side of her neck and fell over the front of her shoulder covering her right breast. She smiled at him, showing her bright, straight teeth.

Galen just stared at her for a moment. They looked into each other's eyes and Galen noticed a slight blush rise to her cheeks. She looked beautiful all of a sudden. Somewhere along the line, a complete transformation had come over her. She did not look "small-town cute" anymore. She looked like a beautiful, sensuous woman. She was a competent, strong-willed female that set fire to his heart. Galen wondered if what he felt at that moment was true love. The thought scared him.

"What?" Audra asked. She broke the eye-locking gaze by looking down at her bare feet.

"Nothing," Galen said, "I was just thinking."

"Oh," Audra said with a disappointed tone. A moment of silence passed. "We'd better get some sleep," she said, moving back across the bed. She tugged at the blankets and fluffed her pillows. She slid beneath the sheets at the far side of the bed. "Yeah, you're right," Galen said. He was still clad in a pair of jeans but wore no shirt or socks. He lay down on top of the blankets and dropped one of his two pillows on the floor. "I sure am tired," she said. "It'll feel good to get a little sleep for a change."

Although she claimed to be tired, Audra's voice seemed full of energy as she spoke. Galen looked over to see her staring at the ceiling before he clicked off the light.

"G'night Audra," Galen said.

"Good night," she returned.

Galen stared into the complete darkness of the room. With the shades over the window pulled the room was as dark as a cave. He tried to dig through his shambled thoughts of Audra. Within the last few minutes, he had a funny feeling in the center of his chest. He longed to reach out to her and pull her close. He could imagine the smell of her hair and the smoothness of her skin. *Am I falling in love?* he wondered. *After so many years, is it happening now?*

He wondered how Audra felt about him. After all, she had gotten upset with him more than once during the last couple of days. Yet, he had kept his temper under control for the entire day today and his mouth had not betrayed him. Maybe he had a chance with her, maybe not. He felt Audra's hand close over his upper arm as he argued the point with himself.

"You asleep yet?" she whispered.

"No," he whispered back.

Audra lay silent for a few seconds. "I'm afraid, Galen," she said. "I hope Paxon can help us." She slid her hand down his arm and clasped his hand in hers. "I want this to be over."

"Me too," Galen said. He squeezed her hand. "More than anything, I want this to be over." He rolled toward her in the bed, unable to see her in the darkness.

"What will you do when this is over?" she asked.

"What do you mean?"

"I mean," she said, "will this change your life in any way?"

Galen thought for a moment. "Yes," he finally answered. "I would have never believed in anything like this if it hadn't happened to me. I guess it already has changed my life. I now know things like this are possible. Do you know what that means?" Audra did not answer. "It means all of those things that I never believed in could also be possible. All those weird things that science can't explain, could be possible. Near death experiences, ESP, ghosts..." Galen was silent for just a moment, and then spoke again. "I guess I'll have to look at all those things in a new light."

193

Again, a moment of silence ensued.

"Anything else?" Audra asked.

"Yea," Galen said. He was not sure if he wanted to bring this up right now, but a certain thought had been on his mind for a while. He wanted to run it by Audra. "I'm thinking about giving up my career as a Paramedic."

No silence this time. Audra spoke immediately. "What?" she asked. "I thought you loved your job."

"I've been at it a long time," Galen said, his voice flat, emotionless. "I've seen so much pain, so much death." He paused for a few seconds. "I just don't know if I can take it any longer."

"But you're so good at it," Audra responded. "I've never seen anyone as good at it as you are, Galen."

"I've served my time, Audra. I just don't think I can take it anymore."

"Would this decision have anything to do with Al's death?" Audra asked.

"Maybe," Galen said. "I don't know for sure." He sat up in the bed and put his feet to the floor. He reached for a cigarette. "I seem to get depressed after calls more often than I used to," Galen said. "It's like this huge responsibility is always resting on my shoulders. Sometimes, the pressure is just too much."

"What would you do?" Audra asked.

"My Dad's got an accounting business near Chicago," Galen said. "He's always wanted me to take it over before he retires. I've been thinking about taking him up on his offer."

"I can't picture you in an office," Audra said. She squeezed his arm. "Are you sure about this?"

"No, I'm not," Galen said. "I just think it's time to take a look at the possibilities."

"It's not your fault that Al died," Audra said. "You did everything you could."

"I know," Galen said. "I didn't say it was."

"You've got to *believe* it and realize that you can't save everyone."

"Don't try to analyze me, Audra," Galen said with an angry edge to his voice. "I'm a big boy and can take care of myself." The tip of his cigarette glowed brightly as he took a deep drag from it, casting a dull red light on the wall.

"How many lives *have* you saved, Galen? Did you ever stop to think about that? Did you ever think about all of the families that are still together because of you, because of how good you are at what you do?"

"Stop it!" Galen hissed. "What about *my* happiness? What about *me*? Who takes care of me when I need help?" Galen's voice began to crack. "Who cares for the care-givers?"

The door to that dark closet in Galen's mind burst open. Painful memories gushed out in a flood of tears. All the pain he had kept to himself for all those years, were released in an hour-long crying spell.

Audra held him close. She placed his head against her chest and stroked his hair as a mother might comfort a child. Then they talked, they kissed and they made love.

.   .   .

The alarm went off at one o'clock in the morning. Neither of them felt they had gotten enough sleep.

Galen switched on the light. "What do you think," he asked, "another hour?"

Audra nodded her head and yawned. "I could use more than that," she said.

Galen reset the alarm clock and turned off the light. He didn't want to delay leaving for much longer because he wanted to get to Savannah.

The extra hour flew by and before they knew it the alarm was banging out its warning that their time was up. They groggily got up from the bed. After showering, they left the motel.

They found a twenty-four-hour convenience store and bought some coffee and rolls. Within a few more minutes, they were rolling along highway 65 toward Nashville.

The sun rose over the hills as they passed through the home of country music. Galen pulled over at a restaurant to have a real breakfast.

They had both been in better spirits since last night. They both felt some deep, dark void in their lives had been filled by the other and the feelings they had for each other was enough to build a relationship. A relationship that they both not only wanted; but needed.

After a satisfying breakfast served by a young girl with a strong southern drawl, Galen went to a phone. He called the Fire Department first to find out about the fire. He was answered this time by a voice that he recognized immediately.

"Chief," Galen said. "How're things going?"

"Galen?" the chief asked, "where the Hell are you?"

"Didn't you get my message?" Galen asked.

"Yeah, I got it," the Chief said, "but that doesn't tell me where the Hell you are."

Galen said, "Actually, I'm somewhere south of Nashville."

"What the Hell are you doin' way down there?"

"It's a little hard to explain," Galen said, "it's a personal emergency Chief, I had no choice."

"I know," the Chief said, "but when the Hell do you think you'll be back?" Chief Atley rarely completed a sentence without using the word 'Hell' at least once.

"Probably a couple of days," Galen said. "I'll keep in touch and be back as soon as possible."

"Yeah," the Chief said. "Get back in a hurry. We've got a Hell of a mess out here."

"What happened?" Galen asked.

"A fuel storage tank over at Huntley's place went up and blew two more all to Hell before we could cool it down. Helluva mess."

"What's going on now?" Galen asked.

"It's still burnin'," the chief said. "Hell, we'll have to let 'er burn herself out. Listen Galen, I gotta get back out to the scene.

There's a guy here that needs to talk to ya'." The Chief's voice disappeared, replaced by another.

"Galen Morris?" the vaguely familiar voice asked.

"Yeah, this is he," Galen answered.

"Galen, this is Clive Jennings, Al Gaston's attorney," the voice said. "I've been looking all over for you."

"What can I do for you Mr. Jennings?" Galen asked, now associating a face with the name.

"I just wanted to let you know that Al has left everything to you in his will," Jennings said. "I need to meet with you to have you sign some papers as soon as you can get here."

Galen was silent for a moment. "What did you say?" Galen asked the attorney.

"Mr. Gaston has left everything he owned to you, Galen. I need to have you sign some papers so we can get this thing all wrapped up."

"He didn't leave it to his nephew?" Galen asked.

"He doesn't have a nephew."

"Sure he does, out east. He told me about him."

"Well, if he did, he didn't leave anything to him. It all goes to you, Galen Morris."

"Okay," Galen said, still unbelieving. "I'll come see you when I get back to town."

"I'll be expecting you," the attorney said. "The sooner the better, Galen."

Galen hung up the phone in disbelief.

.   .   .

John Paxon had things to do. Galen and his girl would be here within the next few hours and Paxon had not left his bottle long enough to plan ahead. He needed a secluded place, a few supplies, rope and a gun. He hoped he would not have much trouble with them, and if he did, the gun would tip the scale in his favor.

He would certainly have to be careful. No one should see him with the two visitors. He remembered the messages Galen had left on his answering machine and removed the tape. He stuck the tape in his pocket as he dialed the school. He pleaded sickness, not having used that for an excuse for more than two months.

He took another nip from the bottle. He went through the house looking for a box to put his collection of supplies in. He took the gun from his nightstand drawer, checked that it was loaded and put it into the box. He grabbed a handful of extra cartridges, (.38 hollow points; he was not playing games with anyone who was unfortunate enough to break into *his* house) and placed those into the box with the gun. He went to the garage where he spotted a coil of clothesline rope hanging on a nail and dropped it into the box. He glanced around his workbench, which had not seen any action in years. Spotting a utility knife, he picked it up and checked the blade. It was slightly rusted, had a couple of nicks in it, but he figured it would still cut the soft rope. He dropped it into the collection box. As he turned to leave the workbench, he noticed a few nylon wire-ties that an electrician had left when he had the new furnace installed in the house. Those also went into the box.

Paxon picked up the phone in his study and looked up his brother's telephone number.

"Hello?" a voice answered.

"Tommy?" Paxon said, "is that you?"

"John?" the voice said, sounding unsure. "Yeah it's me. Something wrong?"

"No, hey, I was just wondering if anybody was living out at the old place anymore," Paxon said.

"Nobody's lived there in over a year, John. If I heard from you more often, you'd know that."

Paxon and his only brother Tom, had grown up on a farm a few miles outside of town. Neither of the boys wanted to continue farming so when their father died their mother sold off the land. She had kept only the house and the out-buildings and lived there for the rest of her life. She had died nearly four years ago.

"Well, you know how busy things are," Paxon said. "It seems like every time you turn around these days you've got somethin' to do."

"Yep, I know what you mean," his brother said. "But you *never* come around John, and you never seem to be home. I bet I've tried calling you a dozen times in the last year and always get that blasted answering machine."

Paxon did not want to tell him he had heard him leave several of the messages while he sat drunk in front of the TV, bottle in one hand, cigarette in the other. He had been too busy doing nothing and had not wanted to leave the bottle long enough to take the time to talk. He had meant to return the calls the following day, in a series of endless tomorrows that found him in the same mood and the same situation.

"I'm sorry, Tommy," Paxon said, in his most apologetic voice. "Let's get together real soon. I've been writing a novel about this local legend. It's been takin' up a lot of my time but I'm almost done with it."

"That's good to hear, John," Tommy said. "Let's do that. You probably could use a good home-cooked meal. I'll have Peggy whip up a somethin' good and we'll sit and talk."

"Sounds good," Paxon said.

The line was quiet for a few seconds before Tommy spoke up again.

"What are you askin' about the old place for, John?"

"I was just wonderin' about it," he said. "I've got to drive over that way on business this week and thought I might swing by it."

Tommy hesitated for a moment. "The place is in dire need of some repairs," he said. "I couldn't keep up with it. It seemed like every time I turned around, the tenants were calling about one thing or another. First, the hot water went out, and then the pump broke down. The roof started to leak and the list just kept

199

getting longer. I didn't have the time or the money to fix it up right, so I've just let it sit empty for a while."

"I see," Paxon said. "Maybe if things work out on this book I'm writing, I'll be able to help you out a little. It's a shame for the place to be sittin' like that. Momma and Daddy put so much into it."

"Yeah, that's what I've been thinking," Tommy said. "I just haven't had a choice."

"I know," Paxon said. "I better let you go. I've got to get to work," Paxon lied.

"Me too," Tommy said, "another day, another dollar."

"I'll call you again soon," Paxon said. "We'll decide when we can get together."

The two brothers said their good-byes and Paxon hung up the phone. He rubbed his hands briskly together like a fly anticipating a meal.

The old place would do nicely. Its seclusion would be perfect for what he had in mind.

He ran through a brief plan in his head. Perhaps he should kill the woman right away. Then he would have one less to worry about while he and Morris waited—waited for death; for the Eater of Hearts to come knocking at the door.

Chapter 19

After their hearty breakfast, Galen and Audra felt much better. Audra drove and Galen fiddled with his injured left hand. He carefully wiped it with some anti-bacterial pads and replaced the dressings while Audra drove them toward Atlanta.

After finishing with the dressings, Galen began to read the files again hoping to discover what Paxon had in mind. It bothered him that Paxon had been so vague over the phone, not divulging his plans on how to stop the thing. He just hoped Paxon was right and whatever he had in mind did the job.

When they arrived in Atlanta, Audra guided the Mustang off the highway and began seeking a gas station and a restaurant. After filling the car and making a pit stop at Hardees, Galen called Paxon's house.

"We're in Atlanta," Galen said, looking at his watch. "Looks like it'll be closer to two o'clock before we get to Savannah. We slept a little later than we expected."

"I'm sure you needed it," Paxon said through gritted teeth. He was angry about their delay. He wanted to get his plans underway, the sooner the better.

"Yeah, we did," Galen said. "Where do you want us to meet you?" he asked.

Paxon gave Galen directions to the old family farm. He explained to Galen that he didn't want to risk anybody being around to avoid any unnecessary risk. He told Galen how to recognize the farm house and to park in the back. "I'll be waiting for you there," Paxon said.

"Uh, John," Galen said as the conversation wound down, "what do you have in mind, anyway?"

"It's kind of hard to explain it over the phone," Paxon said. He took a deep breath and tried to make up something that would get Galen to come to Savannah without making him suspicious. "There are some records about the Eater of Hearts that indicated a way to stop the curse. It was started by a ritual, and there's supposed to be a ritual to stop it." Paxon told Galen other lies about the curse. Lies about how he had met with modern-day practitioners of the African religion and had gotten their input on ways to stop it. "I made it sound like I was asking hypothetical questions," Paxon said. "I didn't want to tell them this was for real. I just wanted them to think I was just curious."

"What does it involve?" Galen asked, curious as to what they had to do.

"There are some religious articles I have here with me," Paxon lied, looking into his box of supplies. "Think of it as an exorcism, Galen," Paxon said. "It's something like that, but not really the same. I'll assure you that we will maintain a safe escape route in case anything goes wrong. We'll make it as safe as possible."

Galen gently bit his bottom lip while taking in what Paxon was telling him.

Paxon could feel Galen's tension and apprehension on the other end of the line. "Galen, nobody knows what will happen," he said. "We're just going to have to give it a try and hope for the best. If it doesn't work, we'll have to think of something else." Paxon hoped that his last statement sounded authentic. By letting him know there were no guarantees he hoped it would sound more believable.

"I have no other options," Galen said. "I hope it works."

"Same here," Paxon said.

Galen exhaled loudly, "Well, I guess we'll see you in about three, maybe four hours."

"Okay, Galen," Paxon said. "Be careful on the way."

"Will do, John," Galen said. "And John, thanks for all your help."

"Anytime, Galen, anytime."

Galen hung up the phone with a puzzled look on his face. He would have felt better if Paxon said he had a way to *crush* the thing, to physically stop the crazy ball. This bit about spells and curses left Galen feeling flustered. He wanted to see it obliterated, to actually see it *die*. He wanted to sweep its remains into a can and enjoy crushing it to powder, watching it blow away with the breeze, never to haunt another living soul. If Paxon thought it could be stopped otherwise, he would be forced to go along with it. After all, Galen had a new outlook on many things since he had learned about the Eater of Hearts. As crazy as it sounded, if this thing was started by a curse, why did he find it hard to believe that it could also be stopped by a counter-curse? The thing was real, of that he had no doubt.

Galen drove the remaining distance. Audra read the map and Paxon's instructions to the farmhouse. They found it with little difficulty.

They traveled for miles down red-clay roads, soft and a bit slick from a recent rain. They watched the woods change to farmland and back to woods as they approached the house.

The house was a large two-story structure with peeling white paint on all of its surfaces. The roof was a complex design of many angles clad in tin instead of conventional shingles.

They drove down the weed-choked driveway and saw a car parked behind the house. Assuming it was Paxon's, they parked beside it. As Galen and Audra stepped out of the car they heard the screech of the old screen door as it swung open. A man of average height and bland looks stood in the doorway.

"Galen?" the man asked.

"John?" Galen said as he habitually stuck out his right hand.

The two shook hands and Audra joined them on the dilapidated porch.

Audra disliked him from the moment she first laid eyes on him. His facial features looked red and swollen. Small veins in his nose showed through his thin skin, running in tiny patterns that joined similar patterns on his cheeks. The man looked ill and his eyes looked like two bullet holes in an old tin can. He lead them into the house which looked much better on the inside than on the outside. "I'm sorry to have made you meet me way out here," Paxon said. "The place has seen better times."

"It's a unique house," Audra said, looking around. The high ceilings and wide wood trim indicated it had been built over a hundred years ago. The first floor was laden with doors and hallways shot through the house as if designed by an explosion. "My grandfather built the house in 1884," Paxon said. "It's been vacant for over a year." He looked around the house. "It's a shame."

A few worn-out furniture remnants littered the large sitting room. The former tenants must have felt they were not worth the time or effort to move. A card table and three chairs sat in the center of the house in what had been the dinning room during Paxon's childhood. They looked oddly out of place, surrounded by the antiquity of the house.

"I trust you brought Gaston's files concerning this thing?" Paxon asked as he motioned them to sit at the card table.

Galen looked at Audra. "They're still in the car," he said. "I'll get them."

"Very good," Paxon said. "We'll need to go over some of his writings to collaborate my findings."

Galen got up and disappeared through one of the many doorways. The house made Audra feel a bit claustrophobic. Instead of being a large, open house, it was maze-like; every room connected by a swinging door instead of open doorways or arches. From the dinning room in which they sat, one wall opened up to a sitting room, another to the kitchen. Two doors were on her right, both closed, that went to parts unknown. A fourth door went to another hallway. It was too tight, too closed up; it seemed to squeeze her.

Galen returned and dropped the ample stack of papers onto the card table.

"My," Paxon said, "there's a lot more here than I had anticipated."

Audra and Galen took the obvious gleeful tone in his voice to mean that he was happy he had so much information with which to help them. His face widened in a grin. "My old friend spent many hours on this subject, I see."

Audra began to tell Paxon what she had learned while reading the papers. "Al left some notes on his computer that said he had bought the object from the wife of the last living relative of Benjamin Richards. The object was passed down through the generations, but really held no meaning to her. Al had learned through his research that after the slave catchers found the runaway slave, they set their hounds on finding Richards. He had also gone missing, and they found him dead with this object embedded in his chest."

Paxon barely heard Audra as she spoke and began to glance through the papers, picking out highlights from each. "It looks to be very well done," he said, the broad grin returning. *Yes, this will work nicely!* he thought, shuffling through the papers. He would now carry out his plan and set the first part into motion.

"How much of this have you read through?" Paxon asked, looking at both of his visitors.

"Audra has read a lot more than I have," Galen said. "She told me the core of the story about Tobias, the slave, and the ceremony."

Audra nodded her head, "I've read through a lot of the interviews that Al did while he was down here and some of his thoughts about the Eater of Hearts. I focused mostly on his research notes instead of the novel. I was hoping I would find the most useful information in his notes."

"Did he mention anywhere in here about a way to stop it?" Paxon asked.

"If he did, I haven't read it yet," Audra answered. For some reason she felt she should not tell Paxon anything. She offered only what he specifically asked for and no more. If she felt the information she could offer would help Galen, she would have spoken up in a heartbeat. Paxon struck her as a con man. She could not figure out why Gaston had ever wanted him to have the thing in the first place.

Paxon pointed out the several books he had brought from the college, more for show than anything else. He had barely glanced through them before his friendly bottle of whiskey had pulled him away.

"I've poured through these volumes," Paxon lied, "and have found a few interesting passages that may be useful."

He handed one of the books to Galen. Galen reached for it and Paxon saw the bandages on his hand. "What happened?" he asked. Galen explained the episode to Paxon, whose eyes lit up with belief. After completing the story, Galen sat down and looked through the book about West African religions.

Audra remained at the card table reading through some of the files.

Paxon was searching his mind for something he could ask Galen to do, something that would get him out of the house, if only for a few minutes. Then he would deal with the girl. Taking care of them one at a time would be much easier. Before he could think of anything, Galen thought of something for him, virtually volunteering himself for the job.

"You didn't bring any food by chance?" Galen asked. "I'm hungry."

"No, I'm afraid that slipped my mind," Paxon responded.

"Maybe we could run into town and bring something back," Galen said, looking at Audra.

Paxon panicked slightly, thinking they both might leave, but quickly responded with an idea. "Audra and I can stay here and go over these files. It's very important that I try to find a passage that deals with stopping this thing and see if it agrees with what I've found elsewhere."

Audra wanted to go with Galen but staying would be of more help. She still did not trust this man but did not want to offend him if he could stop the ball-thing. She looked to Galen, who nodded and asked what he should get to eat.

After deciding on cold cuts and sandwich fixings, Galen got directions to the nearest store. He gave Audra a quick kiss on the cheek and left the house. She heard the Mustang's engine roar to life and saw the car cruise past the house.

Paxon continued to read the files, seemingly paying no attention to Audra. She read through the files, setting aside things she had already read, looking for new information. The house still gave Audra the creeps but she tried to ignore the feeling.

Paxon got up and walked across the room. He bent over and began to shuffle through a box that sat on the floor. "Finding anything interesting, Audra?" Paxon asked, pulling the gun from the box.

"Not yet," Audra replied, paying little attention to him.

"I have," he said.

Audra turned to see what he meant and found herself looking down the wrong end of a gun barrel. Her face dropped its color and her mouth stood agape.

"Get up," Paxon said.

Audra stood up and lifted her arms over her head without being asked. "What are you doing?" she asked.

"Making a better life for myself, dear," Paxon said with a smile. "Now, be a good girl and come over here and sit down." He indicated a spot on the floor in front of an old-fashioned heat radiator. He kicked the box over to where she was sitting and used the wire-ties to attach her wrists together behind her back. He then tied her to the heavy, cast-iron radiator.

"What are you doing?" Audra continued to ask, now helplessly bound to the radiator.

Paxon pulled a roll of duct tape from the box and tore off a six-inch strip. He placed it over her mouth as she struggled to free herself.

"Much better," Paxon said. "The quiet is so peaceful out here, don't you agree?"

Audra continued to struggle; the thin nylon strips around her wrists were biting into her skin. They were impossibly strong and the more she struggled, the more painful it became.

Paxon came near her, intent on putting another wire-tie on her ankles. She kicked at him the best she could but he sat on her legs, pinning them tightly to the floor. He strapped the wire-tie to her ankles, pulling it painfully tight.

"That should do for a while," Paxon said. "And you're such a pretty girl. What a shame."

He reached down and stroked her face gently with the back of his liver-spotted hand. The feeling he had over her at that moment was intense. Such power. He could do anything he wanted to her and no one would ever know. Evil, vile thoughts ran through his mind, thoughts he had never had before. The power he felt made him feel invulnerable. *Anything I want!* He reached down and cupped her breast in his hand. He smiled.

Audra gasped. With her mouth taped closed she couldn't seem to draw enough breath through her flaring nostrils. She tried to calm herself, keeping her thoughts on Galen, who would soon return. She felt both relieved and scared of that thought. Relieved that maybe he could help her, and frightened that he too, may get caught by this crazy man.

Paxon moved his hand from Audra's breast and moved it over the tight jeans on her legs. Although Audra did not know it, Paxon's vile thoughts were all that kept her alive at that moment. He wanted her and would keep her alive for only one purpose. *His* purpose.

Paxon controlled his urges, knowing he had more to do before he could have his way with the girl. Galen would be coming back soon and he would have to take care of him, too. Then there would be waiting. Waiting for the thing. *The Eater of Hearts.*

Paxon was excited by the thought of seeing the Eater of Hearts. Few men would ever witness such an event. He went over to his box and pulled out his friend. The amber liquid sang to him, its beautiful voice calling him. *I'm here John, just like always.*

I'm here for you. He felt the warm liquor splash against the back of his throat. He was relieved. The tension in his muscles relaxed and John Paxon felt strong, felt *powerful*.

Audra had calmed herself down fearing she would suffocate if she didn't. She consciously willed herself to slow her breathing in an attempt to calm her nerves. She sat against the radiator and watched Paxon make love to the bottle.

Paxon took his bottle to another room. He looked out the front window toward the road, waiting for Galen. He sipped cautiously, controlling himself.

After a few moments, the Mustang turned off the road and rolled quietly toward the house.

Paxon met Galen at the back door. He held the gun behind his back, waiting for just the right moment.

Galen entered the back door with a large grocery bag in one arm and a six-pack of Pepsi dangling from the fingers on his injured left hand.

"I trust you found everything you were looking for?" Paxon said.

"Yeah, no problem," Galen said. "I hope you like roast beef and ched-." His sentence was snapped off in midstream when he saw the hideous grin on Paxon's face and the gun pointing toward him. "Paxon, what the Hell..." His thoughts quickly turned in another direction. "Where's Audra?" he asked, his voice hard edged with both fear and anger.

"Oh, she's quite alright," Paxon said. "Now listen to me very carefully. Put your hands behind you and lean over the counter."

"What the Hell are you doing, Paxon?" Galen asked.

"Just do it!" Paxon shouted. The gun quivered slightly in his grip. "I'll explain everything to you later. Lean over the counter, now!"

Galen thought about rushing the crazy man but decided he did not have much of a chance. A bullet was a lot faster than he was and there was about twelve feet between him and Paxon. Galen leaned over the counter with his hands behind his back.

Paxon walked cautiously toward him, keeping the gun pointed at Galen's head. Paxon took one of the wire-ties and fumbled with one hand to tighten it around his wrists. He gave it a sharp pull. Galen winced at the sudden pain and Paxon backed away.

"Okay, now turn around," Paxon said. He would not feel comfortable until he had Galen tied to one of the radiators like Audra. He marched Galen into the other room where Audra sat crying.

Audra had tears in her eyes; sorry she had been unable to warn Galen before he got into the house.

Paxon told Galen to sit down in front of a radiator at the opposite end of the room. Galen complied, his mind furiously racing to find a way out of this mess and wondering what had gone wrong.

Paxon slipped the rope over Galen's head. With Galen sitting down and his hands tied behind his back, Paxon sat the gun on the floor and quickly tightened the rope. He then made a couple of passes around Galen's body with the rope and tied off the end in a good, strong knot.

"There," Paxon said. He brushed his hands together and picked up the gun. He walked back to the card table and pulled up a chair. He took a long swallow; his way of rewarding himself for a job well done.

Galen looked at Audra, her eyes red, her face wet and that obscene piece of tape censoring her mouth. He looked back to Paxon who sat comfortably in a folding chair, taking another sip.

"Just what do you think you're doing?" Galen asked.

"I am doing the only thing I'm fairly certain will work," Paxon said smugly.

"I want to talk to Audra," Galen said. His voice sounded as mean as the growl of a Rotweiler.

"Poor thing," Paxon said. "I couldn't let her warn you, could I?"

He walked over to Audra and reached for the tape. "It really won't make a difference if you scream," Paxon told her.

"Nobody will hear you. I just don't want to hear it myself. So if you scream, the tape goes back on. If not, I will enjoy the company while we wait for the 'Eater' to come and do its job." He peeled up a corner of the tape and began to pull it off. Audra's lips stretched crazily as he pulled it off, distorting her face as if seeing it in a fun-house mirror.

She drew the first long breath she had had in over an hour and then said, "Galen, I'm sorry."

"You have nothing to be sorry for," Galen said. "Are you okay?"

Audra nodded and looked over to Paxon. "Why are you doing this?" she asked.

"Well, where do I start?" Paxon said. He tapped his fingers on his lips and studied the ceiling. "Your friend, Albert Gaston, and I worked together years ago."

Audra and Galen listened to the man ramble on, both trying to secretly loosen their bindings.

"He was a very brilliant man. After a while though, it seemed everything was handed to him on a silver platter. Everything he wrote caused a sensation. His books were adopted as textbooks in most schools and his novels rocketed to the top of best-seller lists. His academic papers were praised." Paxon became quiet for a moment, his eyes full of envy. "He was a gifted man."

Paxon reached over and picked up Gaston's files. "And these words of his will lead me to the same type of success. It will be my start. I can take it from here on my own."

"So you plan to steal his work and put your name on it," Galen said.

"Precisely," Paxon said.

Galen began to laugh.

Audra looked at him as if *he* were the crazy one.

"I'm glad you find humor in that Mr. Morris," Paxon said. "It warms my heart to know you can leave this world in such good spirits."

"It's not that I find it funny," Galen said. "I laugh because you sound like a man who thinks he'll live happily ever after.

211

What will you do after that? How will you live with yourself, knowing you sacrificed two lives for a book? You're still gonna be the same failure that you are now, only worse. You'll be a murderer *and* a failure; a thief and an alcoholic."

"I'm not an alcoholic!" Paxon shouted. "I'm a respected professor and this *will* be enough to give me a start!"

"Paxon," Galen said, "I've only known you for a couple of hours and you can't even fool me. How do you expect to fool all of those people who have known you for years? Do you think they're going believe that after all these years you just suddenly came up with a great book?"

"The book is not all I will have, Galen. I will have the thing itself, the *Eater of Hearts*! If Gaston believed it was made of diamond, I would tend to believe him! That in itself will be enough. It will be worth a fortune!"

"I pity you, Paxon," Galen said. "You're living in your own little world. You'll never get away with it."

"We'll see," Paxon said confidently.

You haven't got any idea of how to stop it," Audra said. "You brought us here just so you can get the ball."

"To the contrary my dear," Paxon said. "I do know how to stop it. I've known all along. I just knew you wouldn't want to hear it."

Paxon looked smug in his knowledge. "It has to have its way," Paxon said with an evil smile returning to his face. "It has to run its course; *it has to get its heart!*"

Fear ran through Galen as he realized what this lunatic had in mind. He fought furiously for a moment trying to loosen himself. He would rather die from a bullet than from that *thing*.

"Don't try to free yourself," Paxon said. Those thin strips of nylon are impossible to break. You'll only hurt yourself worse."

"I cant believe you would kill us over this!" Galen shouted.

"I'm doing the world a favor," Paxon said. "Do you know how many people have died because of this thing already?"

Galen said nothing.

"Several," Paxon said. "Probably dozens. Yes, I've been watching the papers and the news. There have been several unexplained deaths in the last couple of days. Unexplained to most people that is. But we know what killed them, don't we, Galen?"

Galen hung his head, knowing that Paxon, crazy as he was, now spoke the truth.

"That's not his fault!" Audra protested. "He didn't ask for this. What's he supposed to do?"

"I agree," Paxon, answered. "It's very unfortunate this had to happen. But now that it has, I can end it and put myself in a better position at the same time." Paxon paused for a moment then added, "You do agree that it has to end somewhere, don't you?"

"You're a sick man, Paxon," Audra said. "You're a very sick man."

"You know," Paxon said, "I really know very little about this thing, but I do know that it will stop at nothing. It's quite marvelous, really. According to the legend, it can go through anything. Brick, concrete, even steel. It makes no difference to this thing. It searches for its prey relentlessly. It never stops. It's always coming. It toys with the person it is after, chasing them on a hopeless journey through Hell." Paxon looked at Galen. "Is that how you feel, Galen?"

Galen sat motionless, saying nothing.

"Not so funny now?" Paxon said. "Believe me, it's better this way. I will force you to face the thing and it will soon be over."

Paxon took another long pull from the bottle. "I don't understand how it was reactivated though. I'm sure if Gaston had any idea this could happen he would have taken some kind of precaution against it. It's puzzling. I'll think about that."

Paxon reached into his coat pocket searching for another pack of cigarettes and his hand ran across the cassette tape from his answering machine. He pulled it out and began pulling long segments of the tape from the case. "Wouldn't want anyone to

213

ever find this," he said. He lifted the pile of audio tape from the floor and lit his lighter. The mass of tangled tape flamed up quickly and Paxon dropped it to the floor. It sent a small cloud of smoke upward as the tape twisted, shrank and pulled inward - as if alive - from the heat. Paxon stomped it into a mass of ash and remnants with the heel of his shoe. "That's the only evidence that links *me* with *you*," Paxon said, trying to avoid the noxious smoke.

Paxon continued to drink for the next several hours. He would babble from time to time keeping the bottle close at hand. Audra and Galen grew painfully stiff from sitting in the same position for so long. About the most they could do was shift their weight from one side of their buttocks to the other and the effectiveness of that wore off after the first hour or so. Audra had already wet her pants, Paxon refusing to let her go to the bathroom.

Galen continued to work on loosening his bindings but managed only to wear a bloody groove in his wrists.

Paxon was drinking enough to get six men totally plastered. He held his liquor well. He was accustomed to this kind of drinking; he functioned with it daily. He lit a small propane lamp as the room began to darken.

Galen was hoping that Paxon would pass out so he could try to pull the whole radiator out of the floor.

Audra sat quietly, thinking about the loss she was about to suffer. She had hopes for her and Galen. She had pictured them together, perhaps someday, even married. She worried about what Paxon would do to her after Galen was dead. She almost did not care. If Galen died, a part of her would die as well. Let Paxon have her lifeless body, for her spirit would forever be with Galen, wherever he was. She had to admit, however, that the thought of him becoming sexually aggressive with her was sickening.

Galen began to change his mind about the whole thing. Maybe Paxon was right. He might be doing the world a favor, as he knew people had died. That thing was out there, coming for

214

him. There was no way to stop it. It had all been a cruel lie from Paxon. He began to wash all of the lovely thoughts of his life with Audra out of his mind, facing the fact that the world would be safer with him dead.

The next few hours went by agonizingly slow. Each of the three kept their thoughts to themselves. Paxon continued to drink and smoke but showed no signs of passing out.

"How about a smoke?" Galen asked.

Paxon thought for a moment, his eyes revealing the liquor *was* affecting him to some degree. "What kind of man would I be to deny the condemned a last cigarette?" Paxon said. He lit one off the end of another and stuck it in Galen's mouth.

Galen drew deeply on the smoke and held it in his lungs for a few seconds before letting it out. It had gotten dark hours ago but Galen had no idea what time it was. By his calculations, the ball would be showing up early in the morning.

Dawn meant death to Galen. He dreaded seeing the sky turn pink in the east.

Audra had shifted her thoughts back to the ball. Something stuck in the back of her mind; something that she could not pull into a thought. She went over in her head the things she had read, trying to make some sense of it all. Something was lurking there, at the fringes of her consciousness, but she could not grasp it. Audra had a view through a door that faced east and she saw the sky lighten as she wrestled with her thoughts.

Paxon sat with one hand on the bottle. He had slowed his drinking to a sip every now and then instead of the steady pace he had set earlier.

Galen stared at his own feet, rocking them back and forth, trying to get the blood to flow through them.

They all heard a gnawing sound and felt the vibrations course through the hard, aged frame of the house. Their heads jerked in unison toward the sound.

Paxon jumped to his feet, *It's showtime!* he thought and the excitement went through him like high-voltage electricity. He did not know what to do and looked incredibly stupid as he ran around the room. He thought of leaving the room completely but wanted to keep Galen between himself and that thing. He slammed all of the doors closed and went back to the center of the room. The small propane light cast crazy shadows all around. The hideous gnawing, drilling sound continued to close in on them changing its pitch as it chewed its way through the different materials in the house.

"Jesus Christ!" Paxon said, backing away from one of the doors. The door shook violently in its frame, shuddering as the Eater of Hearts tore away at the wood.

Audra screamed. She saw dozens of snakes, ghostly white with iridescent red eyes slither beneath the door. They scattered themselves about the room, covering the floor.

Galen struggled with all of his might against his ties when he saw flames licking from the cracks around the door. They sought every opening, squeezing their way through, reaching for the other side. He saw burning fingers reach beneath the door, black and bubbling, the flesh dropping off them as they probed. They reached for him.

Paxon screamed when he saw the bony, white, skeletal fingers tearing at a hole that appeared in the center of the door. Light flowed through the opening, as the skeletal hand reached through, pulling at the remaining splinters of wood.

They were all aware of the light as it passed through the door, bringing their individual fears to life. The light hovered in the center of the room, seeking its prey. It toyed with its victim. It would show Galen the worst of his fears before finishing its quest.

Galen could feel the heat of the flames on his face. He imagined his flesh starting to burn, first bubbling, then turning black. The burning people beckoned to him, *please, Galen, help us!*

The fear leaped into his throat and he screamed. The ball moved slowly closer.

Audra tried to kick at the ghostly snakes. They crept over her legs and slithered beneath them. One of the snakes coiled on her lap. She struggled to shake it off, but could not move enough to dislodge it. The evil looking serpent lifted its head and bared its fangs. Audra screamed and threw her head back.

Paxon found himself trapped in a corner by the Grim Reaper. His biggest fear, it seemed, was the fear of dying. *It's a mirror of fear, and knows what's in the hearts of men.* The skeletal face sought him out. The dark robe it wore seemed like a shadow. The eyes glowed dimly red like the flames of Hell. It reached for him with a bony hand, its fleshless jaws locked in a perpetual grin. He could see the ball behind it, *through it.* It shimmered beautifully in its own light. The many facets upon its surface scattered the light in all directions. It was gorgeous. It hovered in the air, slowly making its way toward Galen.

In the middle of all that commotion, Audra's lost thought exploded to the surface of her mind. *The gift!* Gaston had left all of his possessions to Galen. The inheritance was like a gift. She looked back at the snake, still poised in the striking position on her lap. "Galen!" she screamed.

Galen was hardly aware of Audra's shouts. He saw Paxon, cowering in a corner, screaming. He turned his head and spotted Audra through the flames. He could tell she was shouting at him, but the heat was growing unbearable. He shouted back at her. "Audra!"

"Galen! Give him the ball!"

He looked at her, not understanding her intent. "What do you mean?" he screamed back.

"Just give it to him! The gift, the gift!"

Galen wasn't sure what she meant, or that he heard her right.

"You own it Galen! It's *yours* GIVE IT TO HIM!"

Galen caught on. "Paxon!" he shouted, trying to turn away from the flames.

Paxon looked at Galen, tearing his gaze from the beautiful ball.

"You want that thing Paxon?" Galen shouted.

Yes!

"It's yours Paxon! Take it!"

Mine!

217

At that moment, the Eater of Hearts changed its course.

Paxon saw the Grim Reaper turn away from Galen. The glow in the eyes of the skull-face terrified him. He screamed again as the Reaper raised his sickle, and as if in slow motion, brought it down into the center of his chest.

Audra saw the snakes recede from her and Galen's wall of flames disappeared before his eyes.

Paxon shriveled in the corner, the ball chewing its way into his chest. His body vibrated madly as the thing clattered against his sternum. After clearing the bones, it entered the softness of his chest cavity. Blood spewed forth from the gaping hole. A gush of air left his chest in a rush as one of his lungs was punctured. Paxon's dead body continued to shudder for a moment longer as the ball tore into his heart, finally coming to rest, its quest now over.

.   .   .

Galen and Audra sat staring at Paxon's crumpled body. Blood had splattered onto both of them, onto the wall, and even the ceiling. The room looked like a map of the universe done in red. Great galaxies of crimson here, small red planets there and the big bang itself lay beneath and behind the dead man.

Galen and Audra looked across the room at each other, their eyes bright against the background of their blood-speckled faces. They sat quietly for a while, each consumed by their own thoughts. Most of their thoughts could be summed up in one word - *disbelief*. They both still wondered if this could be real, or, if they were both sharing a nightmare.

Galen finally asked Audra is she was alright. He knew she was when she answered, "my butt is completely numb."

Galen began to fight the ropes more aggressively, now that Paxon was no longer keeping watch over them. Galen looked around and noticed the card table Paxon had set up. Overturned during the commotion, the box had fallen onto the floor. Galen noticed a utility knife had spilled out of the box, and maybe, just maybe, he could reach it with his foot. He tried several times but could not bring the knife any closer to his hands.

"Audra, he said, "I think I might be able to kick this over your way."

She looked up and nodded. Galen lined up his shot and kicked the knife. It clattered across the uneven hardwood floor and came to rest against Audra's thigh.

"Nice shot," she said as she began to wiggle around to see if she could get her bound hands on it. After several attempts, Audra managed to get the knife into her right hand. It was an awkward angle, but she managed to get the blade against the rope and after what seemed an eternity, the ropes finally let go. She stood up on wobbly legs and waited for the blood to return to her lower extremities. Her hands were still bound behind her by the nylon wire ties. Using the knife behind her back, she eventually managed to cut the rope holding Galen. After a few more minutes of tedious cooperation, they completely freed themselves.

Galen decided they had to get the thing out of Paxon's chest and dispose of it where no one would ever find it again.

They completed the task in only a few minutes, since the thing had ripped such a large hole in his chest. Galen was still afraid of the ball, but wanted to make sure nobody else would experience what he and Audra had.

They washed up at the farmhouse and changed their clothes. They considered taking Paxon's body out and burying it, but decided not to. They wanted to get back on the road back home. There was nothing either of them could think of that would link them to Paxon's death except the messages Galen had left on his answering machine, and they were now ashes. They gathered up the papers and things they had brought, the food and anything else they had touched and loaded them into the Mustang. They then headed for home.

Somewhere in the Smokey Mountains, Galen stopped on a high bridge. He and Audra stepped from the car and looked into the turbulent water below. They nodded to each other and Galen retrieved the ball-thing from the trunk of the car. They watched as it hit the surface and sank into the murky waters. They hoped it would never again be seen by human eyes, but knowing the nature of humans, doubted there was any place on Earth that could hide the thing forever. They drove back toward The Willows, stopping again at the same motel in Louisville and making love again on the same bed.

Chapter 20

Although neither Galen nor Audra said it aloud, neither had ever been so glad to return to the Willows. What had always seemed to them such an ordinary place, was now a *wonderfully* ordinary place. After such an extraordinary experience, both Galen and Audra reveled in the common sights and sounds that made Willow River feel like home.

They both went to Audra's apartment where Galen called the fire department and told them he would resume his regular shift at the next shift change. Audra made arrangements to take a couple of days off, just to pull herself together.

They continued to see each other and were soon discovering what the other was like under *normal* circumstances. They generally liked what they discovered about each other, and would independently realize that nobody was perfect. Audra realized that Galen was who he was. She loved him for who he was. Of course there were little things that Galen did that did not fit Audra's image of the perfect man. To change those small things might also cause changes in the things about Galen that she cherished. She dared not take that risk. She fell in love with the man, and whether good or bad, those little things were a part of him.

Galen came to many of the same conclusions as Audra had. After spending those days with Audra while they ran for their lives, Galen realized he missed having Audra with him whenever they were apart. He could feel her love for him when they were together, which made him love her all the more.

Upon his return to work, Galen faced making some very big decisions. He could no longer say he loved his work. In fact, it seemed more of a chore each time he reported for duty. Once again, Audra was there to help him through this. Galen explained to her that while he did like helping people, and was good at what he did, he did not want to do this for the rest of his career. He told her he saw what he did as necessary, not desirable. How could anyone *enjoy* being the first on scene at terrible accidents and fires? He knew plenty of firefighters who loved their jobs and would never think of doing anything else. Galen was grateful for those people, but never understood them.

Audra told him she would support him in whatever decision he made. She would love him just as much whether he was a firefighter-paramedic or an accountant, or anything else for that matter. Her only argument was that she felt it such a waste of his talent and training to abandon his career at this point. She was still learning to be an Emergency Medical Technician, and had every intention of furthering her skills and volunteering on the fire department.

After a few weeks, Galen moved into Al's house and was soon followed by Audra. They called the curator from the local museum and donated all of Al's artifacts to their collection.

"There's some incredible stuff here," Logan, the curator said.

"Take everything," Galen told him. "I don't want any of this stuff around."

Logan and some helpers loaded a truck and drove it away. The house seemed almost empty with all of Al's strange decorations gone, but Audra wasted no time in trying to fill the void with her own ideas. Her cedar chest supplied a few decorations that made the large house a little more like a home.

Galen had claimed Al's study and had vowed to keep it the way it was. He could *feel* Al in this room. This was the room where Al had really *lived*. He had been at his best in this room and Galen was comfortable with that.

A few days later, both of them with the day off work, Audra noticed Galen searching for something.

"What are you looking for?" she asked.

"Johnny Bench," Galen said.

"What on Earth are you talking about?" she asked.

"A baseball card," Galen said. "Al had a '71 Bench. He showed it to me once."

Galen had collected baseball cards since he was just a kid and had not let a little thing like growing up stop him. One of the cards he had always hoped to have was a '71 Bench. "I can't find it anywhere," Galen said. "I've been through all of his notebooks, his drawers, everything."

"Al collected baseball cards?" Audra asked, surprised.

"Yeah," Galen said. "He thought it was interesting that so many people collected them, and when he found out that I did, we got into a conversation about it. The next thing I knew, Al was collecting cards. He would call me sometimes and ask me to trade with him."

"It'll show up," Audra said. She smiled as she cleaned out the top of one of the closets. She reached back on the top shelf with a rag, wiping out the dust. Hitting something with her hand, she blindly felt around for it. She retrieved a wooden box, very similar to the one the ball had been in. "I wonder what this is?" she asked.

"Don't open it!" Galen shouted. "Whatever it is, we don't need it. Send it over to Logan at the museum."

Audra nodded her head while she smiled at him. "Okay," she said, "I'll wrap it up and send it to him."

Galen nodded and went on mumbling about the baseball card for the rest of the afternoon.

A week later, Audra received a note in the mail from Logan. It read:

Thanks again for all the things you donated to the museum. They will all make wonderful additions to our collection. I was especially surprised to receive that last package from you. I've never collected baseball cards before, but I guess a 1971 Johnny Bench is a good place to start. Thanks again - Logan.

Audra and Galen would be married soon after and she would never tell him of the whereabouts of the '71 Bench.

THE END

Photo Courtesy Barb Light Photography

Donnie Light lives in rural northern Illinois with his wife, Barbara and their cat, Hedgie. He has two grown sons who also live in the area.

Dark Justice is Donnie's first novel. He is currently working on his next book.

Donnie can be contacted at donnie.light@gmail.com and loves hearing from readers. Visit http://www.DonnieLight.com where you can find the latest news on his work. Donnie can also be found on Twitter and Facebook.

Made in the USA
Monee, IL
10 July 2023